MW00804629

To: First loves and Panther Mamas.

Dear Reader:

This is just not a story of a sexy second chance at love but giving yourself permission to fall in love more than once, especially with yourself.

Cindy

Chapter One

Barnes & Noble, Vancouver, Canada
Shelly

"You made me a terrorist?" A pair of sapphire eyes conjured the memory of a young man in the final huff of an orgasm—head back, eyes closed, mouth open. His eyes had flown open with the deepest indecipherable emotion, luscious pools of blue crashing into my soul, wrecking me, just like now.

Jason Mattis.

All the air stuck in my lungs. I might never breathe again. I might suffocate in a sea of killer blue eyes.

"Jake isn't a terrorist," I said, "and he's *not* you."

Any attempt to maintain composure in the presence of this godly man took every ounce of strength.

He straightened his magnificent six-foot frame, still broad and fit, still gorgeous—unlike me. His expression conveyed both pain and hurt. "You and I both know the truth, Michelle. Or should I call you M.R. Taylor?" He glared at me. "Maybe I'll sue you."

I laughed, hoping my voice didn't reflect the shaking throughout my entire body.

Kenny, my PR manager, who arranged this book signing, leaned in. "Sir, if you're not here for an autograph, please stand aside for the others."

"You're done here in ten minutes." Jason glanced at his phone. "I'll be waiting to discuss this." He walked over to the café and sat at a table. It's a crime against all mankind how amazing he looked. He must've sold his soul to the devil.

I looked around. Did the line of women waiting for my signature have any idea the swoony love interest from my book—yes, the one whom I had just told was *not* the inspiration for—was in fact sitting thirty feet away?

I shook out the cramp in my hand from clenching my black Sharpie at his unexpected appearance. *What's he doing here?*

"Whoa." Kenny huffed. "He's not messing around. Who is he?"

"Jason Mattis." I sighed. "The Zen Shredder."

Three-time world surf champion, legend, international cover model...and the elusive man from my past who never truly belonged to me. His girlfriend was a Brazilian supermodel, he'd had liaisons all over the world, and I was just his former "Huntington Hook-Up."

The real man still had a powerful effect on me, and now my years of therapy were in jeopardy.

Fifteen minutes later, Kenny encouraged me to go over the allotted time of the book signing to ensure I'd accommodated all the ladies in line.

I tapped my foot, and my hand sweated around the Sharpie. My mind flip-flopped between dreading the end of my book signing and excitement at talking to Jason. He and I had the most entertaining and sexy banter...a long time ago. Why was he here? Did he live in Vancouver? No, he lived in Brazil. Anxiety struck. Why show up after all this time?

He looked up from his phone, and our eyes met. I averted my gaze to diffuse the sexual chemistry that still flared between us.

After the last fan left, I stood, smoothed my skirt, and adjusted my belt. I popped the cap of the Sharpie on and off like it was the only thing keeping my sanity, as I walked over to him. My current middle-aged state of chubby, thinning hair and veiny hands invoked waves of humiliation since he still looked spectacular.

Insecurities swarmed like killer bees. How did he think I looked now, twenty-five years later? Did he still see the cute blonde I used to be?

Damn it, I *was* cute, confident, and a real pistol back then. I smoked cigarettes in social situations and observed people, gauged their intent like a character in one of my beloved spy novels. But the Marlboro-lite was also employed as a smoke screen to hide behind, masking some deep social anxiety. Jason saw through that the first time I'd met him.

I'd just graduated on the Dean's List from UC Irvine, had a great job as a legal assistant for a law firm representing antiquities collectors, and I was starting law school in the fall. My life was set.

But the beautiful surfer who pierced my soul with his intense stare almost wrecked my plans. His deep blue and bloodshot eyes stared at me for longer than should have been comfortable across the Tennent Surf Company sponsor tent all those years ago.

I'd looked behind me to see if there was a model or bikini he was really staring at. No one. Okay. I smoothed my hair. Maybe I had some weird flyaway? No. All smooth. Looked down at my shirt. Did I slip a nip? Spill something? No and no. I met his eyes again. He smiled, and a bolt of lightning shot across the tent, hitting me square in the crotch. That bothered me.

I raised my palms in the air and mouthed "what?" to him.

He side-eyed me, still smiling, then shook his head and mouthed "nothing." That sweet smile reached his eyes, and I couldn't move. He was the most amazing thing I'd ever seen in the flesh. I forgot to breathe. What's your story, blue eyes? Are you a deep thinker, maybe an avid reader? A philosophizer? A poet?

A tall man in a large, straw, Japanese gardening hat whispered to my guy, and they went to the far side of the tent and around the back.

I padded to the edge and peeked around to see him pull his shirt off. Bless the sheer humanity of him standing in all his rock-hard-stomach, tanned glory. I wanted to play him like a washboard in a jug band. This man was a god. His body put marble Italian deities to shame.

He zipped into his wetsuit, covering his miraculous body, picked up his surfboard, and trotted past me. "See ya." He glanced back over his shoulder at me, smiling.

Yup, Jason Mattis disrupted my well-laid plans that day.

"Since when do you write romance novels?" His words dripped disdain as I sat across from him.

"Since when do you *read* romance novels?" I shot back.

Just like that, we're back to our regular banter. Our sarcastic back and forth was like foreplay and usually ended up with us naked. His voice made my sex clench and pulsate. It hadn't done that in years. Oh, what this man still did to me.

"You read it?" I sat back, pushing my belt tie down again so my belly didn't pouch.

He nodded and stared at me. "That's how I knew it was me. You wrote it word for word, Michelle."

"I did not. Jake's a pilot, not a surfer."

He shook his gorgeous head. "Word for word, *Michelle*."

Gazing at his soft, full, pink lips, I remembered how they'd felt on my wrists, and other places, that first night.

"It was a good story. It should be told." I fiddled with the napkin dispenser, pulling a few out to fold in front of me.

He smirked at my nervous compulsion. "What are you going to do with those now that you've refolded them?"

I slid them across the table and gazed up at him.

He slumped in his chair, looking down at my gift like he was relieved I wasn't angry with him. He placed his hand on the napkins and curled his fingers into a stack. "The book's a success. Congratulations."

"Thanks." I sighed. "I've been working on it for years." I glanced at his left hand resting on the napkins. No ring. "Are you married?" I regretted asking the moment the words left my mouth.

"Not for a long time." He shifted, and his seat creaked.

I nodded, deciding not to press the subject.

"How about you?" he asked.

Surely he knew the answer to that. *Everyone* knew. My *People Magazine* interview had covered my husband's long terminal battle with cancer, my grown kids, nineteen and twenty-one, and even my two cats, Thor and Loki. My sons named them. It's all over the internet, my Google profile, Wikipedia, and my book jacket.

"Not anymore." I shrugged.

"Right, I did read that somewhere. I'm sorry."

"*People Magazine.*" I squinted at him. "You're reading *People Magazine* and romance novels, Jason. Who are you?"

He laughed.

I'd missed that laugh, low and husky and with his whole body.

"Oh, Shelly." He fiddled with his phone. "You made me laugh at myself. Like no one else."

"Stop doing stupid shit, and I won't have any ammunition." I blushed and pulled more napkins from the dispenser. "I admit I've been stalking you a bit too."

"Okay, I'm not stalking you." He still smiled, watching me.

"You sure about that?"

His grin tightened to a straight line.

Neither of us was stalking the other. Mine was *research*. I don't know what his was.

"I Googled you and saw you'd sold your private jet company," I told him. "That seemed serendipitous for my story since Jake's a pilot."

"I thought I wasn't Jake."

"Okay, maybe now that you've been so *pertinacious* about it, it may've been in my subconscious to write him *similar* to you."

"*Pertinacious.* What's that word?" His face lit up, and he snagged his phone. "Per-tin-a-cious. Adjective, meaning resolute, persevering, constant, steady." He showed me his phone screen. "Good one, *wordsmith*."

I giggled. I'd forgotten his fascination with words, how they'd turned him on. Another thing I'd missed about him.

"*Give me a word.*"

"*Salacious.*" *I straddled Jason's lap fully clothed.*

He squirmed beneath me and grabbed my hips, pulling me onto him. "*Oh yes! Another.*"

I liked this game. His reaction made me want to grind hard on him. "*Insatiable.*"

His smile set me on fire. I circled my core over his erection.

"*Hell, yeah! How many syllables is that?*" *He threw his head back.*

I counted on my fingers. "*Four.*"

"*More.*"

"*Avaricious.*"

'*What does that mean?*"

"*Greedy.*"

"*Oh,* pones cachondo.*"

"*What's that?*" *My thoughts spun as he lifted his hips, hitting me in the right spot and making me lightheaded.*

"*It's Spanish for 'you turn me on.'*"

"*You speak Spanish too?*" *I kissed him hard.* "*God, that's hot.*"

"*Spanish, French, Japanese...*"

"*Oh, say something in French.*" *My body flamed from the friction between my legs, and I moaned.*

"Broyer mon amour. *Grind, my love.*"

"*Shit, Jason.*" *I huffed. So close...*

"*Eu precesio de você.*" *He panted as he lifted his hips again and grabbed the back of my head.*

My heart was pounding for the oncoming orgasm, so I'd barely heard what he'd said.

"*What language is that?*"

"*Portuguese.*"

"*What does it mean?*"

He shook his head "*I can't tell you.*"

"Your book was well written. I was impressed and not at all surprised."

"Are you going to sue me?" I pulled the hair off my neck. All hot and bothered from the memory, a hot flash, or just Jason's proximity?

"You tell me, Counselor," he said. "Should I?"

"J, I wasn't that kind of lawyer."

"It's pretty simple. Defamation of character, maybe?" He was goading me, and I wasn't going to lose my argument.

"Defamation? You're the fantasy of millions of women all over the world *and* voted Best Book Boyfriend by Romance Reads, for Christ's sake."

"What a fucking honor. Do I get any prize money?"

Oh Jason, sharp as always. God, I'd missed him.

"Jake isn't you," I repeated. "There's a disclaimer."

"A disclaimer?"

"Yes. The characters in this book do not reflect anyone living or dead and any similarities are coincidental."

"Oh, really? Who else throws up when they have a fever because of a rare heart condition? How many people have you known?"

As I lay on his chest listening to his purr snore. We'd just met that day and he wanted to cuddle. Jason Mattis, the legend, the superstar, was a cuddler. His body was on fire but he didn't let me go. Jason started to shake, his teeth chattering. His skin radiated heat, getting clammy. Perspiration made his skin glow. His head thrashed side-to-side.

I sat up. "Jason." I shook him awake. "Jason, do you have the flu?"

He rolled his eyes and continued to tremble.

"Oh shit, you're burning up." I palmed his forehead and the back of his neck. "Come on, let's get you in the shower." I pulled his arms.

He got up on his own. I couldn't support his entire weight.

I put his arm over my shoulders and helped his slumping, burning body into the bathroom, where I turned on the faucet. I adjusted for cool, not too cold, got in first, and guided him in.

"Burning!" he shouted. "No, no. It's fucking freezing! Fuck, make it stop!"

"We have to lower your temperature." I held his naked body under the water.

He slinked his arms around my waist and hugged me. "Okay, Shelly. Okay."

Resting his head in the crook of my neck, he took deep breaths. Quite a few loud heartbeats passed. "I have to get my heart rate down and holding onto you naked isn't helping."

"You sound better."

"Yeah, now that you've scorched my skin."

"Okay, now you sound like you."

"Get out!" he shouted. "Get out of the shower now!"

I jumped out just as he'd leaned forward and retched, yellow

bile spewing from his mouth. He panted and held onto the side of the tub.
"What can I do, Jason? Tell me."

He just held his hand up to me and retched again. He bent forward, pressed his arm across his stomach, then spat. "Damn it!"

I took a towel from the back of the door and held it, not drying myself.

Jason turned off the faucet and got out. I handed him the towel. He looked up at me with fear and humility in his big eyes, then took the towel from me and draped it around my shoulders. He pulled another one from the back of the door, threw it over his head, and stumbled out of the bathroom, falling onto the bed face down.

"Do you have ibuprofen?" I asked.

"I can't take it. There's aspirin in the drawer." He pointed.

I opened the drawer on the nightstand to three empty aspirin bottles. A fourth had two tablets left. "You're going to need some more."

He held out his palm, and I handed him the pills. His stunning rear end stared at me. The cream color contrasted with the line across his hips, breaking to a golden tan.

"Your skin looks much better," I said.

"You're looking at my ass," he mumbled into the bed.

"Yes. I want to bite it."

He jiggled from laughter. "Where are you?"

"I'm still ogling your ass."

"Come here."

I lay down on my stomach, turning my head to face him.

"What happened?" I asked. "You just have a fever."

"I have a heart condition, kind of a flutter. Fever could send me into cardiac arrest."

What? My stomach clenched.

"You did the right thing. Sorry for yelling at you."

"You acted like a big baby," I teased him.

He didn't laugh.

"Jason, you can't compete today."

He buried his face again. "I have to." He eased himself up.

"You need to see a doctor."

"Are you a doctor?" He went into the bathroom, took a swig of mouthwash, swished it around and spit it out in the sink.

"What? No, you crazy person."

"I only want to see you right now." He took my hand as he crawled back onto the bed and pulled me close to him.

"You're impossible." I rested my head on his chest, resuming the exact position from before the episode. I'd just become his biggest *fan. Before I could say another word, he was asleep.*

Jason looked at his watch and stood. "I have to go."

"You're not going to sue me?"

"There are so many things I want to do to you, Shelly."

"Yeah? To my *fat ass*," I mumbled.

"Yeah." He glared at me, serious as a heart attack. "Especially that."

I swallowed hard in shock. "I don't understand."

"Yes, you do." He closed his eyes and hung his head, as if willing me to read his thoughts.

I imagined some dirty ones, for sure.

"Where are you staying?"

His question surprised me. "The Fairmont downtown until tomorrow."

"Have dinner with me."

"I can't. I'm dining with my publisher." I took my phone out and saw the dinner notification. "You want to come?"

"Do I need a tux?"

"No, Nutball." I chuckled. "Although I'd love to see you in a tux, no. We're just having dinner at the hotel."

"That's easy. I'm staying there too."

"Are you here on business?"

"You're my business today."

"You just flew up here to see me?"

"I have planes. I can go anywhere." He turned to leave.

"Jason?" I called after him. "Jake's *not* a terrorist."

"Good. Cause neither am I."

What did that even mean?

Chapter Two

Jason

I still hadn't been sure that M.R. Taylor was *my* Shelly until seeing her smile, her movements, and especially the way she looked confident and anxious at the same time. I'd know her anywhere. I'd known her since the first time I'd laid eyes on her thirty years ago at the Huntington Open. As I walked out of the bookstore the memory came so clearly.

The last set of the day. I felt like shit. My skin burned, and my head pounded.

Keep it together, man. *Ma was in a hospital bed with a chemo IV in her arm, and Pop had been drowning in a sea of bills. I had to compete, or I wouldn't get paid. Not to mention, Old Man Tennant would scalp me if I bagged out now. He looked ridiculous with that big straw hat. Thank God he didn't make me wear one too.*

Everything irritated me, including the chafing collar of my wetsuit. The first one I'd grabbed when I saw that blonde peeking around the tent.

How cute she was, trying to look cool with her cigarette, like some old movie character with major attitude. She'd give me some smoky, throaty line like, "Just whistle if you need me. You know how to whistle, don't you? Just put your lips together and blow."

Ma loved those movies.

The way she looked at me differed from most chicks. Like she already knew I wasn't some dumb surfer.

The crowd waited for me to do my thing, the theater my sponsor reminded me to do before I got into the water. He didn't need to remind me. Ever since I'd dislocated my shoulder at sixteen, I chatted with the ocean before jumping in. That became a tradition, a ceremonial understanding with the waves so they wouldn't hurt me. Tennant Surf Co. named me "Zen Shredder." Not because I was some hippie kook. But because that's what they saw when I'd taken a moment to bond with the waves.

The cheers started for me to begin my ritual. As soon as I'd raise my arms, palms up to the sky, they'd fall silent.

"Oh, great ocean, I fear and respect your beauty. I wish not to take away nor leave anything behind. Only to dance with you for a short time."

Some places would be as quiet as the dead when I spoke. My hometown would recite the entire thing with me. Fifty thousand in attendance chanting right with me—there's nothing like it in the whole world. I'd finish by turning to them and shouting, "Let's dance!" like from Footloose.

I needed a little more time before the show. The fever worsened, but cheering fans made the best medicine. Breathing in through the nose, out though the mouth, I tried to channel the pounding in my head.

I raised my hands, palms up.

The crowd fell silent. All fifty thousand recited my prayer. Their wish for my safety in the unpredictable waves supplied the fuel I'd needed to get out there and let everything else go away.

"Let's dance!" We all cheered together.

For the first time on the tour, I worried about getting sick. If it got out of hand, I'd end up in the hospital, like when I was nine. My sponsors would find out about my heart condition, and I'd be done for.

The same high level of stress from that day dogged me as I left the bookstore for the parking lot. My phone kept buzzing from unknown numbers. I was disinclined to answer any of them. All I could think about was Shelly and our life three lifetimes ago. Even though I'd jumped on the plane this morning to come see her, I didn't really have a plan. Getting into my rented Escalade, I put the hotel's address into the GPS. Hopefully my Black Card would get me a room, since I didn't book one.

I had to smile, watching her fiddle with those napkins, her energy so frenetic but grounded at the same time. I'd missed her. She hadn't changed since the first night I'd met her.

"You were great out there today."

"It wasn't my best day, though. I'm off for some reason."

She nodded with a hum, like she agreed with me.

"You noticed I was off?"

She turned to me with a bewildered look. "Yeah, I noticed. You seemed distracted."

Yup, burrowing into my brain, like she could read the deep recesses of my mind.

She released my hand and sidled away from me. "But I don't know you. I might've imagined it."

"I was." I closed the distance between us. There's no way I'd tell her about Ma or anything else going on, even though I wanted to. "You were distracting." I took her hand back and kissed her wrist.

Her whole body shuddered, then she pulled away and gathered herself lightning fast. "Oh please," she scoffed. "Jason Mattis, the Cheese Grater. You're a professional. Some chick in a sponsor tent couldn't distract you."

The Cheese Grater?

I laughed so hard I doubled over with my arms around my stomach. "The Zen Shredder," I corrected her.

"Whatever." She rolled her eyes, a huge grin on her face.

What a tease.

Chapter Three

The Fairmont Hotel, Vancouver, Canada
Shelly

Jason called my room a half-hour before dinner and told me he'd be in the bar.

Doing my makeup, I stared into the mirror at the older woman who'd lived a lifetime since she'd waited for her fantasy man to come see her every year. He'd show up every July for the Huntington Open to stay with me, sleep in my bed, make out with me, but not have sex. He'd had an agreement with his Brazilian model girlfriend, Gabriella or Gabby, to not sleep with any other girl. He'd told me all about her, but I didn't care when he was with me. It was the only reckless thing I'd ever done, and it was only because of him. He made me want to be less of a control freak and take chances.

The entire timeline played in front of me like a movie. Year after year, he'd show up, and I'd always take him in. We'd mess around, get naked, and do almost everything but have actual sex for five years.

Jason's sponsors paid for his meals and clothes. He had a per diem to spend and they'd pay for his lodgings, but he wanted to stay with me every time he was in town. He didn't call ahead, he just showed up with a bag and his surfboard…and I took him in every time.

I loved having him around. He liked my cooking and did the dishes. He put everything back where I insisted it go. He asked about my day and smelled like summer. Falling for him would be the end of me, but I couldn't help it. I was all messed up in my head, in the dark, with him breathing in my ear. If I asked too many questions about his arrangement with Gabriella, he'd think I was too clingy. I wanted to see him, talk with him, kiss him. I was the "other woman," one of many at the time. He never made promises. I never expected him to.

The first year he'd won the Open, I wouldn't have known it from him. He'd left, and I didn't hear from or see him until the next year.

I'd kept our affair hidden from everyone so they wouldn't think me a desperate groupie to the legendary surfer.

My once-a-year lover/roommate left at the break of dawn each day to surf, then he spent all day at the tournament. Little did he know, on the Saturday and Sunday sessions, I snuck down and sat alone with a big hat and binoculars to watch him. I didn't need the binoculars though. I knew which one he was, out there with his elegant balance and command of the torrid ocean waves.

An orchestra conductor leading the mighty Pacific, creating music and inspiring poetry. The ocean bowed to him, and he embraced it like he did me. He could also leave the water behind, walk away from the waves, and not think of them when he wasn't surfing. Just like me.

After four years of him plowing into my life and turning everything upside down, something changed in me. I graduated from law school and found a really good job. Several boyfriends between his visits never lasted, no matter how wonderful they had been. The affair with Jason was going nowhere. Just an endless cycle of perpetual spin.

I wasn't supposed to be in love with Jason. My sanity teetered on the edge. I knew if I told him, he wouldn't come to see me anymore. I wasn't ready to end our fun yet.

There were moments when I was sure he'd felt the same way about me. We approached that edge where I'd need to confront him. He'd have to decide, or I'd have to let him go.

After the fourth year, I finally snapped at him. The bar exam was next week, and I needed to study. Not play house with a beautiful twenty-eight-year-old nomad. My real life was starting. I was no longer a frivolous young girl who could invite a man into my life once or twice a year with no promises or future. I needed to think. I needed a plan. It would have to wait until Jason left again so I could clear my head from the mind-searing inferno that dominated my body when I was around him.

The following year, he didn't show up or call. I had no way of contacting him; he'd wanted it that way. In some ways, I was relieved the affair had ended. In others, I mourned the loss of someone who'd become more important to me than anyone ever had.

Staring into the mirror at myself, all made up and determined to finally face Jason, the last time we'd been together played out in my head. I'd been curled up on my couch, pouring over claim briefs of the theft of an ivory Cantonese box worth about $200,000, listening to Billie Holiday, a thunderstorm pounding against the windows, when someone knocked on the door.

Jason. Only Jason. No one else would show up at my house like that.

"My mom died," he said, soaked from the rain and more beautiful than my heart could take.

I threw my arms around his shoulders, wanting to dry him, warm him, and take away his pain. "I am so sorry."

"Can I come in?" he asked.

"Have I ever refused you?" I stepped aside for him to enter.

Even though it was cold and wet, he still wore shorts and flip flops, keeping warm by a soaked flannel jacket, just like the one he'd worn in the last Tennant Surf Co. ad in the surf magazines.

He'd given the camera that over-his-shoulder-look he'd given me the first time I'd ever seen him. The memory still made me pulse.

"Don't you have a rain jacket?"

He came in and went right for the fridge like he lived there. "Yeah, somewhere. I wasn't planning on staying this long."

"How long have you been here?"

"Since June."

My ego whimpered with the knowledge he hadn't called me in six months and had missed our annual rendezvous I counted on, put in my calendar, and looked forward to all year. I wrapped my arms around my body, not knowing what to do with them—or what to do at all.

"She had a recurrence of the cancer, and they couldn't get to it this time."

I didn't say anything.

He sat down on the couch and stared into nothingness. "I missed you."

"What exactly do you miss, Jason?" I snapped. He was pulling me in to his control again, and I needed to stay strong.

"You're wearing too many clothes." He ignored my question, as usual.

He's too beautiful; I couldn't possibly resist him. Okay, I'd give in one final time then say goodbye. I approached the couch, and he reached for me.

He fiddled with the buttons of my pajamas, keeping his impassioned, bloodshot gaze locked to mine in his regular seductive way that melted me every time.

It took little effort to get me naked. He took off his shirt and touched me all over. I'd gained some weight since he'd seen me last, and my belly jiggled. He leaned forward and kissed right below my navel. Picking me up, cradling me close to his naked chest, he carried me into the bedroom, laid me on the bed, then pulled his shorts off. Rather than climb between my legs, he crawled on top of me, elbows on either side of my head, and stared down at me, silent. His eyes darted and circled as he looked at my face, his hardness pressed against my soft belly.

I'd never wanted anything more in my life than for him to be inside me at that moment. I didn't care he didn't belong to me or any of the other girls. He was here with me now, and we both wanted this. I'd waited long enough.

I wrapped my legs around his torso to signal I was open and wanted him, all up to him now.

His cock twitched at my wetness, and he inched closer, his eyes becoming dark and glassy, never leaving mine. Heartbeats passed as he looked down at me.

Yes. *No words were spoken.* Beat. *He inhaled.* You have to choose. *His tip reached my outer wall.* Beat. *When he exhaled, his breath shook.*

His lips crashed onto mine as he slid into me, both of us gasping at the sensation. He pressed his head into the crook of my neck, and he pushed all the way into me. The completeness of lust and friendship consumed me in waves of love and determination to keep him for my own. I'd been on birth control since I was sixteen and didn't want to stop what was happening for one moment.

Hips rocked, hitting my clit over and over, pressing and coaxing more pleasure out of me. He lifted his head, his eyebrows knitted. With every slow swirl, my muscles relaxed and let him in farther, slow and splendid. A light kiss to my lips every couple of seconds, our breathing becoming labored. Thrusts getting faster, he touched his lips to mine, open-mouthed, breathing into my soul. He pulsed into me rhythmically but still slow and soft. As he pushed in farther, a shock went right though me. I called out his name in my explosion.

I opened my eyes to see his chin up and his mouth open, and he huffed as his body shuddered, his breath hitched and huffed again. He lowered his chin and closed his eyes. His motions were slow, thoughtful, and passionate. His body tensed and shook as he released inside me.

He'd lost his battle with himself to have me, to break his rules, he'd chosen me over Gabriella. It didn't matter. He'd leave for the competition circuit, and he'd be back once a year. I needed to break the perpetual cycle.

His eyes flew open with a whole bevy of emotions I couldn't place. That look would haunt me for years after. His eyes burned into me. I teared up.

Don't ever let go, *my mind whispered.*

I wanted to tell him I loved him. I needed him to stay with me forever. That need was as hollow as my heart. He could never commit to me, and I'd never ask. He needed to tell me he was ready to give up everything to be with me. It wasn't going to happen. Not ever.

Jason's a stray dog who didn't belong to me. If I stopped feeding him, he'd stop coming around. That's what I needed to do.

We stared at each other, frozen. We both recognized the end.

My heart shattered into a thousand pieces. The sooner I accepted it, the sooner I could move on. Just a little longer, *my heart whimpered. In that moment, he was with me, inside me, breathing into me.*

A tear dripped down my cheek. He kissed it and held his face to my cheek. He didn't move. His heaving chest felt like he couldn't get enough air. His muscles tightened then relaxed as he breathed in and out, in and out, shaky and agonizing.

After what seemed like a silent eternity, he took another deep breath.

Not another word was spoken as we fell asleep in each other's arms. When I woke up, he was gone.

I'd never forget.

Chapter Four

The Fairmont Hotel, Vancouver, Canada
Jason

I've been in hotel bars all over the world, and the Fairmont had a classy, upscale joint. Aged-barreled scotch and a pretty good musical duet. They took turns singing a cheesy playlist of loungelike, low-octane soft hits from Billy Joel to Celine Dion. The woman's voice was spectacular. A strange pang struck my gut when she belted out "If You Asked Me To."

I'd heard the song a million times, but the words brought me back to the last time I'd seen Shelly—and my chicken-shit exit from her life.

I'd left her without saying a word. Not one word to her, after she took me in every year, cuddled with me and talked to me like I was one of her smart, law school friends and not some dumb surfer.

I remembered my father sitting, holding Ma's hand. The beeping of the heart monitor had silenced, and the only sound was the pounding rain outside.

I'd needed to leave. Six months of hospitals had been enough. I was ready to let Ma go. Standing in the doorway watching Dad cry for the first time ever, I needed to see Shelly. I needed her. I didn't know why.

Five years, showing up at Shelly's apartment the last week in July, like clockwork, in town for The Open. She let me in every time. She wasn't the only girl I'd seen when I'd traveled—there were girls all over the world. Only Shelly was my year-after-year destination, my hometown girl.

So much more than just my Huntington Hook-up. I could tell her anything, my deepest fears, like living a normal life like my dad. We had endless discussions about her classes and the law. She was so passionate.

Even doing nothing with her was fun, like watching TV or reading. I liked her mystery and spy books. We synced the chapters so we could talk about them. Always one step ahead of the story and could figure out who-done-it or what was going to happen next on the X-Files or in one of John La Carre's or Robert Ludlum's novels.

She got antsy about what we had though like she wanted more, wanted me to stay with her.

She'd been my friend above the sexual attraction and cared about what I had to say. Unlike Gabriella, who'd once told me "Keep your mouth shut and look pretty" on a red carpet. I didn't understand our relationship back then. She just told everybody I was her boyfriend to portray an image. I went along with it and everything she'd dictate to me. Including the "no sex with anyone else" pact. That night after Ma finally had her peace, I needed my own. I'd wanted it with Shelly so many times but had to stop because of that damn pact with Gabriella. But her compassion that night, her warmth, and her familiarity was something I'd needed. I needed Shelly.

Why did she continue to see me? Why did she let me in every time? She was a smart girl with a good job, disciplined and regimented. I'd never asked why she let me into her life every year.

I knew why I'd kept returning to her. She felt like home. Her warm and inviting body, her stability, and her routines gave me comfort.

I knew how she took her coffee, the book she'd been reading that sat in the same place on her coffee table, I knew her brand of shampoo and body wash and her scheduled phone calls to her grandparents, Tina and Sal, Howard, and Betsy, taking at least twenty minutes with each of them.

She had a regular schedule each day. Her place was pin neat all the time, not a smidge of dirt or clutter. Sunday mornings she would spend cleaning around me when I'd lay on her couch before leaving for the competition or a flight to the next destination.

She loved her neck kissed, and she shivered when I licked behind her ear. She'd come as soon as I made a sucking noise on her clit. That memory made my dick twitch every time. She gave insane blowjobs. The one thing that made my heart thump over and over was making love to her.

I couldn't stay with her. I had other commitments. She never asked me to change, never asked me why I stayed with Gabriella, and never accused me of using her. I wasn't. I loved being with her. Two strong women in my life was one woman too many. I had to choose.

When Shelly looked up at me with such emotion and passion, I couldn't look away. Rather than going between her legs, I climbed on top of her. When she raised her hips, inviting me inside, I could have stayed with her forever.

I'd quit the circuit, break up with Gabriella, and be with Shelly for good. So grounded with her schedules, her career, and her cozy home. Solid and steady, she'd want a house and a husband who worked nine-to-five in an office, a couple of kids, a minivan, baseball practices, and dance recitals.

We fit together like two pieces of a thousand-piece puzzle that was far from finished.

When she called out my name and dug her fingers into my shoulders, it wrecked me. Being inside her, I came undone. The decision I had to make, the connection to the one person left in this world I could talk to, who'd understood and appreciated me, who even made me laugh at myself.

No.

I couldn't give Shelly what she wanted or needed. My life wasn't my own. City to city, country to country, it belonged to my fans and the sport itself. I was lucky to have those opportunities. I'd never be around for her. I had more years on the surfing circuit, was obligated to unbreakable contracts.

Holding onto her in an overwhelming moment, I knew I'd have to leave her for her own good. Hurting Shelly could never be avoided. Gabby knew what I needed to keep going and fulfill my destiny and my obligations.

Shelly had such a strong look on her face when my eyes opened. She knew. She knew I was leaving, and she wasn't going to stop me. The single tear that ran down her face was the only sign she was sad about it. Before I cried too, I hugged her. This was for the best. She needed more than I could give her. Much better off with Gabriella.

The regular sarcastic, flirty post-orgasm banter silenced. She fell asleep in my arms. I snuck out before sunrise.

It was the best for Shelly…and for me.

My phone buzzed and a text from my daughter read:

Jazzy: *I got the classes I wanted and made it so my first class on Mondays doesn't start until one p.m. LOL!*

I smirked at her message.

Me: *I'm not going to ask why that is.*

Jazzy: *Good. Gotta go. Love you.*

She's going to have the regular college life I regretted never having.

My thoughts turned to the frustrations I'd had trying to run a company, raise a daughter, and having no education about how to do either.

Endless Aviation was a gift for marrying into a wealthy family. It didn't occur to me to tell Gabby's father I didn't know what the hell I was doing for twenty years, but I'm pretty sure he knew.

As the piano player blew his harmonica and played "Piano Man," I gulped my glass of scotch, trying not to think about my tattered life back in Brazil. The burning liquid was exactly what I needed to jolt me back to the present and focus on the smell of strawberry shampoo and the sweet face of Michelle Stringer…or M.R. Taylor. Whatever she called herself, she was still my Shelly.

Chapter Five

The Fairmont Hotel, Vancouver, Canada
Shelly

The sight of him at a table with a glass of auburn liquid he swirled in one hand and his phone in the other made my head spin. I'd couldn't recall ever seeing him drink before. Was something wrong?

His tan skin glowed in the soft lights above, and his salt-and-pepper hair looked perfect. I'd never seen him in a suit. Damn, he pulled that off too. Gray-blue, custom, Italian-cut suit with a white-cuffed sleeved shirt and no tie. He wore no socks with his tan loafers.

I second-guessed my off-the-shoulder top and pencil skirt. I resembled a sausage stuffed into a black-lace casing. My tummy pouched through my tummy-tucking panties. Though I also wore Spanx for extra suckage, my wide rear end took up the entire elevator. At least my Louboutins made a statement, red-soled, shiny, and sky-high.

"Let it go," I whispered to myself as I approached his table. "Hey."

He stood and kissed my cheek. *Damn!* Even an innocent peck on the cheek shocked my traitorous body into pulsing.

"Give me the lowdown," he said. "Who am I charming this evening?"

"No need to put forth any effort, Slick." I adjusted the candle to the middle of the table—where it should be. "Your mere presence charms anyone right out of their panties."

I set aside the past twenty-five years, marriage, kids, PTA, carpools, and three mortgages. I was a twenty-something smartass again. It felt great.

He leaned forward to say something. I wanted him to. I wanted him to ask me what color my panties were or if I was even wearing any. He just sat back and grinned. "I'm not sure that's true."

The humility in his comment was a relief. Glad to know he wasn't a fifty-four-year-old titty-chaser making crass comments, even to a woman his own age.

"What do we do here, Jason?" I fiddled with the candle again. "Do we fill each other in on our lives, talk about spouses, homes, kids?"

"I've got a good take on your life from your Facebook page and magazine articles. So, ask me if you want."

"Did you marry Gabriella?"

He nodded.

"Kids?"

"A daughter. Jasmine's eighteen." He gulped the last of his drink.

"Where are you living?"

"Still in São Paulo, for now. Jazzy's going to school in New York. She got into Columbia for journalism. We moved her there last week."

"Columbia's a great school—hard to get into."

"Unless your mother's a supermodel with a skin-care empire, and your grandfather was a billionaire." He sighed.

I scrutinized him. He was different, like he was broken. "Jason, I'm just gonna throw this out there."

He grinned and adjusted his seat in anticipation of my candor.

"You seem sad. What's going on?" My stomach wrenched as his face dropped.

"You see that?"

I said nothing. He knew I could read him.

"Um..." He let out a humorless chuckle. "Yeah, I kind of am, I guess."

I waited.

"Gabby and I stayed together for Jasmine. Now that she's flown the coop, we're done. We've been finished for years. I'm trying to figure out what I'm supposed to do now. There's other stuff going on, too."

The waitress came over. "Another one, Jason?" she asked, a little too familiar. He nodded. "For you, ma'am?"

I cringed. She called me "ma'am," like I was his mother or something. "I'll have what he's having."

"Whiskey?" He peered at me with suspicion.

I nodded at the waitress, and she left. "Okay, so you're bored."

"I'm not bored." He stared at his glass, running his beautiful fingers over the rim. "I've got a ton going on. But Jaz is gone, I have the house to myself, and I don't have to travel for work anymore. It's weird."

"How about getting a dog?"

Jason sat expressionless and shook the ice in his glass. "Gabby took the dog."

"That sucks." How much had she taken from him to make him this way?

"That's okay, he was more fun when he was a puppy. Now all he does is sleep." He shrugged.

I wanted to help him, fix his sadness. "After Eric died, I was the same way. I found writing cathartic, you know?"

"Cathartic, huh?" His stunning eyes finally peered up at me. "I like that word."

The waitress arrived with a big smile for Jason as she set the drinks in front of us. The smile lingered as she glanced at me. It seemed fake by that time.

He side-eyed me with a knowing smile, just like the first time we'd met. My insides melted.

"I should have married you." He said so casually, as if he'd simply regretted his drink order. But the undertone of the statement shook me. His eyes flashed in the overhead light as he took another quick sip.

For the second time that day, the air in the room pulled into my lungs. Memories and emotions spilled onto the table like Scrabble pieces. I just needed to make them into words, and the words didn't come.

"Hold up." I choked, trying to regain my composure. "There's no way..." Words eluded me.

He smirked at my tongue-tied reaction and looked down, fiddling with his phone. He loved to stump me, surprise me, and render me speechless. "Do we need to go to dinner?"

"Yes."

"I'll settle the tab."

"You're not going to take off on me, are you?"

"You giving me an out?" The wicked grin on his face was ravishing. He was enjoying himself.

"Jason, you don't have to go to this dinner. We can talk another time."

"No, I'll come." He removed his wallet from his breast pocket.

When he stood, I got a whiff of his familiar scent, summer at the beach, warm, sunny, and carefree. Nostalgia hit me like a crashing wave, returning me to a time when I was young and impetuous. I felt younger, sexy—and I wanted to let him know.

"Red lace," I blurted, wanting to lighten the mood. I loved teasing him.

"Red lace?"

I leaned in and whispered in his ear. "My panties."

His shocked expression was rewarding. We had always effortlessly switched from friends to lovers and flashbacks of our teasing took over. He wasn't the only one to render the other speechless. I ran my hands down my ample backside and looked back at him as I walked away. He grinned.

Two familiar figures already waited at our table in the restaurant. Kenny, PR manager extraordinaire, and Rose Becker, my publisher. She'd flown in from New York to congratulate me.

Jason's arrival turned up the temperature in the room...or it was a hot flash? I couldn't tell the difference.

He gazed at me with that same sexy smirk.

I introduced him and prayed I'd sounded coherent. He sat down and did not take his eyes off me.

"Glad you could join us," Rose said. "What a wonderful coincidence you were in town. Shelly told me you are old friends."

"That's right." He flashed his panty-dropping smile, and mine got a bit wet.

The waiter came to my side with an ice bucket, which I would've loved to pour over my head. A beautiful green bottle with hand-painted calla lilies, Perrier Jouët, my favorite and crazy-expensive champagne, stuck out of it.

"Oh, Rose," I said. "This is too much."

The waiter poured us each a glass, and Rose held hers up.

"To M.R." She toasted. "Fifty weeks on NY Times, Best Book Boyfriend on Romance Reads, and you crashed Amazon when the *People Magazine* article came out."

My cheeks heated. I wasn't used to such praise. It was an out-of-body experience having Jason witness my accomplishments.

"I take full credit for believing in you, Shelly," she joked, and we all laughed.

Rose and Kenny had worked just as hard as I had to get to where we were. We were a true team, and she *had* believed in me. Kenny fought the publishing company's budget czar for the old-fashioned book tour, and he'd been validated by its success. The book sold out at every location.

We all drank.

Jason's cellphone rang. "Excuse me. I have to take this." He took his jacket with him.

Dread struck he wouldn't return, based on our history of his frequent abandonment. After ten minutes, he still hadn't. Memories of him leaving me caused an unsettling in my stomach. I needed to see if he had disappeared on me again. Now that he'd just shown up, I needed more time with him. The feelings got stronger the longer I sat with my colleagues and tried to tune out their idle chatter about travel and the weather. Before I knew it, I'd downed several glasses of champagne.

How dare he bail on me.

I needed an excuse to chase after him, to make sure he didn't leave. "That champagne is going right through me. Excuse me, I'll be right back." Ripping my chain-strap Tory Burch purse from the back of my chair, I stormed from the restaurant.

He faced the corner of the lobby, hunched over his cellphone.

"What the hell, Jason?" I demanded.

He pulled me in front of him with my back to the wall, shielding me from the lobby. "Shh." The phone was to his ear. "It's there, dammit. Can't they just go get it?" He paused, listening.

What was happening? I felt like I was in a James Bond movie. Of course, that would make me a Bond Girl. I was okay with that.

"That isn't my problem." He pinched the bridge of his nose then his face turned quickly at the open space behind him, "Where?" He scanned the lobby and the creases in his forehead deepened. "Shit." He hung up and shoved the phone in his pocket. He stood in front of me as if shielding me.

Two men in black suits exited the restaurant.

"They're looking for you." Jason said. "They saw us in the bar."

What? Who?

"Come on." He hauled me toward the elevators, then stopped short when another man in a suit stepped into our path.

"Caesar has a message for you," he said.

"I don't know anyone by that name." Calm and sarcastic, Jason drew me back against him as the man closed in.

I felt his heart racing. Mine was too.

We backed away from him only to turn and see the two men from the restaurant coming toward us.

"M.R. Taylor, the author." The first man showed his phone to the other men.

From his raised arm I saw a shoulder holster under his jacket with a gun. *A gun?*

Jason and I looked back and forth at the men. They knew who I was?

"Come with us, please." The fatter of the two took my elbow. I jerked away with all my strength, preparing to give him a piece of my mind. All of us froze as a big group of Calgary Flames-clad hockey fans wearing jerseys and holding banners burst into the lobby, shouting and singing. The men turned toward the ruckus.

As the group passed right behind us, Jason ducked behind the distracted men, all but dislocating my arm. He dragged me toward the glass doors leading to the valet.

"What's going on?" I asked.

He didn't answer, looking left then right before heading right. We crouched behind a line of cars as he extracted his cell from his pocket. The men went the other way, and we trotted from the valet lane toward the street. The men didn't see us at first, then one shouted in Spanish and pointed as we rounded the side of the building.

"Encuentrame!" Find me. Jason shoved his phone back in his pocket. "Don't ask me any questions right now."

Rather than scared, I was exhilarated. A real adventure with Jason Mattis? The writer in me took in everything—the smells, the sounds, the ache in my high-heeled feet, the grip of his strong hand in mine. I'd wondered what his life was like, and now I was getting a glimpse.

Was this who he was, an action hero? Was I right when I'd written Jake in my book? Was the real Jason some brave spy or something?

My heels clacked behind him, trying to keep up without falling.

He stopped us on the sidewalk about fifty yards from the hotel valet and pulled me out of the streetlight into an alley at the end of the historic hotel building. We ducked behind a stack of cardboard boxes and the men ran right past. His face showed panic not bravery. He shielded me like a precious treasure. Now I was scared. What was going on? I felt his heart. *Pound, pound, flutter, pound.*

His heart was struggling, his weak heart. What was this episode doing to him? I knew his biggest problem was when he'd get a fever, but he was much older now. I was one of the only people who knew about his condition back then.

My back against the cold brick, I panted from running, and his body pressed to mine. He leaned into my cheek and inhaled near my ear, and my thighs flamed. *Did he just smell me?* Who does that outside of a regency romance? There was silence except for our breathing and the dripping sound of some invisible broken water tap. I put my hand on his chest to feel his frenetic heartbeat. He backed up and looked into my eyes. Longing, regret, and gratitude shifted in that split second before he blinked, those luscious eyelashes shuttering his expression.

"Shelly..." He squeezed my arm, about to say something, something important.

Tires screeched to a halt, and he jerked his head toward the street. A black SUV stopped short at the alley entrance. He pulled me over to the car, opened the back door, and shoved me inside. Slamming the door, he came around to jump into the front seat.

The driver looked back at me. "It *is* M.R. Taylor. You weren't kidding."

His accent sounded Mexican. The man was in his late twenties with broad shoulders and dark eyes. Was he Jason's sidekick, like in comic books? Like Robin to his Batman? My heart was beating out of my chest. I didn't dwell on thoughts of leaving the hotel or my dinner or the bottle of Perrier Jouët behind. Just the urgency to escape mysterious men with guns.

"Not now," Jason said. "Straight to the airport, Luis. I've got to get to San Salvador."

"But, you told them where the money is?"

Money? A chill shot up my spine. The situation just went from a fun adventure to something more nefarious. What was going on? Big men chasing us, knowing who I was, was more than I was able to process.

"You *are* Jake."

Jason turned to scowl at me. "No, I'm not."

Luis laughed. "Yeah, that's you. Isn't it, Mattis?"

"You read my book, Luis?"

"Uh..." He faltered. "My girlfriend—"

"Stop," Jason snapped. "He said the feds were everywhere, Luis. What the fuck?"

I'd never seen him so angry.

Luis shook his head. "No, they were supposed to stand down and ghost the bank."

"They aren't ghosting well. Caesar's man said they were everywhere. Now *his* guys are all over *me*." Jason lowered his window and tossed out his cellphone. "One of them got a lock on me from the lobby. I wouldn't be surprised if they were following us."

Was this Jason sexier than my sweet Zen surfer boy? Maybe? Wait, what was my brain doing? This was serious.

"Don't use your phone—it can be tracked." Jason turned to me. "Actually, give it to me."

I took my phone out and hesitated.

"But my calendar, my schedule, when to take my vitamins, my

contact numbers, photos I haven't uploaded to the cloud, notes for my books—is all on my phone." I held my phone like it was the most precious thing in the world to me.

"Sorry. We've got to pitch it now."

"I have to call Rose and let her know—"

"Text her from my phone that you weren't feeling well or something. Come on give it to me."

He held his hand out and glared at me.

"They had guns." I whimpered.

Jason nodded. "I'll get you protection, I promise. Just trust me, please."

A light passed over his face, showing true concern, and I warmed to it. He'd never lied to me or played games. I did trust him.

He opened the window again, and I slapped the phone in his hand with a groan. He tossed it out, and I almost threw up.

"In the glove box is a burner phone." Luis pointed. "Jessie will text the number."

Jason extracted the new phone and started tapping. "Magda will get her protection when we get to El Salvador."

I gasped. "El Salvador?"

Jason turned back and glared at me.

"No, no, I have to be in Seattle tomorrow. It's on my schedule." I panicked at having said schedule disrupted.

Jason didn't answer me. He just tapped on the new cellphone.

We entered a chain-link-fenced tarmac at least a mile from, but still in view of, the Vancouver airport lights. Mist swirled as we climbed out. Stairs lowered from a small white jet with Endless Aviation and ES-ONE typeset. The image of the Endless Summer movie poster on the side glowed orange and gold.

"Wait!" I shouted over the jet's engine. I struggled to breathe through the barbell lying across my chest. A panic attack was imminent—the chest pressure was a sure-fire sign. Maybe flying to another country at the drop of a hat is fine for him, but I didn't even have my passport. My mind flashed to my boys safe at school in Chicago and San Luis Obispo. I knew I wasn't going to see them until Thanksgiving, but I couldn't just leave. Could I? "I can't go to El Salvador."

Jason squeezed my shoulders. "I'm sorry. I didn't mean to involve you in this. You need to come. They know who you are. I need to get you some protection."

I couldn't get enough air into my lungs. Jason must have seen my struggle.

"Shel, just try and breathe." He hauled me up the stairs of the plane, then turned and took my hands in his. "This is a Tantric breathing exercise I use to lower my heart rate."

"Tantric? Like the Kama Sutra?" I shook my head in anxiety and confusion.

"Yeah," He chuckled again, like my panic was hilarious. "Focus. Breathe in, count to three, then out, count to six. I'll do the same. Don't look away from my eyes."

I followed his lead, staring into his sapphire orbs. As soon as our breaths synced, a wave of calm washed over me, warm and soft. My body heated from neck to ears, soothing tense muscles. Buzzing and humming streamed though me like power lines. The way he looked at me made me want to lean in and kiss him. I jerked my hands and eyes away and stumbled backward. My whole body was on fire, and I needed him to stop touching me.

"I'm better, thanks." I dropped into a white leather chair embarrassed at my reaction to his touch, as if he'd seen it too.

Jason sat across from me; a small table sat between us.

My whole body still pulsed.

"We'll need to refuel in San Diego," a tall man with hunched posture, sporting a white pilot's uniform, informed Jason.

"Right. Let's get out of here—fast."

"Yes, sir."

I tugged on my Spanx that had curled around my thighs, digging into my skin. I stuck my thumb into the waistband of my skirt to get some relief from the tummy-tuck underwear and yanked it.

"You're worse than a three-year-old." Jason eyed me. "What are you squirming about?"

"Spanx, Jason, okay? I'm sure Gabriella never had to wear compression shorts to suck in her flab. I do." Post-confession, I felt free to reach into the waistband of my skirt and yank the underwear over my belly, showing him the top of the evil spandex blend.

He put his fist over his mouth, laughing. "I didn't realize how much I'd missed you."

Taken aback by the endearing comment, I sat staring at him. His words and his actions contrasted so much I wanted to strangle and kiss him at the same time.

Just like I used to.

"I didn't miss you." I didn't believe myself for a second. I'd written the Best Book Boyfriend based on his infuriating ass. Hearing he missed me did strange things to my insides, like an old pilot light in a forgotten fireplace sparking back to life. I felt quite warm.

It could be hot flashes, though. I can't tell anymore.

"Yes, you did miss me," he said. "Maybe you didn't for a long time, but now you do."

He was right.

"What the hell is happening here, you crazy person?" I tugged at my thighs again. "Can you at least tell me that?"

"No," he said with a blank stare.

"No? That's it?" That answer surprised me. This cold and angry Jason was a stranger to me.

"Plausible deniability, counselor."

"Why take me with you?" I was still in disbelief of what was happening. But just being in Jason's presence was like feeling the sun again after a long winter.

"I told you, protection."

I opened my mouth to protest again.

He shook his head, his new phone already to his ear. "Hi Mags, we're coming tonight. Yes, I heard about the bank." He paused, listening. "I know, *mi quierda*. I know it's not your fault. We'll try another way. Hey, listen—can you please have Jorge meet us at La Libertad airstrip? I'll text you when we're an hour out." He leaned into me across the table. "What size do you wear?"

"What?"

"I want to get you some clothes, unless you want to continue being assaulted by your underwear?"

Too embarrassed to tell him, I shook my head.

"Come on. It's not that bad."

"Speak for yourself and *your* non-menopausal ass."

He smirked. "Come on."

I sighed with a groan at the end.

"Fourteen or extra-large."

"Bra size 32C, right?"

"Ha!" I threw my head back. "Try 36D."

"I've got M.R Taylor with me." He paused, smiling. "I'm serious. She's coming with us." I heard a muffled high-pitched scream on his phone. He yanked it away from his ear, wincing. "It's a long story. I told you, we're old friends. Can you get her some casual clothes? She's a medium, bra size 36D," he said into the phone, as if my humiliation was nothing. "*Si*, leggings, cardigan, T-shirt, no logos. Perfect! You are the best friend anyone ever had." He waited. "*Si...*" He looked at me. "Shoe size eight, right?"

I nodded. He'd remembered.

When he hung up, I glared at him.

"Why did you tell her to get me medium? I told you extra-large."

"Sizes are different in Central America. Average women are a size twelve. You're a medium."

"Whatever. They'll be too tight. I'm a cow right now."

"That's enough." He scowled at me. "You're beautiful. You've had kids and took care of a sick husband. You took care of everyone in your life for years. You had more important things on your mind than worrying about your weight."

I stared at him in shock.

He huffed and slumped back in his chair as the plane took off. "Jazzy's had issues with her weight her whole life. Believe me, when your mom is a supermodel, you're subjected to a whole lot of body shaming. Gabby refused to be seen in public with our sweet girl after she turned eleven." He showed me a photo of a black-haired girl with chubby cheeks hugging a Basset hound. "Living with someone like Gabby for twenty years puts things in perspective when you see your baby girl struggle with insecurities about her body." His eyes darkened. "Gabby counted every fucking calorie. So many stupid surgeries to remove skin and fat, injecting poison into her face on a regular basis... It was disgusting. The older she got, the worse it got."

He glanced at the photo. "My girl is perfect just as she is, and so damn smart." He put the photo back in his wallet. "Makes me feel like an idiot I didn't finish high school like my parents wanted me to. Maybe I wouldn't be in this situation now if I had."

The pained look on his face was back, the one like when his mom died and when he glared at me at the book signing. He was broken, and I wanted to fix him.

My mother's the same way. She'd even taken a class on Kintsugi, the Japanese art of putting broken pottery back together with melted gold. You can still see the flaws, but they're made beautiful. I wanted to do that with Jason—put him back together. His flaws could still show.

"You'd love Jazzy. Her favorite movie is The Princess Bride." He smiled at me. "She wants to be a writer. Her stories are hilarious."

I smiled back.

"She read your book and is a big fan." His beauty magnified with his adoration for his daughter. I *had* missed him. Not many men had the kind of allure Jason Mattis had, even in this sad and broken state.

I pulled on my waistband again. "Uh, there's a lot of sex in the book. Did she know it was you?" My cheeks heated with embarrassment. I wouldn't even let my boys read it, not that they wanted to.

"God no! I was kind of uncomfortable about the sex parts, even though she's eighteen, a grown woman. She told me she'd read worse."

He shrugged. "I know she's a good girl. I'm protective."

I didn't know this man. He was a grown-up now, an overprotective father. The Jason I knew didn't even have a driver's license. I wanted to know *this* Jason. He was fascinating and still so sexy.

When we landed in San Diego three hours later, the discomfort from my undergarments was intolerable. Luis tapped on his laptop and Jason on his phone, ignoring me the entire time.

Thank goodness I only had to sit for twenty minutes before we took off again.

My body swelled as the air pressure changed in the cabin, and the pain became agonizing; I needed the spandex off my body—now. It was strangling me.

"I need to get this off." I stormed into the tiny bathroom. It had a small shower to the left with a plastic curtain, a toilet with the lid closed, and a tiny counter to the right with a miniscule sink, bigger than most airplane bathrooms, but not by much.

Profanities spewed from my mouth. The damn thing wouldn't budge. I was in tears.

Jason pounded on the door. "Shelly, what is going on in there? Let me in."

"No way!"

"Is it your girdle?"

Shit, why did he have to call it that? "It's not a girdle. They're Spanx."

"What?"

"Fuck. Yes, it's my girdle." I pictured my grandmother in her underwear and almost gagged.

"Come on. It's not like I haven't seen you."

"Ugh." I exhaled in exasperation and defeat and opened the door.

He squeezed in and closed the door behind him. "What's the problem?"

I sobbed. "I can't get it off."

He pulled a Swiss Army knife from his pants pocket and lifted my skirt.

Most women might've been nervous or scared by that aggressive action. Jason was far from scary to me. His touch brought back so many familiar emotions.

He lifted the seam away from the skin of my right thigh. After slicing the fabric with a finger-sized serrated knife, he closed the knife then placed it on the counter.

Total concentration showed on his handsome face when he

gripped both sides and ripped with such force, I jerked toward him. I had to put my hands on his shoulders, and my heart raced in excitement. He ripped the fabric all the way up, freeing me from the torture device, then stood upright and peered at me.

I panted from the sheer exhilaration of his action.

"Better?" he asked, as if he had just handed me a handkerchief in a gesture of chivalry instead of annihilating my undergarment.

"Uh." I looked down at my left thigh, and he dropped to his knees, took the knife from the counter, and repeated the same action, I was free.

He threw the mutilated fabric aside, and I glanced down at him. He was looking at my panties, and without speaking, he gazed up at me with those eyes. His finger stroked the skin at the waistband as my beathing increased. He hooked the finger under the elastic and pulled them down my thighs without a word.

"I lied." My voice shook. "They're not red lace."

He didn't seem to care. Blue eyes glazed up at me as his warm hand made its way up my left thigh, then his thumb stroked and parted the folds, finding the spot that was aching for the first time in many years and pressed. He'd always known how to make me crazy.

"Jason." I huffed.

His touch brought back the first time we were together all those years ago when he touched me in that way, putting me under a very powerful spell.

He'd explored me in a way no other man had before. He knew exactly how to make me come undone when he dropped to his knees, and his talented mouth caused my knees to buckle. I reciprocated the life-changing gesture with my secret talent of a four-pronged blowjob; deep throat, tongue stroke, extra suckage, and ball fondle that he was very slow to recover from.

That's right sex-God, I've got moves too.

"Mind-Blown Michelle." He lay on his back with his arm over his face, panting. Then he sat up and looked right in my eyes. "Now, come snuggle with me the rest of the night, and tell me how I'm going to leave you tomorrow."

"You're leaving tomorrow?" I studied his beautiful, high-cheek-boned, golden-tanned face, messy brown hair with gold highlights, and mile-long dark eyelashes. My heart thudded in my chest, neck, and sex.

"Yeah," he sighed. "Right after the trophy ceremony. I'll be back next year."

Hearing confirmation he'd be gone a year saddened me. I only had one night with him, and it wasn't enough.

"Jason, what do you want from me? I mean, you have a girlfriend, and now you're telling me you don't want to leave me. What am I supposed to say to that?"

He stayed silent and focused on the ceiling, his lashes fluttering. I wanted to know what he was thinking beyond the joking and teasing.

"Am I supposed to wait for you to come into town and be your annual 'Huntington Hook-up' or something?" I scolded him.

He rolled toward me. His gorgeous blue eyes flashed.

"You don't wanna be that? Good name by the way." That smile could light up the darkest night.

"You're something else," I snarked. "It's a good thing you're so hot or I wouldn't be here at all."

"That's all you want me for, to feed your erotic fantasies?"

"How can you be a fantasy when you're lying here next to me? I'd say you're an erotic reality." I stroked his semi-erect cock with my pinky.

"You keep doing that, and I may have to fuck you into next week."

"No, you have a girlfriend. Remember?"

He faced me. "I'm exhausted and need to get some sleep. Okay?"

"Okay," I said. "I'll catch a cab."

I wasn't upset or embarrassed. I wanted him, and I got him in a way where I felt no regret, thankful for his "no sex" rule.

"No, you stay and snuggle," he ordered in the most adorable way. It made me smile. "I may want another taste of you later." He curled me to his scorching body and wrapped his arms around me.

"All night?" I asked.

"Yes. Can you stand it?" He squeezed me. "Naked all night. Maybe forever. We'll be nudists."

"You're nuts, Jason."

He chuckled. "My mom says that all the time."

"I'm glad I'm not the only one who thinks so. But can we not bring parents into our bed tonight?"

He laughed. "You're amazing, Shelly." Jason gave me another squeeze then fell asleep.

"I remember you." He whispered into my wetness, sending a puff of heat that shot an opposing chill up my spine.

"Are you talking to my pussy?" I asked between gasps.

He chuckled, his breath vibrating my sensitive nerves.

His thumb circled my clit. My head spun as a bolt of heat shot to every extremity, then I exploded. I steadied myself by gripping the counter and the shower curtain. My knuckles whitened as my knees gave out.

He stood and looked me in the eye. "I remember *you*." He kissed my forehead and slipped out the door of the tiny airplane bathroom, sucking his fingers.

Shit that was hot. "Jason Mattis." I sighed after the door closed.

~ * ~

I gathered myself and reveled in the sensation of being liberated from my binding underwear. Gushing from the gift of the "Mile High Club" orgasm, I felt drunk, high, and light as a feather. The day was glorious. Even though I was being kidnapped and taken to Central America, I was with Jason Mattis. Sexy-as-fuck Jason Mattis.

When I exited the bathroom, Jason was sitting back in the chair with the table.

"Jason," Luis said from across the aisle, looking at the screen of his laptop, "Caesar's giving us an ultimatum."

Jason leaned across the aisle as I sat across from him.

"'You have twenty-four hours to get me the money. I don't care where it comes from,'" Luis read. His accent gone, now he sounded like he was from Texas.

Jason sat back. "Eight million dollars in twenty-four hours?"

"What about Sebastian?" Luis asked.

I wanted the whole story. It sounded like a great nugget for my next book.

"No!" Jason snapped. "He'll tell Gabby, and she'll hold it against me when it comes to Jasmine. I can't risk my relationship with my daughter. We find another way."

"Who's Sebastian?" I asked.

Jason shot me a look like he'd forgotten I was there. "My-brother-in-law." He sighed and picked up his phone. "I can come up with one mil. That might buy me some time." He stared at me for a heartbeat then looked back at his phone. "Maybe I can just go into the bank and get the money. It's *my* safety deposit box."

"You know what'll happen if you do that. It's just as bad as your confessing involvement. That will screw us all." Luis shook his head. "Wait until Caesar gets his money, then the rebels can—" He stopped and glanced at my attentive face.

"Jesus!" I shouted. "Are you funding a coup?"

Jason and Luis looked at each other.

"No, *Señora* Taylor." Luis' accent returned, and he sat frozen. "It's the people. The people want to get rid of a corrupt government, that's all. We aren't involved with that."

That's all?

"What's Caesar's money for?" My writer's curiosity peaked. Jason shook his head. Luis shrugged.

"Oh, come on." I glanced back and forth between the two of them.

"Whelp, I'm starving." Jason diverted the conversation and rose from his seat. "Let's see what we can find around here."

He went to the back and opened a cabinet. "Shelly? Veggie lasagna, lemon chicken, or bean-and-cheese burrito?"

"Burrito." My brain processed everything that was said, but I needed more information.

"Luis?"

"Lasagna."

"Okay, that leaves chicken for me." Jason withdrew three plastic containers and placed them in the microwave drawer.

I summed up the plot. Eight million dollars for some guy named Caesar lay in a safety deposit box at a bank, watched by federal agents, and none of his guys will go get it. Caesar wants to get paid for something that will help rebels incite a coup. I couldn't have written anything better. If I were writing this story, I'd need to fill in the missing pieces.

Weapons? Yes, the money was for weapons. Caesar was either an arms dealer, a corrupt general or gangster, or, even better, a rival politician of the current leader. No, then he wouldn't need to get paid for the weapons…unless someone was paying *him* to launch the coup. Maybe another government, like *ours*? With wide eyes, I peered at Luis and considered his on-again-off-again accent. *Hmm.*

He caught me looking at him and I leaned across the aisle. "Where are you from, Luis?"

He smiled and turned his attention back to his laptop. "Laredo, Texas." He didn't look at me. His accent vanished again.

"Were you a policeman in Laredo? A detective? Border officer? Not ICE."

He looked up at me in shock and confusion then back to the laptop.

"Before that an athlete, maybe a baseball player? You have the build of a pitcher, tall, broad shoulders, and an eagle eye. My son Connor's a pitcher."

"Eagle eye." He chuckled.

"CIA?" I whispered.

His smile dropped into something phony. He wouldn't look at me. That was all I'd needed.

Jason carried the containers and utensils to the table and slumped into his seat. He caught my eye. "What's on your mind, Shel?"

I smiled, shrugged, and shook my head as I peeled the plastic top off the steaming burrito.

"She's piecing everything together," Luis said.

"Is she right?" Jason asked as if I wasn't there.

Luis nodded.

Jason scowled at me. I flashed him a guilty smile and shoved the stuffed tortilla in my mouth.

"So, are *you* going to give me eight million dollars so I don't have to crawl to my brother-in-law and destroy my daughter's image of me?"

I felt guilty. He'd messed something up, and I wasn't helping. I wanted to help. I put my hand on his across the table and squeezed. "I want to help. I don't have even one million, let alone eight. I mean, maybe my house—" *What am I saying?*

He shook his head and rubbed his big thumb over my hand. "You can't help me. I'll have to go see Caesar. Okay, Luis, send the message. I'll go to his office tomorrow. 11 AM."

"Jason, what about me?"

"Don't worry. My friend Magdalena has a house just outside of town. She has the protection of the Silvas. You'll be safe there."

"Who are the Silvas?"

"Gabby's family," Jason answered, refocusing on his phone.

Gabriella Silva, Brazilian supermodel, sister to Sebastian Silva, Jason's ex-wife.

I knew about Sebastian Silva, a famous gangster in São Paulo, Brazil, the successor to his father who'd died in 2002. Silva's thugs had stolen millions of dollars of insured items from auction houses. The firm I used to work for lost millions in claims because of him. This was the best story I'd ever heard. The writer in me was aroused.

"Get some sleep. We should arrive around five in the morning. It's another hour to Magda's." Jason's face softened.

What the hell was he into? This was his life? No wonder he didn't want to talk about it when we were together all those years ago.

Chapter Six

La Libertad, El Salvador
Shelly

"It *is* you." A petite woman with long black hair and red, claw-like nails threw her arms around me. "M.R. Taylor, in my house." She backed up and bounced on spike heels, her hands pressed together at her chin, like a child who'd just entered Disneyland.

I smiled. "It's nice to meet you, Magda." I was running on an hour's sleep, without brushed teeth. I tugged on the strapless bra that had numbed me from any feeling on my torso.

"Come with me; I have clothes for you." She hooked my arm with hers, leading me up the most ostentatious curved staircase I'd ever seen.

Bulbous white spindles with a marble handrail matched the marble floors and stairs. An enormous crystal chandelier hung over the expansive foyer. As we ascended the stairs, morning sunlight hit it through a window over an oversized oak door, sending little rainbows spanning the cathedral ceiling. It was like the lobby of an elegant hotel in Paris.

"Now, tell me. If Jake returned to Maria instead of staying with Sarah, would he have gone to jail?" she asked.

I'd left a cliffhanger ending in the book. "You'll have to wait for the next book." It was a canned response. I was so tired and uncomfortable.

"Ooh, I can't wait." She squealed. "I may have to torture you to get it out of you."

"Magda," Jason called from the bottom of the stairs, "that's not even funny."

She turned to him and gave him a scowl. "Oh, I almost forgot." Her face all smiles when she looked at me. "Tessa wants me to bring her over to meet the book club."

"Contessa Rivera?" Luis chimed in, peering at Jason.

"Yes, she wants us there by eleven o'clock this morning." She turned me by my shoulders to face a long hallway. "You know Tessa, no one says 'no' to her."

"Who's Contessa Rivera?" I asked.

"Caesar's wife."

I stopped walking and glared at her. "Caesar, as in the eight million dollars?"

"Yes." A single word, said as if he were a mere nuisance, just the meddlesome husband of her friend who could ruin her party.

"So…Tessa is the wife of the man Jason owes money to, who has thugs following him, and we're going to a book club at their house?"

"Yes," she repeated, exasperated. "Don't worry. Tessa is my best friend."

"Don't worry?" I felt nauseous.

~ * ~

"Hey." Jason knocked after already opening the door and poking his head inside. "You decent?"

"That's a matter of opinion." I couldn't help still bantering with him.

"Always." He walked into the room with a sheepish grin.

"So, you were right—everything fits. She has great taste. Expensive, but great taste." I tugged on the heather-gray Stella McCartney cardigan. The jogger pants with cargo pockets, loose T-shirt, and brand-new white Adidas were all so comfortable and chic *I* felt like eight-million bucks.

"Jason, tell me everything, please."

"I can't." He sat on the edge of the bed with a groan. "You already know too much. I can't risk it ending up word for word in one of your books."

I wanted to be offended. Problem was, he was right. I used as much real-life experience in my books as possible.

"I need to hear back from my handler about what to do next. I'm trying to keep you out of this as much as possible. With you here…" He shook his head.

"At least tell me who Magda is."

"Her family has oil money, and she married who I can only describe as the Secretary of State for the country. The leader of the rival political party of the current President. Magda and Gabby have been friends since they were teenagers. She's more my friend now—she and her husband, Roberto. They're good people."

I nodded. "How did you get wrapped up in this?"

He exhaled for a long time and bent forward, running his hands though his hair. He looked up at me with his pained eyes pleading. "All you need to know is that I fucked up. So did Luis. He's a rookie and assumed I knew what I was doing. We're trying to fix this."

"Great." I peered at myself in an antique mirror. "I guess I have a tea party or something to go to." I turned back, scowled at him, then walked away from the ornate, gold-painted, free-standing mirror, perusing the ridiculous room.

I recognized what the decorator was trying to do with the garish furnishings in dark wood and rich fabrics. It was an over-the-top attempt to recreate a Spanish Regency atmosphere. I examined a box on the credenza and vases made into lamps on the bedside cabinets. They were real, from Ferdinand VII's reign before the fall to Napoleon. Most antiquities from that period were either shipped to the Americas or stolen by the French.

"I hope this will be suitable attire," I said to him as snarkily as possible.

"You look great, Shelly."

I crossed my arms and leaned on my left leg, jutting my hip out. "So, what was all of that 'I remember you' business back on the plane? Not that I'm complaining."

The vision in my head made me heated and a little embarrassed. Maybe it had been too long since any man had touched me like that. Eric never pleasured me that way. After being together for as long as we were, sex between us was familiar and regimented. I was the one to initiate, not knowing how sick he was for years.

Eric was such a man, avoiding going to the doctor until he was riddled with cancerous cysts on his prostate. By then it was too late. I'd spent years going between anger and sorrow and everything in between. Abandonment by the two men I'd ever loved was the biggest theme in my writing. My fans read into that bitterness, some telling me they'd felt it only when they'd read it twice, others felt it right away. An unrequited love that needed resolution.

Jason stood and approached me.

My stomach squeezed, and my sex pulsated. My damn treasonous body!

He stopped as our toes touched. I dropped my arms and my breasts pressed against his chest.

He took my hands in his. "This is just bad timing." Gazing into my eyes with that look, the look that made me too agreeable. "I missed you." He leaned in closer.

I pulled my hands away, stumbling back. "I'm married. I have kids and a house and a…" My psyche messed with me. I knew Eric was dead, but my brain couldn't process that fact. Jason was going to kiss me, and in my mind, I was still married to someone else. Even though I knew what was happening, I couldn't stop it.

My therapist said in moments of extreme stress my brain would search for a place of security. My previous life presented itself, and my mind thought it was real.

"I'm happily married, for over twenty years." Tears welled. "I'm married. I'm…" My whimper turned to sobs.

I never cry. I'm the shoulder everyone else cries on.

I covered my eyes, and he embraced me, squeezing me closer, face in his chest. I'm a strong and brave woman. I'd carried everyone in my life. I'd stood in the face of many adversities. Why was I terrified of this man taking my heart, now? What did he want?

He'd put me in this situation. I was fine with my adoring fans, exploring different cities on my book tour, and with my inner book world where I was in my twenties again, thin, adventurous, with my whole life ahead of me. I was in control of my life for the first time in years.

My writing kept me sane, kept me company. My memories of three lifetimes ago made me happy.

Why was he back in my life? I needed him to be the fantasy I had created, not the sad, broken, and beautiful self-professed "fuck up" hugging me so tight I could hear his damaged heart flutter.

I pushed him away with as much force as I could.

"I am married!" I shouted at him. "Why did you come to see me anyway? Why? What did you want me to do?" I was on the verge of a panic attack. "You kept leaving me, you just kept leaving! Now I have to go to this book club with these women whose husbands are…I missed the local T.V. interview—I am supposed to be in Seattle right now! It's on my schedule!" I paused as my chest heaved and tears stung the corners of my eyes. "I'm married." I whimpered again. The battle in my head was making me woozy. I leaned on the credenza to steady myself.

"I did get you into this, and I'm sorry." He said and sat back on the edge of the bed. "Shel, you're *not* married." He was so calm. *The Zen Shredder.*

I froze, eyes and mouth wide open at his blunt response. There were no words.

"Have fun with your fans." He stood and left, rubbing the back of his neck.

How was I going to get through this day?

~ * ~

Jason

"Change of plans," Luis said as soon as I got to the bottom of the grand staircase. "Caesar wants you at his house at noon."

"Fuck." I braced my hands on my hips. "He's going to kill me, isn't he?"

"Probably not." Luis rubbed the stubble on his chin.

"It'll be his thugs. They'll drag me into the jungle, strip me naked, hang me from a tree, then shoot me, right?"

There goes the heart again. Thump, flutter, thump. Breathe.

"He wants his money."

"Great. So, he'll just torture me in the dungeon of his house."

"How does that get him his money?" Luis asked. "This is business to him, J. You read his dossier. Tell him he will get his money."

"*How* will he get his money?" We stood silent. I stared at him. He was the *spook*, the all-powerful CIA agent. His colleagues could do anything they wanted. How did he not know what we should do?

"I'm working on it," Luis said. "I can't stay here, though. I'm going to town to meet with my people."

"What about me?"

"Stall him. Charm the fuck out of him. Do whatever you need to do. Just give me a few hours." Luis strode out the large oak doors, leaving me alone in the grand marble foyer of Magda's house.

Find your Zen place, Jason.

I closed my eyes and heard the big oak door close. A vision of Shelly sitting on her couch reading calmed me. That vision had come to me many times over the years. It'd never occurred to me to use it to find a calm place. It made so much sense now. She was my rock. She'd grounded me. Now I'd kidnapped her, and she was pissed at me.

"Jason?" A familiar male voice called from the library. "When did you get here?" Roberto approached and embraced me. The man stood a head shorter than me, graying beard, thick, black-rimmed glasses, custom-tailored Italian suit with silk tie, and a black leather briefcase.

I felt much better. Roberto was one of the few people in my life who was there for me. He and Magda had my back.

I'd met Roberto when Gabriella's grandmother died twenty years before. Gabby and Magda had been best friends, attending the same boarding school in Argentina, and we'd vacationed together, spent holidays together, and our daughters were best friends.

"This morning. I've got some business to attend to." I wasn't sure if Roberto had been aware of my current situation with the money for Caesar.

"Let's talk." Roberto motioned for us to go into his home office.

He knew something. Roberto didn't miss much. I sank into a red leather club chair with a groan. I was exhausted.

He unbuttoned his jacket and leaned on the front of his desk, crossing his arms. "You're in a bind, my friend."

I nodded.

"Magda's trying to help you?"

I nodded again. "I have to see Caesar."

"What are you going to tell him?"

"I'm going to ask for more time to get his money."

Roberto pursed his lips. The man's a genius at problem-solving. He's a planner, a strategist, an analytical master. I cursed myself for not going to him first.

"You're my brother, but I don't want to get involved with Caesar or the CIA." He paced. "What was the money for?" He already knew the answer—this was a test of my loyalty.

"I'm pretty sure the PNM." The People's National Movement. "I delivered a shipment for the Company. They told me it was the last errand for them. They'd leave me alone afterward."

He nodded. Magda *had* told him everything. I never would've gotten him involved on purpose.

When I'd arrived at the house with the bag of money a month ago, I'd told Magda the whole story. She was wonderful about it, no judgment, no scolding, she just got on the phone and before I knew it, we were in a private room at the National Bank of San Salvador loading a large metal box.

Luis had located a field officer back in São Paolo who'd informed him the money should be handed over to a businessman named Caesar Rivera.

Magda and her friend, the bank president, convinced me to keep the cash in a safe deposit box for Caesar to pick up. I'd found out later the "businessman" was an arms dealer whose guns I'd transported to rebels in the jungle. We hadn't told Roberto anything about it at the time.

I thought I'd been doing one last "favor" for the CIA, and then they wouldn't have me arrested for tax evasion back home. But when the fat, sweaty man at the end of a jungle runway handed me two nylon gym bags full of Ben Franklin's sardonic smirk with no further instructions, I called the only person who could help me. My best friend Magda. She'd obviously told Roberto everything. She always did.

Roberto Garcia was a servant to his people. He abhorred the

current leadership's corrupt practices and outwardly criticized them. He would never get involved in whatever craziness I was into. I also knew Roberto couldn't support a coup. He'd obviously heard about the PNM and knew what they were planning.

"Leave me out of this, do you understand?" Roberto snapped at me.

I was trying. I didn't say anything. I just turned to leave then paused. "One more thing. I had to bring someone with me. Caesar's men saw her with me in Vancouver."

"You brought some girl here?" Roberto asked.

"Not just any girl." I went to the bookshelf, found Magda's section, pulled the hardcover from the shelf and handed it to him. "Magda's current favorite author."

Roberto took the book and turned it over then opened the front cover. "You're serious?"

"They're going to the house for a book club with Contessa. They're all big fans." I shrugged.

Roberto threw the book onto his desk and rolled his eyes. *"Esto es un maldito desastre!" This is a fucking disaster.* "Figure this out, and keep me out of it." He pushed past me, picking up his briefcase, and stormed out of the library.

I needed to keep Roberto far from my dealings with Caesar. The man was in line to be the next president if the coup was a success.

The Garcia's were my closest friends and a true power couple. They held influence in many circles, including the local and surrounding governments. Rob and Magda would do everything they could to help me, I knew they would. Magda had told me she could handle Caesar through her friendship with Tessa, and I had to believe her. She'd never lied or deceived me, a true friend. I didn't have many left.

Damn! Now I'd gotten all my people involved and made an even bigger mistake bringing Shelly into this mess.

Seeing her again, being close to her, smelling the same shampoo she'd used all those years ago, flooded me with wonderful memories of her. Memories of her rigid schedules, her salty food, and the smart mouth I wanted to kiss as soon as possible.

Chapter Seven

A road in El Salvador
Shelly

"Magda, I'd like to call my boys and tell them I'm all right. Jason didn't want me to use my cell."

Especially since it's on a highway in Canada.

She handed me her phone. "Dial the country code first. 011 for El Norte."

I called Dylan first, he was in his senior year at Northwestern University. It would be 1:30 PM in Chicago. No answer. I left a message.

"Hi, Honey. I'm in—uh—Mexico for a long weekend to get some rest. Aren't you proud of me for being spontaneous? Okay, the cell service is bad so email me if you need to. Love you."

The identical message was left for Connor at Cal Poly San Luis Obispo, where he was playing baseball.

Oh, the lies. My guilt was sky-high at the deception to the boys and to Rose. At least I'd sent a very short text to her saying I wasn't feeling well. She was sure to have read right through that after seeing Jason in all his silver-fox glory—Kenny probably called the police by now since I wasn't answering my phone and didn't meet him for breakfast. Hopefully Luis would clear everything up with the authorities. He told me he was in 'clean-up' mode as we landed in La Libertad.

Leaning on the door of the big black SUV, I rested my chin on my fist to look out the window.

The highway cut through lush green hills, and I finally got a good look at El Salvador. Fluffy Balsam trees made my nose sting a bit with their strong sweet scent, and flat farmland held perfectly straight rows of whatever they grew on the flatlands. Maybe lettuce? Cucumbers? The familiar scent of the Pacific Ocean relaxed me a bit. It smelled like home. We must be close to the coast.

Magda picked at the cuticles of her acrylics, making her look like a teenager as she nibbled on the edge of a nail and looked out the window. This was just a normal day for her.

Everything since we'd left Vancouver was going so fast. My emotions spun. Now that we were quietly sitting for a while, my head reeled with organization. My thoughts tried to categorize themselves by importance.

I must've been too quiet for Magda.

"You are in deep thought?" Magda asked me. "Would you like to talk, or do you want to think?"

I smiled at her. She looked like Selma Hayek with long, wavy black hair and big brown eyes.

"I want to get out of my head." Nothing was going to make sense. I just had to take a break, or I'd have another panic attack. "Tell me, how are you still friends with Jason after he and Gabriella split up?"

"Eck, I don't talk to her anymore." Magda waved her red claw in the air. "I don't like what she did to Jasmine. It destroyed our friendship. I love Jason—" pronounced "YAY-sone" "—for his dedication to Jasmine—" pronounced "Yaz-MEEN "—and I wanted to help him. She's best friends with my daughter Cassandra. They're in New York together at Columbia."

"That's wonderful." I stared at her. How sophisticated and silly she was at the same time. I already liked her very much and wanted to be her friend.

"So, he's a dedicated father, huh?" I asked my new friend.

"*Si.* When he moved out on his own, he took Jasmine with him. She'd spent her teenage years with him. That was—" She nodded her head. "I helped as much as I could."

"He was a single father?"

I couldn't imagine him having so much responsibility. I don't even remember him having a pair of pants.

"He was all alone raising Jasmine. Although Gabby's mother, Celia, lurked in the shadows just to go against his rules and tell his daughter he didn't know what he was doing. Ugh, that family! Horrible people, all of them."

It was hard to imagine Jason with a teenage daughter—make-up, menstrual cycles, and boys.

"That man is pure love, he is." She scrutinized her long nails. "He wanted to take care of his mother, then spoil his daughter. Did you ever meet his mother?"

I nodded. "She was already sick."

Jason's mother had been recovering from her second round of chemotherapy for cervical cancer when he'd brought me to meet her. She'd sat propped up on a floral couch with throw pillows of various sizes, bundled up in the dark, stuffy room, multiple blankets strewn across her legs, and a knit cap on her head.

"Is this the smart one with all of the fancy words?" she asked him as if I was not there.

"Yeah, Ma. Isn't she pretty, too?" Jason put his arm around my shoulder.

"Very." She became a bit breathless. "So, the Brazilian is out?"

"Uh." Jason paused and looked at me. "Not quite."

His mother scowled at him. She'd not asked us to sit, and Jason didn't offer. We just stood there looking at his thin, pale mother.

"Mrs. Mattis, I noticed the pair of Cuturica-style wedding flasks. Are they Croatian?" I pointed to a shelf in the entry hall.

Her eyes opened wide. "Yes, they are. How nice of you to notice. Jason's dad's parents gave them to us on our wedding day. I was hoping to pass them along soon." She'd scowled at Jason again.

"Someday, Ma," he said.

She threw a small throw pillow at him. "Marry this one before I die, Jason."

Jason's face got dark. "Now we talked about this. You aren't going anywhere. Cut it out."

We sat on the matching lumpy floral loveseat and watched an old movie with his mother, who'd fallen asleep ten minutes into it. We stayed for the duration, and the nurse convinced Jason to carry her to her bed for the night.

We left, and his face turned sallow, distant.

"I need to come back and spend more time with her," he said as we pulled away.

I drove as usual since he did not have a car. "Can you take the year off?"

He was silent for a long time. I didn't press.

We ascended the ceramic-tiled steps of my 1920s duplex in North Huntington. When we entered the apartment, he turned me around and kissed me on the lips.

"Thank you for being you." He kissed me again. "She hates my open relationship with Gabriella. She's never met her but doesn't like her." He pushed my hair back from my face. "She liked you, though."

I wanted to put such a tender moment in a drawer, to pull out and wrap around me like a warm scarf whenever I was cold and missing him. "You didn't answer me about taking time off."

"I can't." He plopped down on my couch with a groan. "If I don't surf, I don't get paid. If I don't get paid, neither do the doctors or the live-in nurse, the rent, or the bills." He waved in a circular motion.

"You pay for everything?"

"No, my dad's a long-distance truck driver. He makes okay money, but his health insurance sucks. When I started making money winning competitions, he wanted to put it all away for college. Then Ma got sick and needed the money for medical bills." He patted the spot beside him, and I sat. "Joining the circuit made enough money to pay for everything. Pop didn't have to be away so much."

"But you do," I said.

"What's done is done." He sat back, looking at the ceiling. "This is just how it is."

He'd made sense, rational and selfless. He loved his mother, worked for her. One of the good guys.

He'd worked through his own illness to make sure his mother had the best care. I admired him so much for that and how Magda gushed what a dedicated father he was with Jasmine. He *was* pure love. He loved the women in his life and took care of them. I was the caretaker to the *men* in my life. The boys, my brother, Eric, and even Jason, for a short time. I suppose we were much alike that way. It had never occurred to me Jason was, at his core, a caretaker. That wasn't what our relationship was about.

"What's going on, Magda? He's in deep with this, isn't he?" I asked.

She didn't speak, staring at me, then shook her head. "No, Shelly. Don't."

"Don't what?"

"I see the wheels turning in your head. You want to do the whole 'Mama will fix everything' thing. Just don't."

I exhaled and slumped in my seat. How did she know me so well already? Maybe she was the same way. Maybe she was an intuitive person like my Aunt Helen who claimed to be psychic. I remembered my aunt calling me once to tell me to get my tires checked. It was weird. I didn't listen, and the next day I got a flat tire on the 73 freeway. I'd never doubted her again.

"Tell me, please. I promise I won't do anything. I just want to know what's going on."

"Fine. About five years ago, a U.S. intelligence agent threatened him with back taxes and jail in El Norte if Jason didn't give him information about his brother-in-law's business. Jasmine had just started living with him full-time, and he didn't want to jeopardize that. So, he did whatever this guy told him to do. A few months ago, the agent told Jason he only had to do one more favor for him and then he'd leave him alone."

"A favor?"

"That's what he called it. Jason had one of his planes fly a shipment here to Salvador up in the mountains. Some guy gave him a bag of money but didn't tell him what to do with it. When he got to my house, Luis got word it was for Caesar."

"Eight million in a bag?"

Magda nodded. "He put it in a safety deposit box at the National Bank in San Salvador. I called the manager, a friend of mine, and asked for the utmost secrecy. He or someone at the bank must have told someone, and now the *federales* are watching the bank. None of Caesar's men will go in to get it."

"Caesar wants his money." There were too many characters, my editor would tell me. This wasn't my book; it was Jason's life. He wasn't a suave action hero. He was a pawn, blackmailed by a rogue CIA agent into working for him.

"He's Jake, isn't he?" she asked with a knowing grin.

I smirked.

"I knew it! You wrote him just right in the book, Shelly. Oh, the romance." She sighed. "I miss it so much. First kisses, butterflies in your stomach, first time making love... We had that when Roberto and I first started out. I was so in love with him. He had a plan. Now it has become something else, like a partnership. I will love him until the end of time. He's my soulmate, but I miss the romance." She stopped and gazed at me. "Jake and Sarah got to fall in love over and over. So romantic."

That had been the common perception of the book by many of my readers The real-life relationship was more regimented. I knew when he'd be coming, when he'd leave, and what to expect—like no sex. No future was discussed. We'd just let it be what it was...until I'd wanted more.

He'd left.

"It's beautiful, you and Jason finding each other again. It's incredible you're here with him. He's been alone so long."

I'm not with him. This isn't a vacation. He kidnapped me, and gangsters are chasing me. The same gangsters who'll be at the house we're heading to for a book club.

"Magda, this whole thing's crazy. You see that, don't you? I haven't seen Jason in over twenty years, and now I'm pulled into his insane world. I'd never known what his life was like. He'd always come into mine. I know why he didn't tell me anything back then. This is all too much for me."

"You are still attracted to him though." She ignored my rant.

"It doesn't matter, it's too crazy for me. All of it."

She paused for a second, staring at me. "Can't you just be open to what happens?"

I opened my mouth but couldn't speak. That wasn't me. I had my routines, my schedules. That worked for my life. In the past ten years, I'd had to learn to take what was thrown at me each day with Eric's illness, and now with my multi-city tour, where I woke up in a different bed every morning for weeks at a time. I'd still make sure to keep familiar things around me, like my hygiene routines with my own soaps and lotions. I'd brought my own coffee and stevia sweetener. I had an app on my phone with ocean waves to help me sleep, and I had a mini diffuser with the scent of calone to mimic the smell of my home on the beach in California even when I was in Canada.

I'd changed since Eric's passing. Therapy helped me accept things I had no control over. Control was a big issue with me. I finally knew who I was and what I was capable of handling whenever life threw curves at me. This was different. This was guns and millions of dollars. I was now in the middle of a possible revolution.

I still had feelings for Jason. The sexual chemistry was so strong.

"Of course I'm still drawn to him."

"That man has so much to give a woman, and he's been restrained for far too long," Magda added. "He's one of my closest friends, and I love him; I want to see him happy."

"Magda," I scoffed, "we're in a serious situation here. I'm not going to think about what's going to happen with Jason and me." I paused and peered up at the back of the men in the front seat with their earpieces and military-style, crew-cut hair. "How dangerous is Caesar? Will he kill Jason? Will he kill me?"

I'd hoped she had some secret plan, or someone did.

"Jason will get the money. Right now, he's not safe and Caesar can be—impatient."

"Can't you do anything? Or your husband?"

"We must keep Roberto out of this. He stands the most to gain when the rebels set their plan in motion, and we can't let it look like he has any connections." She put her hand on mine. "I'll talk to Tessa. That's one of the reasons we need to go today. They all should just leave this to the women. We'll figure something out." She squeezed my hand. "Do you love him?"

Maybe she was trying to calm me down or somehow divert my anxiety by talking about Jason. I rolled my lips inward and shut my eyes. I couldn't answer because I didn't know if I could love any man ever again. They kept leaving me.

"Do you?" She was his friend and was looking out for him.

"Magda, I don't know if I can do this again. Jason has heart problems, and we're getting older. What if he gets sick again? I don't know if I could take it. I've been through so much already with a sick man in my life."

"Excuses." She glared at me with piercing eyes. "You loved your husband?"

"Yes, very much. It was the hardest thing I'd ever had to do getting over him."

"Do you wish you wouldn't have married him?"

"Never. I loved him, I loved my life, I love my boys. I'll never have any regrets."

"So, that is important to you?"

"Not having regrets? Yes."

I'd thought about that a lot. I discussed it with my therapist. I even wrote it into the second book.

"I refuse to leave this world with regrets" was a passage in the last chapter. I repeated it for Magda.

"For me?" she said. "I would let a man love me for as long as we had together rather than push him away and have regrets."

She was right.

"You will end up together. I see it."

Just like Aunt Helen.

I wasn't as sure.

~ * ~

Fortified metal gates opened for our convoy, and a long gravel road curved to the right, flanked by enormous, tall, trumpet-shaped trees with pink flowers. The last curve revealed a striking Antebellum Plantation-style mansion, white Greek columns and all.

Was I in Georgia or Central America? I pictured Scarlett O'Hara sweeping out the front door in her big hat and hoop skirt.

The cars in the curved driveway shocked me back to the 21st century.

A gulp of saliva stuck in my throat.

"You look nervous." Magda turned to me.

"I am," I said. This no-nonsense person appreciated honesty, so I gave it to her.

We exited the car and met on my side.

"My friends are just like any of your other fans. Trust me, they'll be more nervous to meet you. We don't get celebrities in Salvador. This is exciting, you know. We all watched your Spanish interview on Instagram Live with that Chilean podcaster. I want to have a book podcast. What do you think?" Magda babbled. She seemed nervous too.

"You're never bound by your place in life to try something new." She hugged me, pinning my arms. "You're so right."

We crossed the threshold into the high-ceilinged foyer that housed hundreds, maybe thousands of crucifixes. All shapes and sizes, reaching all the way up the walls. Twin grand staircases arched toward each other. At the top, a five-foot cross hung, gold and bejeweled, shining from the skylight.

"They're collectors, huh?" I asked.

Magda gazed at the centerpiece at the top of the stairs. "Caesar's obsessed. He spends his free time tracking down the rarest and most coveted relics. He's flown all over the world to acquire them."

An image popped into my head of a thick, gold, ruby-encrusted crucifix. I'd had to litigate its theft before I left my job to take care of Eric full-time.

The man who'd filed the claim, Juan Morales, was another avid collector of Catholic antiques. He was able to acquire the rarest crucifix in history, the Cross of Castillo. It was said to have, encased within its base, the largest piece of wood from the original crucifix of Jesus himself. The cross was the most elusive and sought-after religious piece, priceless to collectors.

Through my investigation for the insurance company, I was able to track it down for Juan and get it back. His drug-addict nephew, David, had taken it from the study during a family dinner and was not hard to find before he'd sold it on the black market.

Juan was so thankful he'd invited my family to stay with him at his house in Aspen. Our families became good friends. When Dylan graduated high school, he'd spent the summer with the Morales family in Mexico City.

I knew his daughters well. We kept in touch via Facebook. I'd planned to attend Juan's funeral last November, but my book tour schedule was already set.

Ava, Juan's oldest daughter, had never been as enthusiastic about her father's passion for Catholic relics. She might be willing to part with the Cross of Castillo if I asked.

Jason's problem churned in my brain. If I called Ava, maybe she'd give me a special price. I'd have to do it while I was there.

Maybe I could convince Jason to negotiate with Caesar for it to be repayment, or collateral until he got the cash from the bank. The cross was priceless to Juan and any collector.

"Magda!" A tall, skinny woman threw her arms in the air. "You didn't lie to me. It's really her!"

"*Tu perra,*" Magda cursed. "Of course I wasn't lying."

Contessa had the same claw-like nails as Magda. She took the hem of my cardigan. "Ooh, Stella McCartney?" She rolled the fabric between her fingers. "I heard her collection had arrived at the Galleria. I must go later."

Some of my anxiety abated. She was just like the affluent women I knew back in California.

Tessa tucked my arm through hers, grinning as she led us through a hallway under the staircase to an expansive terracotta patio. Two black-and-white-striped umbrellas shaded a round table.

Two women jumped to their feet when we approached.

"Can we speak English, ladies?" Magda asked. "For our special guest?"

They nodded. "Of course."

"Yes, yes." Both smiled, clutching my book.

"I'm delighted, ladies." I pretended to be comfortable in my current bizarro existence.

"You know, M.R." Contessa poured some concoction from a crystal pitcher. "We never get authors to come to our country, even though we have literacy at ninety percent. Same average as in *los Estados Unidos.*" She sipped her drink. "We have reached out to many publishers with no success."

"I'm sorry," I said. "Ninety percent literacy? Impressive."

"We aren't a Banana Republic, you know," she said. "Right, Magda?"

"That's right." Magda's voice was angry. She banged her fist on the table, clanking the glasses. "We're advocates for education and equality."

I nodded. More than just a book club, these were educated, intelligent, and motivated women. I smiled and sipped my drink. "Tell me."

The woman across from me set her glass down. "Our *husbands* may be political rivals, but *our* mission is as clear as this crystal pitcher." She grabbed the handle. Her cluttered charm bracelet tinkled like wind chimes. "Education is the key. Reading is our passion, and we've taken our program to the farms and every rural village for decades. Putting our own safety at risk to do so."

"To our husbands' determent." The tanned, bottle-blonde beside her snorted.

"Security is at our disposal for the rest of our lives, being cabinet members' wives. What are we supposed to do, have them follow us to go shopping?" the first woman asked.

The charms caught the late morning sun, reflecting light onto her peach hoodie. I recognized two of the charms right away—a silver book and a clay volcano.

"Fascinating." I sat back.

"So, can we be characters in your books?" Contessa asked. "Just do not use my real name, eh?"

I laughed. "You are unique, for sure. Please, ladies, call me Shelly."

Tessa's face fell, and her eyes darkened. "So, Shelly, what are you really doing here?"

I shot a look at Magda, who shifted in her chair. Contessa was the wife of a notorious gangster. No doubt she'd be suspicious of my sudden appearance in their small country. It wasn't on the schedule posted on my website.

She knew something was amiss.

"She's with Jason. You know, our *güero* friend?" Magda adjusted her hot pink Lululemon jacket.

The women softened their postures.

"The surfer?" Charm-bracelet woman put her hand to her chest.

"Jason was the inspiration for Jake, wasn't he, Shelly?"

They all gasped.

Contessa's hand slammed the table, making me flinch. "I see it now...the hair, the eyes."

I could've kissed Magda for her diversion.

"I've been waiting to hear the story." Magda winked at me and took several pieces of fruit from a platter in the center of the table.

I chuckled and popped a piece of mango in my mouth. I was starving.

"Yes, please." Contessa sat forward.

"He crashed my book signing in Vancouver, and he was pissed."

"Pissed?" Magda's eyes lit up.

"Yes, he asked why I'd made him a terrorist."

The blonde threw her head back and laughed.

"Wait, Jake's not a terrorist. He's a patriot." The charm woman seemed concerned.

"I wouldn't call him a patriot. He's too selfish for that," I said.

"Agreed," Magda added.

Contessa laughed at that.

I told the women about how we'd met, and a brief history of how he became my Jake. They hung on my every word. Having met the real man and read the book, I withheld most of our sexual relationship, including the recent Mile High Club orgasm. There was enough in the book for them to get the connection between me and the elusive man of my dreams.

After my third glass of the rum-spiked lemonade, I'd asked for the restroom.

"I'll show you." Magda stood.

When we were in the house, she pulled out her cellphone. "Jason's coming here," she whispered. "He just texted me."

"Magda, I have an idea."

She took a small step back and frowned.

"Can you Google the Cross of Castillo?"

She tapped on her phone and then showed me a Wikipedia entry that had several photos and a brief history. "A cross?" Magda knitted her eyebrows.

"I can get it as a stall tactic for Jason, a diversion for Caesar until Jason can get his money. Look." I pointed to the phone screen. "It's priceless to a collector like him. Do you think Caesar would want it?"

"It looks like something he'd want, yes. How much would you have to pay?"

"I need to call the family. Can I use your cell?"

She handed it to me. "You can get it?"

I nodded as I held the phone to my ear and went into the bathroom. "Go back, I don't want them to get suspicious."

She headed back outside.

I closed the door.

"Ava Hill's office, Amy speaking," Juan's daughter's secretary answered.

"Hi, Amy. Michelle Taylor calling for Ava. Is she in?"

"I'm sorry, Mrs. Taylor. She's on vacation and has gone off the grid until Monday."

Just like Ava and her husband to disappear from all society. They had no children nor stressful jobs. They'd done this a few times.

"Will she check in any time? It's urgent."

"Oh, Mrs. Taylor, wait—she's on the other line. I'll tell her you need to speak with her."

"Yes, please." I waited, tapping my fingers on the marble countertop.

"Shelly, how are you? It's been forever." Ava's deep voice was a blessing to my ears.

"Oh honey, I'm sorry if I sound blunt. How much do you want for the cross? I've got someone who *must* have it. I can arrange five-hundred today via wire transfer."

Ava was silent. I don't know where I came up with that number. Jason said he could get a million. I'm a lawyer and like to negotiate. Christies Auction House priced it at two million. To collectors like Juan Morales and Caesar, it was priceless.

"I don't have it. After David tried to steal it, we sent it to my father's estate in Mexico City. My stepmother commissioned a show of his collection at a gallery there for January."

"Would they miss the cross?"

She laughed. "I don't care. My stepmother can go to hell. He left the entire collection to me."

"Can I accompany my buyer? I'm in Mexico for a long weekend to unwind before hitting the road again." *Oh, the lies.*

"It's stuck at the Port of Manzanilla awaiting customs. They've had so many delays I was going to hire a local attorney, but you'd be my first choice."

"I'll do what I can. I've got to get it as soon as possible. My friend is leaving for…uh…London."

"Can you wait until Monday?"

No! It couldn't wait until Monday—five days away.

"Is everything okay, Shelly? You're kind of freaking me out here." Her voice dropped even lower.

"I promise to tell you everything when you get back." I waited. She knew I wasn't a crook or a cheat. If I promised to do whatever I could to get her property released, I would.

"If you want it, it's yours. I hate that thing anyway. Take the damn thing. You can try and talk to the guys at the customs office. You know your way around, and my dad said you're a pit bull with those lazy people."

"I'll make some calls. Have a great vacation. I have to get back to my suntanning."

"Who's this guy with five hundred large in cash?" Her tone turned playful.

"I promised not to say. I met him here on vacation."

"Good for you. Have some fun, Shelly. You deserve it, and *get some.* You know what I mean."

I snorted in protest. *Shel, you're not married.* "Maybe. Miss you, girl. I'll call you when I get back. I should be in Denver with my book in June. Leave a few days open for me, okay?"

"Wouldn't miss it, 'M.R. Taylor.'" She giggled. "Hot book, by the way. Jake Matthews? Ooh baby!"

I needed a plan. I found Jason's number in Magda's phone, sent him a text with the link to the cross, then returned to the book club.

Chapter Eight

Jason

    Magda: I can get this cross. Can you stall Caesar with it until you can get his money? – Shelly.

I read the text twice. Shelly? What was she talking about? I opened the link, and my stomach dropped into my shoe. What was she doing?

She'd worked with antiques for her job. So, she'd know about this. I had to smile. My brilliant Shelly was trying to help me.

I missed her more than ever. Too many years without her confidence and sharp brain. I missed her body. It was different now—so soft. I wanted to grab every part of her and kiss it. She differed from Gabby in so many ways.

I forwarded the message to Luis and waited.

Seeing Shelly for the first time in so many years had stirred some strong emotions I hadn't felt since I'd broken my promise to Gabriella and made love to her. I was also a young, selfish jerk who wanted the glory, the women, and to be free.

I dragged her into this, and instead of just being angry with me, she's trying to help. I needed her to somehow balance my world, and now she's proving that to me.

~ * ~

Luis: *Will Caesar really want that cross?*

Jason: *Shelly thinks so. He has a bunch of these things in his house. I'm staring at them now. There must be hundreds of them.*

Standing in the grand entrance of Caesar's mansion, looking up the walls at the collection of crosses reaching up to the top of the cathedral ceiling, one thing was for sure—Caesar would want the Cross of Castillo.

Luis: *Still working on something here. See if he'll take the damn cross. We're running out of time.*

"Get in here, *Gringo*," a deep voice ordered from a doorway to my left.

I slid my phone in my back pocket and took a deep breath. Women's laughter rolled down the hallway under the curved staircase. *Shelly.* I wanted to grab her and jump on my plane back to California. I wanted to tell her I'd be whatever she wanted me to be, just to stay with her and her stable life. I took a deep breath and entered a dark room. Caesar sat behind the biggest oak desk I'd ever seen, his fingers steepled to his lips.

I sat in a leather chair across from him.

"You play golf?" Caesar sported a collared pink shirt, a white-brimmed cap, and a white glove on his right hand.

"Not very well." More crosses hung behind the man's desk. "Caesar, I'd like to show you something." I leaned forward. Caesar flinched, laying his hand on something hidden from me behind an ornate silver box. I held my phone up to show him it wasn't a weapon and handed it to him across his desk.

The gray-haired gangster donned black-framed readers. Holding the phone a good distance from his face, he appeared more grandfather than criminal. "The Cross of Castillo?"

"It's the most elusive relic of its kind in the world. It's priceless." I recited the Wikipedia description. "I can get it."

"Why?" Caesar handed my phone back and took off his glasses.

"To make up for the money in the bank."

He watched me squirm with an amused expression.

I sank into my chair. Magda had warned me about this chair. As an intimidation technique, Caesar had the springs removed to make the damned thing as awkward and uncomfortable as possible.

"One's cash, that's business. The other's a priceless artifact, that's personal." Glaring, he pursed his lips like he'd come to a decision. "How about you get me both?"

"Caesar..." My nerves frayed. "You said you'd be open to options."

He grunted and crossed his leg, leaning back farther in his big leather chair. "I thought the Cross of Castillo a myth. The largest piece of the original crucifix of the Savior? If it exists, of course I want it." His ice-cold stare sized me up.

Luis had given me the full dossier of Caesar's business empire. It was built on his immeasurable savvy and ability read his adversaries.

He'd worked his way up the ranks, watching and listening rather than showing bravado. He'd read books by Steve Jobs, Richard Branson, and Rupert Murdoch, absorbing big business acumen as well as brute-Mafioso tactics.

I wasn't in the presence of a sociopath. He was one of the great businessmen of the world. My brother-in-law was a common hoodlum compared to Caesar.

"Get me my money, and then get me the cross."

This wasn't how I needed this to go. If only Luis would get back to me about the money at the bank. If only my new handler in São Paolo, Matt Sutter, got word from his CIA bosses I could retrieve the money without screwing us all. Maybe I wouldn't have a heart episode and live to tell Shelly everything.

"Caesar, I'm trying to get your money. Would you be willing to take the cross as payment instead?"

"No, *Gringo*." Caesar smacked his desk.

My insides jumped and my heart thudded. I was a terrible negotiator. I'd never make a deal with this mastermind.

~ * ~

Shelly

"There he is." Contessa slurred and held onto the door as she swung her body into the room. "I know who you are, Jaaaaake!"

The other ladies giggled.

She crossed the room and crawled into Caesar's lap like a cat, hanging onto his neck.

"It's a little early for this, kitten." He wrapped his arms around his wife.

"Did Jason tell you he's famous?" she asked.

Jason raked his hand through his hair.

"For what?" Caesar glared at him.

"Not *him*. He's a character in my friend's book." She raised her head from his chest. "Shelly, come meet *El Jefe*."

He frowned. "Tessa, that name is for just for us."

She purred at him, smiling, and crinkling her nose.

Jason shot me a look of sheer terror as I entered the dark office.

"Papi, this is M.R. Taylor. She wrote that book I read to you. You know, from certain passages. You know the one." Contessa nuzzled Caesar's neck.

"The—" He started, then jumped as his wife fondled him in full view. "Okay, that's enough, Tessa." Clearing his throat, Caesar stood and adjusted his shirt. "So, I have *you* to thank for this, M.R. Taylor." He waved his hand at the blushing and giggling Contessa.

She was drunk. They all were. I was a bit, too. We'd downed two pitchers of whatever that rum drink was.

"I guess I wrote a pretty steamy book. Women our age are at a different point in our lives than men the same age."

Jason shot me another look, this time of shock and embarrassment.

"That's right," Contessa said. "Women reach their sexual peak in their fifties while men peak at eighteen."

"This conversation is inappropriate for mixed company." Caesar extended his hand to shake mine. He didn't seem surprised by his wife's candor.

I laughed. I liked Contessa for her lack of decorum. She was real and honest, rare qualities in women of certain societies.

"Excuse us Caesar." Jason drew me by the elbow into the foyer, past the other ladies and down the hall under the stairs.

I thought he was angry, that he'd yell at me again.

Instead, he pushed me into the bathroom and closed the door, slamming me against it. He cradled my cheeks in his hands and crashed his lips to mine in desperation, sucking my bottom lip into his mouth, then the top.

I saw stars, and my knees buckled.

He buried his face into the crook of my neck. "Thank God you're all right. I want to take you home. I'm so sorry." He held onto me like the ground was shaking, and I was the only thing keeping him from falling.

"Jason, calm down. You'll have an aneurysm."

"I just…" He backed away to sit on the closed toilet.

I turned on the sink faucet, wet a hand towel, and put it on the back of his neck.

My oldest son, Dylan, had had panic attacks in high school about getting into Northwestern, Eric's alma mater. I didn't care about that stuff. Eric did, and he'd put so much pressure on our eldest son, causing the boy's anxiety. Jason was already too far gone for his sexy little Tantric-breathing trick. This warranted a mother's care.

He took my hands and slowed his breathing.

"What did he say to you?" I asked.

Jason looked up at me, those damn eyes, shiny and bright. His pupils dilated, and he squeezed my hands. "Now he wants both the money *and* the cross."

"I can't get it until Monday. I'd need the paperwork from Ava."

His phone buzzed. Jason showed me the text.

Luis: *I got them to call off the watchdogs. Go get the money.*

He sat for a few moments. "I'm okay." His flushed cheeks paled, and he stood to splash water on his face. Taking a few more deep breaths, he drew me into a tight hug. "Okay, let's get the fuck out of here." His demeanor changed. Determination shoved aside frantic anxiety. Time to finish this business with Caesar. He opened the door to find Magda standing there, her arms crossed.

"What are you two doing?" Magda swayed, drunk.

"Get the cars. We're leaving." Jason's newfound confidence was infectious and made him look younger, taller, and stronger. He marched into Caesar's office.

The man swung his gold putter like a pendulum.

"I am going to the city in the morning to get your money. The coast is clear." Jason huffed.

"What about the cross?" Caesar leaned on the golf club and crossed one ankle in front of the other, fist on his hip.

"You're getting your money," Jason said. "Get the cross yourself."

"I don't think so." The man took a few steps closer to Jason and stopped.

I watched in terror from the foyer.

"You get me that cross in twenty-four hours or I will hunt you down like a dog, *Gringo.*"

"Can I go now?" Jason asked through gritted teeth.

The man stepped back and gave a sarcastic bow. "Twenty-four hours."

Jason grabbed my hand and dragged me out to the first SUV. He opened the door as Magda hugged her friends.

"Thank you, Tessa." I waved from the door of the car. "I'll see you tomorrow."

"Bright and early, *amiga,*" she said.

Chapter Nine

Shelly

Magda passed out as we settled for the hour ride back to her house.

"Why are you seeing Contessa tomorrow?" Jason asked from the front seat.

"We're reading to the students at a school near a coffee plantation in the hills." The rum and the kiss combined to produce a euphoric state. Caesar getting his money meant Jason was off the hook, and I could relax a little.

Now we just had to get the cross from the Port of Manzanilla, Mexico, by tomorrow. *No problem.*

"That's an interesting development. Do you want to go read to kids?" he asked. "Are you sure you're up for that? I mean, it's not on your schedule," he said sarcastically.

"It is now." I straightened, proud of myself for going with the flow like Magda and my boys told me to. "These women are incredible. They've taken their money and influence and made sure it wasn't wasted. I respect that." I stared at his luscious pink lips and wanted to kiss him. The moment in the bathroom wasn't enough.

"Five-hundred? That's what you told them, right?"

I nodded. "I can get the paperwork and bank transfer number on Monday."

"You know where it is?"

"The Port of Manzanilla, Mexico."

He handed me his phone. I typed "Port of Manzanilla" and handed it back to him. He studied it. "Contessa's from one of those mountain towns."

"Really? She's not an heiress like Magda?"

"Nope. She was raised on a plantation. Her parents were laborers." He didn't look up from the phone.

"That's amazing." I studied Magda. Her mouth was wide open, and she drooled.

"Are you drunk?" Jason asked.

God he was gorgeous. I shook my head. "A little buzzed." I leaned forward and put my lips to his ear. "From the kiss."

He pulled his ear away and glanced sideways at me.

I pulled back and mouthed, "What?"

"Nothing," he mouthed back, shooting me that mind-blurring smile I'd missed so much. He rested his forehead against mine, stroking my hair for a heartbeat. When he let go, I sat back. He faced the windshield again. That simple gesture, his gentle stroke of my head, heated my body in serenity and emotions I'd not had in many years.

~ * ~

We pulled up to Magda's house in the early afternoon. Jorge, Magda's bodyguard, lifted her out of the car and cradled her as she slept, carrying her into the house.

Jason waited until they were inside. "Get in. We're going to get it."

"What?" I climbed into the passenger's seat.

He peeled the SUV out of the gated drive. "ES-One is fueled up. It'll take two and a half hours to get to Manzanilla. I just got the flight approved with air traffic control. The internet's amazing that way."

"How are we going to get it?"

"You are." He flashed me the smile that made me want to do anything he said. Preferably something that didn't involve clothes.

"*Me?* How?"

"Property seizure, Counselor." He shot me a reassuring glance.

That *would* be the best way to go about it. The customs people at these big ports were overworked and understaffed. Ava had said they'd been delaying her shipment. I knew how to get property released. I was a pit bull, like Ava said, when I'd needed to be with the folks at the ports, and they didn't want to lose their jobs. I knew how to threaten legal action without threatening legal action. It was fun.

"Okay, let me think. I need a story." I tapped my index finger on my bottom lip. "Give me your phone." I'd felt exhilarated, just like when we were running from the thugs in Vancouver.

The act I was about to perpetrate would've gotten me disbarred. Since I hadn't paid my Bar Association dues in ten years, I wasn't going

68

to worry about the repercussions.

The sleek white jet sat like a beacon of hope. We ascended the stairs, and Jason entered the cockpit.

I followed him. "Is the pilot meeting us?"

He sat in the captain's chair and donned the headset.

"You think I've owned a jet company for twenty years and can't fly?" He winked at me. "Go do your thing. I'll do mine."

The sexy pilot had just given me an order, and damn if I didn't feel pulses of arousal for this hot, confident Jason.

It took longer than I'd thought to tap into the server synced to my laptop at home. I accessed my letterhead and composed a letter of intent on the tiny keyboard of Jason's phone. I finished as we descended into Manzanilla.

"How are you feeling about this?" he asked.

"Like, I'm going to either freak out or throw up."

"You got this, Shelly. You've done this whole thing before, right? It was your job."

"Yeah." I sighed. This was illegal on so many levels. Even though I'd been given permission by Ava to go and try to get the cross, swarms of flying monkeys churned my stomach.

Get it together Shelly. "I *have* done this many times," I said with phony confidence.

Showing up at a port demanding release of property was a major part of my former career. I'd visited ports and storage facilities all over the country. I was good at asserting authority.

"What if they don't speak English?" I asked.

"I've got that covered for you."

"Okay, let's do this."

We went to the rental car desk, and Jason flashed the smile and spoke with innocent flirtation to the girl behind the counter in flawless Spanish; she even blushed at one point.

We got into a white sedan and set the GPS. He held my hand from the airport to the port, giving me more comfort than I could've imagined.

We rode in silence, and I tried to predict which scenario was most likely to present itself. The highway looked just like any American city, with industrial buildings on either side tagged with colorful graffiti. The sight of something familiar loosened my tight shoulders.

Sky-high, bright-orange container cranes came into view from the off ramp. They were a good thirty stories up, manned by a single operator who transferred containers off and onto ships. Multicolored containers stacked six to eight high waited to be claimed. Trucks lined up to be loaded or unloaded. All ports looked alike.

The Spanish GPS prompted us to turn onto a gated road. Amidst looming stacked containers stood a small temporary building, like at a construction site. We exited the car and familiarity washed over me. I knew what I was doing. The forged documents were in order. Unless there was some reason on their side to withhold the property, we should be walking out with the cross.

Inside the flimsy building, a small fan blew on one bearded, sweaty man at a metal desk.

"*¿Señor, eres el administrador de aduanas??*" Jason's silken voice made me smile. He was smooth as hell.

"*Si,* I am the manager," he answered in English.

"I'm the attorney for the Morales family. They wish to take possession of their property. I have permission in the form of this document." I showed him the phone. "I'm happy to seek a judge to get an injunction. However, I'm sure we can handle this problem ourselves."

"Problem?" The man gulped.

I employed intimidating legalese to knock the lazy civil servant off his game. "Your department's inefficiency has caused a delay in the release of the family's property." I glared at him. "I'm here to expedite the release."

"Let me see where... The Morales... I'll have to find... It's in the queue for processing. There are several barges... I'll have to..." The man began typing on his keyboard. "Do you have an invoice number?"

"The family was never issued one, *Señor,*" I improvised.

"What was the point of origin?"

I paused. She hadn't told me that. I was sure it would've been from the Port of Los Angeles. "San Pedro, Los Angeles. Three weeks ago."

"Ava Morales was the shipper?"

"Yes."

"Ah, yes." He pointed to the screen. "This property is awaiting customs, *Señora.* I will have to get an agent down here."

"Make it quick." I was panicked by this point. "Can you show me where it is?"

I needed to see the container. I felt that if I had a visual of where the container was, I could argue the speed of the extraction faster.

He came around his desk.

I glanced into Jason's eyes as we followed the customs man out the door. The look he gave me, full of admiration and respect, made me tingle. We climbed into a bright orange golf cart and headed toward the water, stopping by a break wall of large stones that jutted into the bay.

Several flat barges were tethered together, reaching miles out to the horizon.

"That's it—container 6075." He pointed to one solitary barge, a dirty white container atop it, sitting anchored to the south of the harbor with a sandy beach adjacent to its location. It had to be two miles from shore.

I was horrified. The items in that container were worth millions of dollars and it was just floating out there? "How long before an agent can get here?"

"I'll call now." He walked away with his phone.

"Are there locks on those things?" Jason asked.

"If it's out there it won't be secured. They may have already inspected it. Often they don't replace the lock if it's secluded like that."

"I'm going out there. We're running out of time." Jason took off running back the direction we'd just come from.

The man returned to me with a deep frown. "He can't get here for another four hours. If you want to leave a contact number, we can call you when the property is released."

"He's not coming, is he." I crossed my arms and adopted the tone of a teacher catching a student in a fib.

"He said he'd try…"

"I'm getting a judge—"

"No, *Señora*, please."

I peered out at the Pacific and the container that held Jason's freedom from Caesar. "Ask him again."

I could have the man go over the inventory items one-by-one. That would buy Jason time. Depending on how many items were in the container, doing a thorough inventory would take time, especially if the place was as disorganized as it appeared. They could be modern and have a computerized list, or it could just be some random piece of paper that sat in a pile on his desk, in a file cabinet, or… I'd even seen piles of inventory sheets strewn across the floors of these customs offices.

Such disorganization made my stomach churn.

We made our way back to the little building, and I asked for the invoice with an itemized list of the contents of Ava's container. As I'd predicted, he needed to find it. He wasn't sure if it had been imputed into the computer system or if the loose document was around his messy office.

"Call me Shelly." I extended my hand for him to shake.

"Manny."

I cracked my neck like I used to do before I kicked ass in a deposition. "Okay Manny. Let's get to work."

I sat down at the outdated and slow computer and cleared my mind to a place that heated my head. I was with Jason Mattis, in Mexico, trying to save his life from a gangster. The reality of it all was not what my mind was focusing on. My mind was on the young girl who would have given anything to be in a position with him like this, helping him, rescuing him. Maybe I could have freed him from Gabriella's possession if only I'd made more of an effort.

~ * ~

Jason

I named my surfboards after women, like boats. My first one was named for the person who'd bought it for me, my mother Lauretta. I even had Shelly, Michelle, Gabriella, Jaz, and Jasmine.

"Hi, beautiful," I whispered to my old girl as I pulled out the forty-year-old, yellowing, dinged shredder board from the cargo hold of Endless Summer-One. In the back of the jet was a small bedroom with a chest of drawers containing T-shirts, shorts, and underwear. There was one pair of board shorts too.

I changed into them and took Lauretta down to the car, picturing the barge offshore in my head. The paddle out was about two miles. The Zen Shredder could handle that.

GPS routed me to Manzanilla Beach, a world-famous surf spot. The dirt road had big holes. The sedan creaked all the way down, bouncing Lauretta around.

I winced at having to pay damages on a damn rental car. I was already in debt to Caesar for eight million and Ava Morales five hundred thousand for the cross.

The bottom opened on a dirt lot littered with several older cars, dusty and dented. Smoke billowed from a bonfire, and a few young men sat around it. No surfers were left in the water. The afternoon low tide made for bad surf. I bounded into the water. Throwing Lauretta out in front of me, I jumped on to her belly-first and paddled like a machine toward the solitary barge north of the surf spot. I had to get there as fast as possible, then back on the plane to hand that stupid cross to Caesar.

I made it portside of the floating platform. The sun's rays reflected off the calm, rippling water. Climbing onto the barge, I pulled Lauretta by the leash, placing her on the edge of the splintering wood.

Shelly was right. The lock hung open to the side of the latch opening the container door.

The inside smelled of rotten fish and sawdust. Metal and wooden boxes of varying sizes lined the walls of the narrow space.

Fuck. Where to even start? I had no idea where it was or what it looked like.

The first metal box was about three feet high with a rubber top. I peeled it off and moved wood shavings around until I saw the edges of picture frames and pulled one out recognizing a famous Frieda Kahlo painting, the one with the parrots. Impressive. Gabby's mother obviously had a replica. This one looked real.

I replaced the top and wandered around toward the back. On top of a similar container was a smaller metal box. This one was sturdier and thicker. I opened it to find a cedar box with a family crest. The name read Castillo. My breath hitched as I slid the panel open. Inside more wood shavings lay a black-velvet sack. Lifting it from the box I already knew. The outline of a cross was apparent. I pulled the drawstrings apart. An emerald-cut, blood-red ruby caught the light from the open door.

The Cross of Castillo was a foot long and a half-foot wide at the arm tips of the rounded solid gold cross. I held it and bounced it up and down in my palm. It was lighter than I'd thought it would be, even with six quarter-inch rubies mounted to each end. The gold had faded around the base from hundreds of years of palm sweat holding it in praise. A solid gold figure of Jesus hung in effigy on the front, framed by the red jewels. The ornate vision I was holding before me did not disappoint in its garish appearance.

"Wow, this thing is ugly." I put it back into the wood box.

Now to get the hell out of there. I tucked the box under my arm and jumped onto Lauretta.

Once, I'd paddled out to a swim platform in the Ionian Sea off the coast of Greece, about two miles. My shoulders needed a few days to recover. That was ten years ago. Would the adrenaline from this covert mission hold off the pain until we could get back to Magda's? I needed to get back to Shelly.

~ * ~

Shelly

"I'm sorry, *Señora* Taylor. We've been short-staffed, and the security guards' union is on strike."

Manny sat on the floor, surrounded by stacks of papers. I doubted he'd find the invoice before Jason got back. I focused on my task to find anything in the computer to justify my acquisition of the property. Who was I kidding? We were flat-out stealing the Cross of Castillo.

"I'm getting closer—here are the ones from this month." He grinned.

"If I find the exit documents from San Pedro, we can use them." I exhaled, exasperated by the incompetence. The lazy disorganization of these customs managers spanned the world. It was a wonder anything got to their destination.

"Here it is." I sent it to the printer.

Manny stood with a groan and yanked up his pants.

I pulled the document off the printer. The Cross of Castillo was valued at two million dollars. That seemed a gross undervalue for such a cherished piece. Who was I to argue with Christies? They knew their business.

An original Salvador Dali, a signed Picasso, and a Frieda Kahlo were also listed with much higher values. The Picasso alone was valued at three million.

"These are some expensive things," Manny said over my shoulder. I noticed his putrid body odor for the first time. "I don't know why it was put so far out by itself. With the security officers on strike, it would have been safer here on the shore."

I turned to him with a scowl. "This is unacceptable. Ava Morales will have someone's head."

"Whose head would that be?" A tall, dark man in a black uniform radiated an authoritarian arrogance that wafted into the already stuffy room. I shuddered at his nefarious stature. He reminded me of the villain from Romancing the Stone, mustache and all. A cold wave of fear crawled up my spine and landed in my throat.

"Agent Nogales, this is the attorney I told you about, *Señora* Taylor," Manny's voice shook.

Something wasn't right. "Agent Nogales." I extended my hand. The new arrival towered over me. "I've been instructed to take possession of my client's property. I'll need the container brought to shore and processed."

"As you can see, *Señora*, it is after five and the crane operators have gone home." The man put his hands in his pants pocket, revealing the full gun belt resting high on his waist.

"I can do it. I started as a crane operator when I was eighteen." Sweat dripped into Manny's eyes. He wiped it away with a big smile.

"Great, then I won't have to charge you after hours for the court order." I locked my knees and raised my chin, defying the fear.

"Okay, I'll go." Manny ran out of the office, leaving me alone with the Colonel Zolo character. The only thing missing was a cigar for effect. He chomped on gum instead, glaring at me.

"Whelp." I waved my arms. "I guess we just wait, then."

"There was a man with you. I saw him on the security cameras. Where did he go?"

A stomach-twisting gag reflex hit the back of my throat. "He had to return the rental car."

He drew his gun and pointed it at me. "*Señora*, we haven't verified the inventory of that container yet. If your friend got to it, that would be most unfortunate...and illegal."

"Verify the inventory?" I scoffed. "You're going to rob it."

"Let's go." He grabbed my elbow and dragged me out of the building toward the break wall.

We arrived just in time to see Jason paddling out from the beach.

"Oh shit." I gasped.

He yanked me around to face him and clenched his jaw. "Illegal, *Señora*." He spat out his gum and hauled me back to his car.

I was dizzy and nauseous. I'd never seen a real gun, let alone one pointed at me.

"Get in." He pushed me into the driver's side. I climbed over to the passenger seat. He held the gun on me, locked the door from his side, and threw the car into gear. Screeching tires and the smell of burnt rubber followed.

"You *gringos* are not leaving here alive with that cross." He sneered.

"What cross?" Attempting Jason's breathing technique, I couldn't remember if it was in through the mouth or out through the nose. I just gave up and breathed.

"*¡Cállate!*" He shook his head and spittle flew from his mouth.

We pulled onto a service road then down a bumpy dirt road down toward the beach. I held onto the bar above the door, and he put the gun into the side panel of his car door. *Thank goodness.*

Our rental sat alone at the bottom of the clearing. Jason paddled back toward shore.

Oh God, this is getting out of control.

Nogales got out, took his gun, and waved it for me to get out over his seat again. My shoelace caught on something. I flopped halfway out the door, my hands bracing against the ground. Gravel scraped my palms. The impact of my chest hitting the edge of the car seat knocked the wind out of me, and for a second, everything went black.

"Get up!" Nogales shouted as I came to.

Still dizzy, I pushed myself up, released my shoe from the gearshift, then tumbled to the ground.

He pulled me up then yanked me down to the sand. Jason, surfboard tucked under one arm and a wood box under the other, froze at the tall customs agent holding a gun to me then turned it on him.

He gripped my elbow. I distanced myself as much as possible.

"Hand it over, *Gringo*," Nogales ordered Jason.

I met Jason's eyes, pleading with to him not to do anything

stupid.

He stood frozen, staring at me.

Pop. Something whizzed between me and Nogales. He dropped my arm.

"Run, Shelly!" Jason shouted over another two. *Pop, pop.*

Nogales turned toward the noise and shot back.

Jason and I ducked behind the surfboard and ran for the car. I lunged to the passenger's seat and tucked my head between my knees. He threw his surfboard in the back and the box between us then he jumped into the driver's seat. We peeled away up the dirt road, flying over the potholes. I grabbed under the seat with my cheek pressed my thighs.

Crash!

Glass shattered. I gasped. The bumping stopped as we made it back onto the asphalt road.

I peeked at Jason. He clutched the steering wheel, his knuckles white, total focus on his face. His jaw twitched, and he bared his teeth.

"What was the glass shattering?" I sat up and looked behind us.

"The side mirror. Fuck Shelly, they were shooting at us!" He took a deep breath.

"Who was shooting?" I asked.

He exhaled. "I don't know. Don't you? Who was that guy?"

"The customs agent."

"*The customs agent?*" He peered at me. "Jesus, are you all right?"

I nodded. "Are you? How's your heart?" I put my hand on his chest.

"It's a little tough right now."

"Need me to drive?"

"No, we're here."

We pulled up to ES-One. I trotted up the stairs and straight to the cockpit with the box. Jason was hot on my heels with his surfboard. He called the tower, and we were cleared as soon as the engine roared to life. I panicked, desperate to flee Mexico. As soon as we were airborne, I'd feel better.

"You're not hurt?" Jason stared at the setting sun as we awaited final clearance. His face glowed orange, and his eyes looked like clear water.

I studied my dirty and scraped palms. "I'm fine. Who could possibly know we have the cross besides the customs agent?"

"Maybe it has a tracking device?" Jason asked as we surged forward for takeoff.

"Ava didn't mention one. It would make sense, since her crazy cousin, David, stole it." I opened the box and removed the cross from the velvet sack, searching it for chip or sticker with a GPS code. With lack of good lighting from the setting sun, I couldn't find anything. "I'll have to look harder when we get in the air. I don't see anything now."

A tracking device could be as simple as a fingernail-sized sticker with a microchip you could buy in bulk from Amazon and sync to an app on your phone. I'd have to examine the cross, the velvet sack, and the box.

My stomach lurched as the jet's wheels left the ground, and my body pressed into the seat. As soon as we got into the sky and leveled out, my adrenaline faded. Not eating, lack of sleep, and a slight hangover from the rum drinks at Tessa's was making me tired and cranky. "I'll be so glad when this is over."

Did I want it to be over? Would I just go back to my life and Jason to his? Somehow Magda's words seemed more important. She said she'd take the chance to be with a man for as long as they had together. No regrets. I wanted him, in *my* life, not his. It was the same problem we'd had before.

"Shel, can you please get us some food from the galley? I'm starving."

He'd asked so sweetly; I would've made him a five-course dinner if he'd wanted.

"Yes, let's eat something." I made my way back to where I'd seen Jason pull containers out when we were en route to El Salvador the first time.

"Only burritos left," I called.

"Cool. I'll have two."

I placed three containers in the microwave drawer and set the timer. I washed my hands in the sink and pulled a pebble out of my skin. While waiting for the food, I wandered around the cabin. A few framed pictures hung on the wall. One was a magazine clipping of Jason holding a huge trophy. His messy brown hair and thousand-watt smile made me happy, seeing the boy I used to know.

Next to it was of Farrell's Ice Cream Parlor, not a photo. The familiar front of the menu with its Victorian façade and red-and-white-striped awnings—*the* place to have your birthday as a kid in Huntington. The famous Pig's Trough Sundae was a staple for the birthday boy or girl. Your hands were tied behind your back, and you had to get to the bottom without using a spoon. You'd receive a ribbon that read "I made a Pig of myself at Farrell's" if you got to the bottom. I must've had at least four birthdays there.

I pulled the frame off the wall, retrieved the containers from the microwave, and headed back to the cockpit.

"Farrell's?" I turned the frame toward him then placed the two steaming containers on the dashboard.

He released the yoke to open one of the containers, inhaling the tortilla. "I loved that place. We'd go for my birthday, my mom's, and even my dad's." He smiled and talked with his mouth full.

"Did you do the Pig's Trough? That was my favorite." I took a big bite. The innards burned my tongue. I was too hungry to care.

"Are you kidding? No way. It was all about the "The Zoo," the one with the sparklers. They would beat the big snare drum when you finished it. Awesome." His Southern California surfer-dude accent emerged for the first time. "Do you remember an old waiter named Charles? He had a handlebar mustache?" Jason spoke with is mouth full of burrito.

"I do remember him. His name was Charles?"

"He was my dad's cousin. He made sure I had extra sparklers on my Zoo." He grinned and turned toward the windshield.

"Can I open this?" I asked about the frame.

"Yeah."

I opened the picture frame and extracted the old menu.

Jason wolfed his two burritos, rose from the captain's chair, then headed for the back of the plane. "Time to change out of these wet trunks."

I stayed in my seat and perused the old menu. "I always got the spaghetti with meatballs. I never ate it all—tried to save room for the ice cream."

"Did you get the jawbreakers in the candy shop?" he called back from somewhere.

"Until I got braces." I giggled.

He returned, looking sexy in T-shirt and cargo shorts. I diverted my gaze back to the menu and turned the page to see a photo of the man with the handlebar mustache. "Oh my gosh! It's Charles!" I held up the image.

"Yeah, he was a great guy. When his kids moved away and he retired, he started there. All the kids loved him."

"What did he do before he retired?"

"He owned The Spaghetti Bender in Newport."

I widened my eyes. "No way!"

"What?" he asked.

"My dad loved that place! That was him?"

"Yeah." He chuckled. "Although we went there so many times,

I can't eat lasagna anymore."

I sat back and sighed. Talking with Jason was so easy, and it was wonderful having memories with someone who'd grown up in the same town as I did. He looked sad again, just like when we had drinks in Vancouver.

"I have to tell you, Shelly, I'm pretty homesick. It's been over twenty years since I've been back."

I sat sideways in the copilot's chair with my legs tucked up to my chest and stared at him. Waves of love surged, powerful and familiar once upon a time, only to be torn away like the receding ocean tide. He didn't belong to me. I could pretend all I wanted. I was a battered seashell tumbling with the ebb and flow.

Now his warmth bathed me. We had so much more than just post-adolescent lust. We were good friends who'd connected on many levels. Jason was so much smarter than he appeared. I wasn't the only one who knew that. It appeared that Magda also acknowledged he was so much more than some dumb surfer. I wanted to talk for hours with him about old things and new things. What book was he reading right now? Had I read it?

"What's going on in that big brain of yours?"

He knew when I had something to say.

"I was so in love with you," I confessed in a moment of enlightened honesty. I'd learned to say what you want to say because you might not get another chance.

He glanced over to me. "You never told me."

I sighed. "I couldn't."

He lowered his head. He knew I hadn't wanted to cross the line where he'd stop coming to see me. When he spoke, it was a whisper. "That last night we were together, I was ready to throw it all away and stay with you."

My insides crashed into my feet, blood, bones, nerves—all of it.

"I was ready to quit the tour, take some office job and be what I thought you wanted," he continued, his voice low and cracking.

I was so confused. He'd left me without a word. Even though I knew I had to let him go, hearing his words brought me to the verge of tears. He and I would not have worked back then, no matter what he'd said now.

"I *never* would have let you do that."

I wouldn't ever make him quit his life for me. He didn't only belong to Gabriella, he belonged to the sport of surfing and the fans all over the world. It would have been selfish to make him give all that up.

"I know you wouldn't have." His eyes focused on mine; he

extended his hand to me. "Come here."

Feeling that old magnetic pull, I took his hand and sat sideways on his lap.

"It's different now. All of that is done with. I burned those bridges long ago." He wrapped his arms around me and put his head on my shoulder. "We can be together now. I want to be with you. I'll build the fucking thing out of steel, so it'll never burn down."

Nodding, I didn't even realize I was crying until I caught my breath. I believed him.

He pulled his head back and gazed up at me, that look I'd only seen from him once. The look when he gave in and made love to me, the one I had in my subconscious for so many years, full of emotion. I had to kiss him, claim him, make sure this wasn't just some young girl's fantasy.

Taking his strong jaw in my hands I tilted his lips up to mine and touched. It wasn't enough and, in an instant, we were plunging our tongues inside each other's mouths and pressing our chests together in desperation.

Beep, beep, beep

We broke apart. My heart stuttered at the blinking red light on the control panel.

"It's just the alert for the landing gear." He smiled then held my cheeks in his warm hands. "To be continued."

I returned to the co-captain's seat and strapped in for landing, wiping my eyes. "You know, watching you fly this plane is all kinds of sexy."

"Oh yeah?" He focused on the windshield and fiddled with a switch on the control panel. "Watching you in all of your 'I don't want to have to get the judge' action was really freaking hot, too."

We both laughed.

Our confessions made me forget all about the Cross of Castillo and whoever was shooting at us—and the tracking device.

Chapter Ten

Shelly

Magda's house was dark when we pulled up. The only light on was in a room to the left with the door cracked.

"Rob?" Jason called and opened the door. "Hey." He motioned for me to join him, placing the box against the wall.

I stepped behind Jason as he entered the classic, dark mahogany library. Floor-to-ceiling bookshelves, a leather-trimmed desk, two red leather, winged-back chairs anchoring a coffee table, and a matching leather sofa skimming the right bookcase wall. I blinked, awash with love and admiration for the true reader who owned the space.

"Roberto, this is Michelle Taylor." Jason nudged me closer to the man.

"Shelly," I corrected him.

Intelligence, calm, and justified pride mixed with an indescribable magnetism embraced me just as his space did. This was no ordinary man. He was a leader, a silent and strong presence. Regal.

I bowed as he shook my hand.

Both men laughed at me.

Cheeks burning, I rose.

"Come, sit." He waved us toward the sofa.

"I apologize. I don't know what that reaction was." I perched next to Jason on the couch.

"I've gotten that reaction my entire life," Roberto confessed.

"Since you were a boy?"

"Since birth."

When we were all seated, I got a good look at him. Dark slate eyes, full of empathy and intuition, bored into me. His gaze should have unnerved me. It didn't. It made me curious.

"Why?" I asked. "I mean, you're obviously aware of it. Do you know why?"

"No, I do not. My mother told me it may be because of a *divino*, as she'd called it. She told me I had a responsibility to make sure I used it to help others and never let my ego get in the way."

"So, you went into politics?" I scoffed.

He laughed. "Civil service. *Politics* are for the ego." He held his slim finger in the air.

I shook my head, thinking. He was a man, not divine.

"What do you do with your ego then?" I asked. "You must want *something*."

"Shelly, that's not..." Jason bumped my knee, and I glared at him.

Roberto leaned forward and rested his elbows on his knees. "No, it's all right." His eyes shone. "I read a bit of your book. You have a gift for reading people, their wants and fears. Your characters, how they interact, are so specific and defined. It makes me believe I know you already and all your unique contradictions."

I sat back, prepping myself for a good exchange of wit. It had been too long since I'd had an exhilarating battle. Sparring with my professors in law school about proof and gut feelings was my favorite sport. "Hmm, interesting." I liked my contradictions, being a blonde California Girl was a superpower I'd relished. People underestimated my intelligence. Studying people offered many perspectives and using said knowledge of them gained me an upper hand—useful when practicing law.

"I know nothing about you." That wasn't true. I knew what kind of man he was. Thanks to the remnants of the rum, the adrenaline of being held at gunpoint and then shot at, and the confessions Jason and I had made to each other, I felt empowered. It had been a long time since I had engaged in a tit-for-tat with another academic who could challenge me. I was digging it.

"I think you do, Michelle." He grinned like the Cheshire Cat, pulling that cord in me to fire up my skills and debate my conclusions.

"Okay, let's see—" I said.

"This should be interesting." Jason crossed his left ankle over his right knee.

"—I think you want to be President. Not for you, for the people. Your hard-working family never left their village, sacrificing everything to ensure you had the best education possible to grow your *divino*, or *whatever*, and ensure the world saw it, too. In your studies, far from your family, every person you met recognized your light with little effort on your part, validating you." I leaned forward, mirroring him. "How am I doing so far?"

He sat up, laughed, and clapped his hands.

"Full-ride scholarships, I assume. Where did you go to school, Harvard?"

"Oxford." He didn't argue my assumptions. "And, you, M.R. Taylor, have crawled out of your darkness to reveal a butterfly, eh?" He squinted at me. "But the butterfly doesn't have the colorful wings you thought she should have."

A boulder dropped in my stomach. Were my insecurities about my age and appearance so apparent?

Roberto approached to sit on the edge of the coffee table, so our knees touched. His power covered me like a blanket. "A butterfly is a beautiful creature, M. R. Taylor—worshipped, honorable, determined, and stunning in any color."

My jaw dropped for the second time that day. I'd felt justified, strong, and beautiful. He wasn't flirting with me. He filled me with the confidence I needed—the confidence eluding me. "Damn. Maybe you *are* divine."

"No." He returned to his desk. "I assure you, I'm just a man. Dinner is at nine. We're having Mariscada. It's like Cioppino with lemon and cilantro. Our chef is excellent. If Magda was at her book club, she'll need it. The soup combats hangovers." He chuckled.

Roberto loved his wife. All evidence pointed to a deep affection and familiarity only a long relationship could cultivate. Like the bougainvillea that grew on the outer walls of their house, covering the structure, protecting it year after year with vibrant color and strong vines. She was a lucky woman.

"Thank you," I said.

He peered at me in confusion. "For what?"

"For having me in your home." I unconsciously bowed again.

"Shel…" Jason pulled me out the door. When we were alone, he brushed the hair from my face and tucked it behind my ear. "Have you recovered from your *tocado por dios*?"

"What's that?"

"Touch of god."

I scoffed. "Will he be President after the coup?"

"Who knows?" He cupped my face with his soft hands, gazing into my eyes, and in that moment, Roberto, Caesar, Magda, Contessa all disappeared.

His desire matched my own. Even though I was exhausted and every muscle in my body hurt now the adrenaline had abated, there was so much anticipation in his face I experienced a new energy source.

"What are you waiting for?" I asked him.

He took my hand and led me up the stairs. At my door, he stopped and faced me. "Just know I will never be able let you go again if we do this."

"Promise?"

He opened the door and led me in. No lights, we stood in the dark. His silhouette came into focus after my eyes had adjusted. A crack of light streamed in from the velvet drapes.

"How do you want it?" he whispered, and he put his arms around my waist. "Hard and fast, or slow and agonizing?"

"Shut up and strip." I tugged the hem of his shirt upward.

"Are you sure you're not still drunk?" he asked as he pulled his T-shirt over his head. "Because I don't want to take advantage."

"We have dinner in two hours in the house of a man who claims to be 'divine.' I'm still a little buzzed on rum from a book club meeting at the residence of an arms dealer in El-Fucking-Salvador, we just stole the most elusive antique crucifix in history, got shot at, and I'm making the biggest mistake of my life opening myself up to you again, so before I come to my senses, just get me naked."

He leaned in, sucked my bottom lip, and stripped our clothes off so fast, I didn't realize it until we were both bare.

I stopped him with my hands on his chest, needing to slow down and appreciate his beauty. His body differed from what I remembered. His shoulders and arms were still broad and muscular, and his chest had a light dusting of short-cropped hair, silver, and light brown. The abdominal ripples were gone, and his torso was more solid, still without an ounce of fat or flab. He was more beautiful now than when he was a boy—strong, aged like a limited-edition cognac, smooth, and sweet. Dizzy, I drank him in.

I touched my lips to his chest, and he shuddered. I'd had visions of us together over the years, the memories morphing into scenes of a movie I wasn't sure were real. I'd seen them from an outside camera angle and not in the moment, making me think he was just fantasy I'd invented about a rock star or some another unattainable man I couldn't have possibly touched, kissed, or made love to.

"I've been dreaming about this," he whispered.

"About being with me?"

Jason nodded and threaded his hand through my hair at the back of my head and pulled me to his lips. "I can't believe you're here with me."

My breath hitched in an inward gasp. "Are you real?" I pinched the skin on his shoulder.

He chuckled, wrapped his arms around me and backed me up to the bed. He bent forward and grabbed my thighs out from under me.

I fell back on the red velvet duvet with a giggle. I grabbed a handful, bracing myself for the "Jason treatment" I knew was coming.

He kissed and nipped at my inner thigh, his thumb stroked my folds, and he lingered on an exhale, sending a puff of heat to my core. "I've been thinking about *this*. For a long time." He exhaled as he spoke.

He touched inside me with the tip of his tongue, caressing a spot that made my body shudder and my legs tingle. I arched off the bed and grabbed his hair. He was slow and seductive, opening my thighs wider. I looked down to see his pink tongue give me one long, slow, flat-tongued lick, stopping at my clitoris, which he circled with the tip again. I gasped, and bursts of light exploded behind my eyes.

He traced my labia with two fingers to spread my wetness into my hole and entered with the curl of his knuckles. My body heated and tingled.

When he leaned in again, I looked down at him. He stopped, glanced up at me, and grinned as he opened his lips, surrounded my clit, and sucked. My head fell back, and my eyes shut; a light pierced me behind my closed eyelids as heat rushed through me and inflamed every nerve ending, followed by fireworks I'd felt everywhere.

"Jay-son!" I moaned. "Oh god!" Heat flushed through me. It had been so long. I almost cried at the exquisite feeling of his focus on my pleasure.

Still smiling, he climbed on top of me. His lips and stubbled chin wet with my juices, he licked from my collarbone down to my right breast, cupping it and pulling it up from its slouching position on my side.

"Oh, Venus and Neptune," Jason sighed to my breasts.

"What?" I chuckled, lifting my head to see his serious face.

"Don't you remember I named them?"

A sliver of a memory came to me, and I laughed. "Oh my god."

"Oh girls, I missed you. Oh yes, and you're much bigger now." He fondled and kissed each one, repeating the tongue tip treatment that had just sent me flying. Caressing my right nipple until it hardened, he held it in his teeth and tugged. He rubbed my left breast, circling my areola. He squeezed my breasts together and nibbled one nipple then the other.

I wanted my breasts to be the perky vixens they used to be. He seemed unfazed by their post-breastfeeding state. He improvised by holding them in place on my chest where they were supposed to be and worshipped them. My butterfly wings blushed with vibrant color from the attention.

He rolled me on top of him and put his arms above his head as I straddled him.

"Ravage me, Shelly." He smiled.

I laughed. "Gladly."

Sex was fun with Jason Mattis. He'd switch in an instant from teasing to focused.

I took hold of him, rubbing the tip up and back. He grabbed onto the bolsters of the headboard, and I pulled his beautiful hard cock vertical and lowered myself onto it. I needed to stretch more often, because a sudden, sharp pain shot up my right hip from the kneeling position I was in.

"Ouch!" I grabbed my hip. "Fuck, I'm old."

"Oh no." He sat up. "Are you all right?"

I rolled off him and rubbed my sore joint.

"Yeah, it's just that position." I winced.

"I got this." He jumped off the bed, then took my ankles and yanked me to the side of the bed, spread my legs and wrapped them around his hips.

"You lay there and let the doctor make you forget about your pain, baby."

"Leave 'baby' out of this." I huffed as he entered me, kissing and nipping my neck. "Oh!" I gasped in ecstasy.

Inching inside, then jerking back and forward again, deeper into me. It felt so good, I thought I'd faint.

"Oh Shelly, you're going to take all of me." He pushed all the way inside me, hitting a spot that bucked my hips. He was much bigger than Eric. His penetration shot heat up my thighs and back to where our bodies joined.

I yelped. He'd hit my G-spot. I gasped and clawed his back.

"Hold on, hold on. Don't come yet." He panted. "Oh, you feel so good." His voice hitched, and his breath shook as he plunged, his hips moving up and down, hitting my clit and G-spot at the same time.

"Please! Please!" I needed more friction.

He started pumping harder and faster, pressing his lips to mine as his hips thrust, blinding me with a burst of light brighter than the sun. His face was the same in his orgasm as the boy I used to know. Here was the man reminding me I was still sexy and beautiful. My explosion came at the same time his did, and we shouted each other's names. He collapsed, panting, on top of me, his body on fire and wet with sweat, a hot weighted blanket giving me security.

"I'm never leaving you again." He buried his face into the crook of my neck. "I promise, I promise."

There it was. The promise I'd been waiting a lifetime for. I believed he was going to keep it. "Good." I squeezed him tighter with my arms and my legs, trapping him. "You aren't leaving this spot right now."

His body jiggled with laughter. "I don't think my legs can move anyway. Ow, shit! My arms. I paddled for miles with that damn cross on the nose of my board."

Aside from his body being sore, I was more concerned with his heart. That amazing sex was intense. My heart was thumping. "Are you going to be okay?" I put my hand on his chest.

His heart pounded then fluttered.

I gasped.

"I'm great." He smiled. We were motionless except for our heavy breathing. He was still inside me, and we gazed at each other with appreciation and an intimacy I'd never had with another human being. No words needed.

My bottom hung off the side of the bed, my legs wrapped around him. He struggled to stand and groaned.

"Yeah, I think I *need* help." He propped himself up on his shaky arms on either side of my head, leaned down, and pecked my lips. "You're amazing, you sexy thing."

I'm pretty sure my fifty-two-year-old cheeks blushed.

He bent his knees and caught my thighs from falling off the edge of the bed, lowering them until my feet touched the floor, a silly grin on his spectacular face.

"That was fun," he said. "You need the bathroom first?"

It felt like we had been together for years in sexual bliss. Knowing each other's bodies, desires, trigger points, and after-sex habits.

I nodded and padded my way into the en suite, pulled a few tissues from a box and folded them. I went back to hear him grunting to get onto the bed and handed them to him as he lay down on his back.

"Thanks." He wiped his soaked, soft cock.

"Here." I put my hand out and he handed them back to me.

After I cleaned myself up in the bathroom I returned to the bed and climbed back on top of him. He wrapped his arms around me, and we took one long deep breath together.

"This is good," he said. "This is right."

"It sure feels that way," I answered. We fit into each other, naked, sated, belonging and happy. We'd fallen asleep after he set an alarm for one hour.

~ * ~

"Has it really been twenty-five years since you've seen each other?" Roberto asked as he used a tiny fork to extract a mussel from its shell.

Mariscada *was* better than Cioppino, the cilantro and lime an exquisite mix, the shellfish so fresh it had no briny smell, only a salty, lime flavor. I wanted to recreate the recipe back home.

Jason turned to me, grinning like we shared a secret. I hadn't stopped smiling since we'd come down to dinner. There was no hiding what we'd just done. Magda and Rob ignored our flushed cheeks and sexed essence.

"Uh, about that. Right?" I answered, not taking my gaze from the most beautiful man in the world who'd just promised to never leave me again.

He nodded and took my hand, rubbing his thumb over my knuckles.

"I met Shelly thirty years ago. She was my hometown girl and the smartest I'd ever met—"

"You were already with Gabriella," Magda interjected, extracting a clam from its shell. It was not accusatory, just matter of fact.

I pulled my hand away from Jason and adjusted the napkin on my lap at the mention of Gabby. I was the other woman all that time—one of many.

"You know we had an open relationship, Magda." He sounded offended.

She looked up from her bowl. "She let everyone in her life know where they stood, eh?"

I sat up, hoping she'd elaborate.

Her eyes met mine. "Shelly, just so you know, Gabby was excellent at giving people orders. She was so good at it you'd think she'd had the answers of how you should live your life. Isn't that right, Jason?"

"I thought she *did* have all of the answers, for a long time." He shrugged, his confession so honest and raw I felt his pain.

That was their relationship. She'd manipulated him for years, and he just did whatever she'd told him to. Magda wanted me to know. Was this the best way to tell me?

"You and Jaz are so much better off without her." Magda went back to her food. Roberto and I glanced at each other in discomfort, and we all ate in silence for a long time.

"So, where is this village we are going to tomorrow?" I asked, breaking the silence.

Magda told me about the school and the programs her book-club ladies had started.

I wasn't listening. I put my hand on Jason's thigh and rubbed. He looked at his lap then side-eyed me. My hand made its way between his legs, and I leaned forward on the table with my chin on my palm to hide what my other one was doing. I was on some psychotic mission to prove myself better than Gabriella. Something I should have done many years ago. The battle for Jason should have been launched long ago, and I had a crazy need to be the better lover in Jason's mind.

Jason showed little emotion as I palmed his growing erection through his jeans. He just smiled and wiped his lips with his napkin.

His hand found my thigh and he stroked his thumb over my crotch sending tingles over my entire lower half.

The cook went to Magda, interrupting her story, and asked if we wanted dessert or after-dinner drinks.

"We have the cheesecake Cassie sent us from New York I've been dreaming about." Magda's face lit up at the mention of it.

"Great." I said, trying to stay engaged in the dinner conversation as I continued my assault on Jason under the table.

"With fresh strawberries?" she asked the cook. "*Gracias*, Lina." The cook took her bowl and Roberto's into the kitchen, Magda stood and took our bowls and followed her. Roberto picked up his phone and looked like he was reading an email or text.

"Jason, can you show me where the bathroom is?" I asked.

He jumped out of his seat and took my hand. "This way."

As soon as we were in a hallway, he pulled me into a sparse room with only a twin bed, a servant's quarters that was unoccupied.

"Jesus, Shelly," he whispered and pushed his hands down the back of my pants, grabbing my bare ass and pressing my body to his.

"I'm a better lover than Gabriella, right? Admit it."

He kissed my neck and fondled my ass cheeks. "You are."

"You realized this when?"

He pulled away. I had taken our flirtatious tryst and made it serious.

He hesitated. "I—don't want to relive any of that. "

"When, Jason?" I needed to know what I was to him back then. Was I just another girl in his travels? If I was, why did he come find me now? What kind of hold did Gabriella have on him? Was it her money? Her beauty? Her fame? Why didn't I fight for him?

"Tell me about Gabriella." Did I want to know?

He shrugged. "We've been together since we were seventeen. She travels, I travel, and we meet up twice a year for a month to chill at her family's house in Leblon. That's a rich area. Her family has a lot of money. I've been with her for a long time."

"But what's she like?"

"I don't know." He shrugged. "She's a model—beautiful and she knows it. She knows how we're supposed to..." He cupped my face, touching his nose to mine. "I don't want to talk about her. I want to be with you right now."

What was the deal? What hold did she have on him?

"She's got one of those big Brazilian booties, right?" I rose to attempt a dance, sticking my backside out. Yes, a joke and a distraction.

"Jesus, you're an awful dancer." He drew me onto his lap. "Your mouth, though—" he touched my lips, "—your mouth is awesome. I want to hear what it has to say, kiss it and suck on it. I want to watch you suck on me." He growled.

Guilt overtook me at that moment. Our time together had been in its third year, and my life was changing.

"I kind of have a boyfriend right now,"

"What? You're just telling me now?" He stared at me, betrayal in his eyes.

"Yes, I'm telling you now." Anger and frustration swelled at his reaction. "You have no right to give me that look. You're still with Gabriella."

His mouth opened and closed.

"Don't tell me that's different," I scolded.

"I won't," he said in defeat. "Did you tell him about me?"

"God no," I answered, surprised he'd even ask that question. I hadn't told many people about our affair because of its non-traditional nature, and I didn't want small-minded people thinking of me as a desperate groupie or harlot. My parents thought we were just friends. We were friends. Sometimes it felt like he was my best friend. I told him everything, except how I'd felt about him.

"Are you going tell him?"

I shook my head. "Did you tell Gabriella about me?"

"I did."

I sat in shock waiting for him to elaborate as he took my foot and kissed my toes. It tickled, and the more I pulled away the tighter he held.

"What did you tell her?"

"I told her I hung out with a brilliant lawyer-chick when I was in Huntington." He nibbled my big toe, sending sparks up my leg.

"A lawyer-chick?"

"She was totally jealous when I told her how smart you are."

He feathered kisses up my calf, and my body heated up like a furnace. I ignored it.

"You wanted to make her jealous?"

"I don't play games like that, Shelly." He released my leg.

"Did you?" I wanted to know what their relationship was like.

"She..." He hesitated. "I told her we weren't serious, we're...friends."

I sat up and glared at him. The way he looked at me, his insistence my pleasure came first, how he kept coming back, and his obvious jealousy of my sort-of-boyfriend—all telltale signs he had feelings for me. Maybe he stayed with her because he'd met her first? Maybe she was a manipulating bitch. A beautiful Brazilian model's money and influence would dazzle a simple truck driver's son. Was girlfriend just a loose term and not a formal definition of what they were? Were things different in Brazil? Whatever their deal, it was getting to me.

"We're just having fun, right?" He'd held back, because of her. "We're friends, right?"

I sighed. He was right, and no way I could make this any more than just a fervid affair, not with Gabriella still in his life. Being jealous or arguing about the definition and how I wanted it to be more would drive him away.

"Yes, Jason, and we are having a lot of fun," I relented with a forced smile.

"I promise, I won't play any games." He put his hands on my cheeks and looked into my eyes. I sighed and nodded. That ended the conversation

"You were amazing, Shelly, always." He stepped back. "I was a dumb kid. Gabby kept pulling me back into her world. She was different and worldly, and she taught me a lot. A better lover? Never."

We stared at each other for a few seconds in silence.

"I know what you're doing." He tipped my chin up to look him in the eye. "We won't have any regrets between us, okay? Right now, all I see is you, and all I want is you. I'm in the here and now with you. I will *never* want anyone else." Jason pushed his hands back down my pants, over my bottom, under my panties.

God, that's what I'd needed to hear years ago. But then, I wouldn't have had my life with Eric and my boys. He needed to leave me so I could have something real and steady and reliable. He would have had to change his life to be with me back then.

I'd broken my biggest rule with myself—*no regrets*. Maybe lack of sleep, being held at gunpoint and falling in love again was making me a little unhinged. Maybe I felt guilty for wanting a second chance with Jason after I'd let him go so many years ago.

"Are you here with me, now?" He searched my eyes. "Get out of your head, Shelly. Be here with me now. That's all that matters."

"I am. I want to be."

He leaned in and kissed me. "Just be with me," he whispered into my mouth, pleading with me.

One of his hands went around the back of my head, and his kiss intensified. I'd felt the strength of his feelings in that kiss.

"Eu preciso de você."

I pulled away. "You said that once before to me. What does it mean?"

"I need you." He leaned forward and put his head in the crook of my neck, wrapping his arms around my waist. *"Eu preciso de você.* I need you."

I had to let go of the past to feel what was happening with him now. My emotions and his emotions connecting our undeniable attraction and so much more was happening.

I closed my eyes and nodded. He made me feel sexy and attractive for the first time in years. My insecurities and loneliness were gone with one Portuguese phrase.

"Shelly, Jason!" Magda shouted from somewhere. "Cheesecake!"

We both giggled at Magda's beckoning.

"Come on, we have to go eat cheesecake." He chuckled.

Chapter Eleven

Jason

The buzz of my cellphone snapped me awake in the early-morning light. I rolled over in bed and glanced from Shelly's naked curves beside me to the opposite nightstand. Brilliant and beautiful, she was mine. Her gray-rooted, dark-blonde strands cascaded over her shoulder and down her bare back. Serenity and infinite adoration flooded me.

I got up and walked around the other side of the bed. Her bare breasts pushed together as she hugged the pillow on her side. I wanted to touch them, suck her nipples, and touch her between her legs until she made that little high-pitched moan.

First things first. I checked the incoming text.

Luis: *Matt wants us in the office by 0900. Brace yourself. He's been up since 4:00 AM*

Matthew Sutter was the new lead agent in charge of "Operation Shredder," which was solely about my cooperation with the CIA.

Matt, an ex-marine, had grown up surfing Oceanside, California, the side yard of Camp Pendleton, where his father was the commanding officer. Luis told me the assignment had been a dream for him and he'd been a fan of mine since he was a kid.

What he'd inherited six months ago was a broken mission marred with careless mistakes by his predecessor, Mark DeSantos. DeSantos was so obsessed with taking down the Silva organization and Sebastian, he threatened and intimidated me into doing his bidding.

Matt told me on our first meeting DeSantos' actions to take down a Brazilian gangster was not the CIA's responsibility. No records showed any threat to the U.S. from the Silva organization or Sebastian Silva.

I was convinced that DeSantos and my brother-in-law had a soured business relationship, and the CIA agent did some dirty deals. Luis neither confirmed nor denied my assumptions.

By then I was shackled and had to do the agents' bidding, for fear of either going to jail for tax evasion or Sebastian finding out about my cooperation—whether I'd given any real information or not.

I was in for a fierce tongue-lashing by the new Senior Agent who'd been in Virginia, lobbying to have the whole operation closed.

Luis and I had screwed up to get the money from the rebels to Caesar. Matt was back early, pissed the money still sat in a safe deposit box, and Caesar's men won't retrieve it.

My phone battery was at five percent. I needed to find a charging cord ASAP. Pulling on my jeans, I abandoned our love nest to search for a cord. The big house was quiet at six AM. I found a charging station on the kitchen counter by the cappuccino machine. Getting a bit heated thinking about what I'd wanted to do to Shelly to wake her up, I opened the enormous refrigerator, found what I was looking for, then went back upstairs.

She'd turned onto her back with her arms over her head. I held a strawberry under her nose and her eyes fluttered open. She peered at me with her darkened hazel eyes and croaked, "What is that?"

"Did I ever tell you you taste like strawberries?"

"You're crazy." She rubbed her eyes. Her hair was a wonderful mess.

"Don't tell me you forgot about that." I grinned. "Bite."

She leaned in and took the tip off with her teeth then furrowed her eyebrows.

I threw the covers from her and took the juicy insides of the strawberry circling it around her nipple then leaned in a sucked.

Shelly writhed. "Oh god." She shivered.

"Mmm, breakfast."

"You're certifiable." She giggled.

"That's me, honey." I repeated the act on the other nipple. "Now where? Let's see."

"Oh god, Jason." She dug her fingers into my hair as I ran the fruit down her belly to her triangle of dark blonde hair, following the juice with my tongue. I stopped and gazed up at her. She was delicious, and this was only the beginning with her. I was going to spoil her rotten.

She looked down at me and knew what I was going to do.

"No, you are not." She huffed.

"Oh yes, I am." I ran my thumb across her folds, pulled them apart, then rubbed the juicy side of the fruit around her clit. I licked it clean as she squealed.

"No," she protested, "sticky."

"Yes, sticky." She hated messes, never a dirty dish in her sink or spec of dirt anywhere. I traced her labia with the fruit, circling and circling and circling, my tongue not far behind, and her muscles clenched as she let out a breathless moan.

"Oh god!" She yelped as she came, panting and grabbing my hair. "Okay, stop now, please."

I sat up and popped the strawberry in my mouth, grinning as I chewed. "Good morning, lover."

"Shit," she said with her hand on her forehead, still panting. "What are you doing to me?"

"I'm giving you some overdue loving, lady."

She nodded. "Okay. Okay. That's good. Fine, thank you."

"Are you going to be all right?" I went into the bathroom and turned on the shower.

"Eventually," she said, not moving her hand from her head.

"Come take a shower with me and I will wash away the rest of the sticky."

"I need a few more minutes, Jason. Please."

"You're missing out." I pulled a fluffy white towel out from the cabinet and threw it over the shower wall. "I've got to get going anyway. I'm going into the city this morning."

"Tessa is picking us up at 8:00 AM. You go ahead, I can't move yet. Thank you. That was amazing. You're nuts."

"You'll have to get used to it. Cause this is going to be your life from now on."

"Just give me a head's up when you are going to assault me with fruit next time. I'll be more prepared."

"Nope." I got in the shower. "What fun would that be? And Shel? You could *use* some fun."

~ * ~

Shelly

A black Chevy Suburban and a white Range Rover pulled up the curved drive of Magda's house at 8:00 AM.

Though I could've slept for another day, I'd promised Contessa to meet the village children. Jason was safe. He could get Caesar's money and had the cross. We'd started, or we were continuing, something with so much chemistry, intimacy, and friendship I couldn't have written any better romance. I had renewed passion and inspiration again from Jason, *my* Jason.

"Come ride with *me*, Shelly." Tessa beckoned a red-clawed hand at me from the door of the Range Rover.

I glanced at Magda and the two other women. It felt like I'd been chosen by the popular girl to sit next to her at the lunch table, drawing scornful jealousy from her minions.

"Come." She beckoned me.

I climbed in next to her. "How long is the drive?"

"Two hours." She chomped on her gum. With her oversized Gucci sunglasses, Adidas track suit, and layered diamond tennis bracelets, she looked more like one of the Housewives of Orange County than the menopausal wife of an El Salvadoran arms dealer. She was intimidating and fascinating.

I wanted to know her better, dig into her psyche. "Jason told me you're from one of the villages."

Without looking at me, she growled. "What else did Jason tell you?"

I'd upset her. Maybe she didn't want anyone to know. Maybe she was ashamed of where she came from amongst her wealthy friends. I backpeddled from the comment and hoped she hadn't taken it as an accusation she was not as worthy as her friends.

"That was it." I fumbled through the evening bag I still had from my kidnapping in Vancouver.

"Magda has a big mouth," she said, still looking at something above her. Maybe she was going to take a nap. I couldn't tell with the big sunglasses.

"Sube el aire acondicionado!" she ordered the men in the front seat. The air conditioning blew stronger at our feet.

"Fucking hot flashes," she said.

I chuckled. "Me too."

She turned and took her glasses off, grinning. "So, Jason, eh?"

I felt a little better. She loved my book and was a fan of mine. I nodded, more relaxed. "Perpetually, for about thirty years, with a twenty-year pause for real life."

She shivered with a wicked grin. "That's so sexy. You must write a book where the character is a woman our age finally getting her fantasy lover." She stopped and frowned, glaring at me.

I was concerned she'd turn on me, and she was scaring me a little bit. Maybe this trip to the school was a ruse, and she was taking me into the jungle to have me shot.

"Oh wait. You *have* that." She did a goofy little dance and hummed some tune that sounded like Bamboleo. Tessa had a silly side, and I loved it.

I laughed. Now I *really* liked her. She leaned back on the headrest, looking at the ceiling again, smiling and chomping on her gum. She'd shown what a contradiction she was and reveled in it.

We sat for a few more minutes, and I squirmed. I had so many questions for her. I couldn't read her like I could with most people. That was so intriguing.

"Tessa, how did you meet Caesar?"

She grinned and turned to me. "Oh, Caesar." She sighed. "He is still so handsome, no? He will be sixty in February, and we have been talking about his retirement."

"Yes, very handsome." He was too damn terrifying for me to notice if he was or not.

"He always was, you know. The girls in the village all wanted him."

"He was from your village too?"

"His family moved there when I was fourteen. He'd started school late." She adjusted her position to tuck her leg under her as if we were at a sleepover, gossiping about boys.

"I was always reading. I love books, poems, newspaper articles, anything with the written word. My father would tell me my face was too pretty to be stuck in a book. He meant it as a compliment. I did not think so." She pulled a tube of lip-gloss from her hot pink tracksuit jacket, swiped the wand across her bottom lip, then blotted. "Since I was the smartest in the school, the teacher asked me to help him with his reading." She put her head back again and smiled. "Oh boy, did we kiss and kiss and kiss." She shuddered again and giggled.

I smiled at her sweet story.

Her face dropped as she looked up at the ceiling. "I couldn't stop him from leaving school and going to work at sixteen, though. He wanted to make money to take me away." She paused. "He did not have a choice, you know."

"Was his family in danger from gangs or the cartel?" I asked.

"I know you mean well, Shelly, but we do not speak of such things."

I felt her threat in my fluttering stomach.

She closed the air vent at her foot. "He left, that's it."

"For how long?" I asked.

She hesitated. "It felt like forever at the time. Eight years, I think?"

She'd waited eight years for Caesar? How was she so devoted? I'd thought about if I'd waited for Jason for that long instead of moving on. Our situation was different, though. He'd never promised me anything back then.

"When did *you* get married?" Tessa asked.

My thoughts turned to Eric—how he'd romanced me. We'd traveled together, and over the years had bought a couple of houses, gushed over our babies, and cuddled on the couch each night with a glass of good wine, planning our future. He'd shown me unconditional love and support, giving me everything I'd needed for twenty years. I had no regrets. I wouldn't change a thing.

"I was twenty-eight and he was thirty. He was a great man." I pursed my lips. "Funny and smart. I loved him very much. Losing him was…" I sighed. "How old were *you?*"

She sat for a few minutes looking at me. She was deciding, wondering if she could tell me something. I felt it. I put my hand on hers in a show of encouragement. She removed her glasses.

"Caesar was accused of killing my cousin for stealing from his boss. He ran away." She took a deep breath. "I knew he would come back for me, someday. He'd promised."

"Where did he go?"

"I did not know for many years. He finally told me he'd gone to San Salvador and got a job as a dishwasher. The owners of the restaurant were a family with…connections." She glared. "He charmed them to join their organization. That's how he got involved with his current business venture."

"How do *you* feel about the business?"

She shrugged and replaced her glasses. They were a shield she donned, her protective armor. I was grateful for her trust in telling me about Caesar.

"He told me a long time ago when he came back to the village for me, he would rather be on the side that sold the products instead of the side that used them." She faced me and took off her sunglasses again as if she was pleading with me to understand. "You people in El Norte do not realize we have *no* choice. We either play the game or we die."

I needed to understand. I'd read about the gangs, cartels, and corrupt governments in Central America, and the people left to fend for themselves. Eric loved the documentaries and had a fascination with the dictators, cartels, and revolutionaries—Pablo Escobar and Che Guevara. He would've loved to have met these amazing people.

She put her armor back on. Now I understood her better. I admired her with a wave of warmth in my chest. "I envy you and your devotion to Caesar. It's truly romantic."

"Are you for real, Shelly?" she snapped. "You've had *two* great loves. I'm the one who should be envious. If I ever lost Caesar, I'd never find love again."

It started raining. I stared out the window at the lush green trees and the imposing volcanic mountains as they grew closer and bigger.

Was Jason a great love? Was Eric? Was I allowed to be in love with both of them?

Jason and I had been so young, consumed by passion and lust. Now, being with him again, there was something familiar and satisfying in the feeling of an aching need soothed. A long-ignored itch scratched. The promise he'd made me and the passion we still had fed some strong emotions inside me.

Can one be bound by the finality of only falling in love once and forever, like Tessa?

There are so many kinds of love, having children taught me that. I loved my boys differently because they're so different.

I was in love with Eric in such a contrasting way than I was with Jason. Yes, damn it, I was allowed to fall for two different men. I was going to allow myself to fall in love twice in my life.

I pondered this in silence, and I could tell my new friend was awash in her own thoughts. No awkward pause in our conversation at all, just a true respect between two deep thinkers.

I felt a new kind of love for this sister sitting next to me, a kindred spirit. "How in the heck did you and Magda become friends?"

"Magda… People say we were sisters in another life—or an old married couple." She laughed. "We love and hate each other. We met volunteering at the library over in Libertad thirty-some years ago. We started the book club just to see each other, because our husbands… You know."

The men were on opposite sides of the law. It would not do for Roberto to socialize with Caesar.

"They don't hate one another. They just can't fraternize. Maybe one day, when they both retire, they can sit and have a bottle of Mezcal and play golf."

"What do you think of Roberto?" I needed to know from someone else if they'd felt his magnetism. "I mean, do you think he—"

"Has the *divino*?" She cut me off.

I nodded.

She pursed her lips. "I saw and felt his light when I first met him. Hearing from his wife, though… Trust me, he's just a man. He turns into a whining infant when he has a cold and is a slob in the bathroom."

She jumped when her cellphone rang. "Speak of *la punta* herself." Tessa tapped on her phone. "Talk clean, bitch, you're on speaker."

"You're talking about me. I can feel it with my powers," Magda said in a serious tone.

"What powers?" Tessa rolled her eyes.

"You know what I mean, Con-te-ssa." Magda said.

Tessa mouthed the words "powers" at me. "Yes, we were talking about how I love and hate you and how the men will someday drink Mezcal and play golf. I'll sell my daughter to your son to ensure a forever bond, like we discussed."

"They're thirteen and eight, a most agreeable age," Magda said, sending a volley back at her friend.

I threw my head back in laughter. "I love you ladies." I wiped the corner of my eye.

"I have daughters too. Shelly, you have two sons. Let's make a love connection, eh? I have money," Magda added. "I'll pay you to take them."

During our three-way conversation, I learned Magda had five children, spanning from twenty-two to thirteen. Tessa had four. Her oldest was twenty-seven and her eight-year-old was an accident. "That's what happens when you and your husband still like each other." She sighed.

Chapter Twelve

CIA Headquarters, San Salvador
Jason

"It's 0900 hours and I've got *two* headaches." Matthew Sutter stomped into the conference room, the floor shaking beneath his six-three frame. He threw a pile of files onto the table between Luis and me, and papers went flying. "This one is you, LaAceituna." Sutter pointed to the back of his head, glaring at Luis. "This one—" He stabbed the space between his right blond eyebrow and his buzz-cut hairline. "This blinding, searing, gonna-have-to-lie-in-a-dark-room-listening-to-whales-fucking, is you, Mattis."

I'd never seen him like this.

He paced, rubbing his temples, then stopped and put his hands on his hips. "You kidnapped some Harlequin writer?"

"I wouldn't say kidnapped..."

"You kinda did," Luis said.

"The Feds in Seattle told me when she didn't show up for her book signing. Her publisher said the last time she'd seen M.R. Taylor was with you, Mattis."

"There are photos of the two of you in a hotel in Vancouver. Explain that," Matt continued.

I didn't say anything. What could I say? He already knew everything.

"She's fine then? You and the Garcia's aren't holding her against her will?"

I shot him a side look. "Come on, Matt, you know Roberto."

"Tell her to call her publisher," Matthew ordered. "I'll call off the alphas."

"Okay." I texted Magda.

"That was the *first* call from the FBI." Matthew plopped into a chair at the head of the long table. He extracted a photo from one of the files and flung it across to me. "This guy just flew in this morning and rented a car. GPS placed him parked outside Roberto Garcia's house. Know him?"

I'd never seen the pale, scrawny man. I shook my head and handed it to Luis.

"Doesn't look familiar," Luis answered. "Who is he?"

"David Morales. He's on the Bureau's watch list as a possible terrorist."

"A terrorist?" Luis asked.

"He threatened Christies Auction House in Denver and the Met Museum in New York over some antique crucifix on loan from the owner's collection, uh…Juan Morales." Matt scrutinized a paper.

Luis and I looked at each other in panic.

"He'd stolen it once before from the Morales family."

"Now he's here?" Luis' voice shook.

There *was* a tracking device on the cross somewhere, and this must be the guy who was shooting at us. I rubbed my chin. Dare I tell Matthew that part?

Matt squinted at us. "What do you know about this?"

"The Cross of Castillo is at the Garcia house," I said.

"Why?"

"Because Caesar wants it."

Matthew slammed the paper onto the table in exasperation. "Caesar wants it. Fuck, of course he does. Why the fuck not?" He glared at me; his eyes narrowed. Closing his left eye, then his right, he buried his face in his hands. "What's this about?"

Luis got up and turned off the lights.

"It was to stall Caesar until I got him the money. Now he wants both."

"Fine. Fucking great. Give it to him." Still covering his eyes, Matthew sat back in his chair. "Did you go to the bank yet?"

"You told me to come here first."

"Mattis, go get the fucking money. Let's finish this thing." Matthew crossed his arms on the table and bent over to cradle his head on them. "Now."

I stood, ready to leave then stopped. "Wait, what happened at Langley?"

"The operation's closed. You're done with us, and we're done with you. Get your girl and go home to Huntington. It was nice knowing you." Matt spoke from between his crossed arms. "Get Caesar his money first."

We left CIA headquarters and drove to the other side of town.

Luis and I sat in an unmarked sedan across the street from the bank, watching and waiting. For what, who knew? A man in a suit sat on a bench with a newspaper. Since nobody read newspapers anymore, that was suspicious. Another man, in basketball shorts, a tank top, and big white headphones, jogged up and down the concrete steps of the Romanesque building. Its fresco of fake marble deities sprawled across a pitched awning held up by white columns the size of tree trunks.

"I counted eight times that guy ran up and down those stairs. He's been doing this all day, every day *for months*. That is a bullshit post. I'd quit first," Luis complained.

"I thought they were called off."

"Only for you. If it were any of Caesar's guys they'd spring into action."

I took a deep breath in and out, then another.

"Okay, Zen Shredder, go get the money." Luis patted me on the shoulder.

I exited the car as a black SUV pulled up in front of me. The door opened to a gun pointed at my face. *Shit!*

"Get in, *Gringo*." Caesar's voice came from the dark inside the car.

I turned to Luis, who'd gotten out of the car and flashed his badge and gun.

Caesar laughed. *"No te preocupes solo quiero hablar con el, Agent LaAceituna."*

I just want to talk, Agent LaAceituna.

I motioned for Luis to stand down and got in the back seat with Caesar. The black leather seats were cool, and the air conditioning felt great on my face. My temperature rose, and my heart struggled. I was so close to putting all of this behind me. What the hell did Caesar want now?

"My wife loves your lady friend, *Gringo*. She made me promise not to hurt you."

"That's fortunate." My consciousness teetered. "I'm getting your money. The cross is here. Are we good now?" My heart worked too hard. I needed to slow it down with breathing.

This is business, don't show weakness. I'd read *The Art of War*.

"How do I know you won't tell the *federales* about our arrangement?" Caesar waved the gun around. "I could just kill you as soon as I get my money. That would be the cleanest way. I like things clean."

"I'll give you anything you want if I can just go back to California and be done." *Thump, thump*. My heart pounded. Could they all hear it?

Caesar sat stoic for a moment then laughed.

"Anything?" He hit his man in the front seat on the shoulder. "The *gringo* says he'll give me anything."

"What else do you want?" My heart thumped, fluttered, then thumped again as I stared at the gun.

"I'll let you know."

Fuck, I'd gone from whipping boy for the CIA to being Caesar's bitch. "Tell me where and when to bring your stuff, Caesar, and leave me and Shelly alone."

"Shelly, yes. I like her book. She's provocative. I'm a fan." He rested the gun in his lap. "She's your girl, eh?"

"Yes."

"Tessa says you were her inspiration for the character in the book."

Claustrophobia threatened. *Stop wasting time talking. Just get the money so I never see Caesar again.* "Tessa would never forgive you if anything happened to me." Pain shot up my left arm. If I didn't slow my heart rate, I'd land in the hospital.

God, this needed to be over soon. Was it too much to ask to sit on the couch with Shelly, rubbing her feet, listening to funky jazz music...maybe Bob Marley? Just chilling?

Focus on that. Calm...need to be calm.

"Out of my love for my wife, you are safe for now. Miguel will call you with the drop-off location." Caesar waved the gun one more time. "Go get my money."

I opened the door to a cool breeze on my face, took some deep breaths, then headed for the bank.

The newspaperman and the stair runner approached me.

"Didn't you guys get the memo?"

They just stared at me. The newspaperman spoke into his earpiece. The entire security team from the bank rushed out and down the stairs.

Luis ran across the street toward me.

The doors to the SUV opened with machine guns pointed at the security guards—and me too.

Oh Shit!

Luis held up his badge and rushed to me and grabbed me by the arm. "Let him go."

A standoff between the guards and the men in the SUV held steady and Luis pulled me up the steps to get away from the conflict. I felt like I was in a bad Brazilian gangster TV show. We got to the top and there was not a sound except for a cawing crow on the telephone line above.

Luis picked up his phone and put it to his ear. "Matt..."

I could hear Matt yelling. 'Where are you guys?'

"We're at the bank. So's Caesar. We're being courted by security guards and *federales*... Okay." Luis shrugged. "Okay, we will." He took the phone from his ear. "He said just go and get it."

"Are they going to let us?" I pointed to the guards staring at us from the bottom of the stairs, guns still pointing at the SUV.

"I think they have to."

Car doors slammed, and the SUV sped off.

I should've been more relieved than I was.

Newspaper Dude and Jogger ascended the stairs.

"There was a miscommunication, *Señor*. Please continue," Jogger said.

"This is fucking weird, Luis."

Luis nodded. "Let's get out of here ASAP."

Without further conflict, we entered the bank and retrieved what we'd come for.

Who was working for whom? There was something between Caesar, Matt Sutter, the local *federales*, and the bank. They were all in this together somehow.

I didn't care anymore. This was the one last key to freedom.

~ * ~

Shelly

The patting sound of rain and the swoosh of the windshield wipers were background noise as Tessa and I chatted about motherhood, aging, writers like Jane Austen, Steven King, and Chilean author Isabel Allende, and TV shows like *Downton Abbey* and *The Walking Dead*.

We veered off the main highway to a narrow dirt road, and the Range Rover bounced and hitched, unsettling my stomach.

We reached the outskirts of a town at the foot of one of the many looming mountain peaks. All I could make out were unfinished, wood-framed structures, along both sides of the road. Roofs made from corrugated metal sheets made 'pinging' sounds from the rain. Plastic sheeting walls like black garden trash bags billowed in the wind, keeping rain out of the houses. The obvious contradiction between rich and poor in El Salvador was striking to me in that moment, sitting in an eighty-thousand-dollar car.

As we got further into the village, the houses turned into painted stucco exteriors of yellow, violet, and sky blue, contrasted with the gray sky above, and popped. Framed glass windows and terracotta-tiled roofs showed the prosperous side of the village. I wondered if the woman I was with had something to do with that. Red blooming bougainvillea climbed up the sides of the buildings as we approached the center of town, recognizable by the commercial structures and a cobblestone road. A grocery store, bakery, *tortilleria*, and café with empty tables lined up against the building's outside walls.

There were no sidewalks, and the street was narrow. Our car had to stop multiple times for a pedestrian to pass with grocery bags or baskets of purchased goods, scurrying to get out of the way and out of the rain.

Our convoy turned and headed out of the village as the buildings became more spread out. The car stopped in a muddy lot at the end of the cobblestone road.

The two men in the front went around to the trunk and extracted large golf umbrellas with "Calloway" printed on them. One opened Tessa's door, and the other opened mine, holding the umbrella over my head.

"Come, Shelly," Tessa shouted. She trotted to a two-story, bright-purple building with tiny windows dotting the exterior. Her bodyguard hustled to catch up to her.

To the right, a paved basketball court slicked with rain and to the left, a rectangle of manicured grass with a goal at each end. It was not so different to some schools in the U.S.

We shook off the rain inside the sparse entrance of the school—a hallway with closed doors to the left and right and a corridor under a staircase in front of us.

Our entourage went down the corridor to a large room with curtains partitioning sets of desks, and white-shirted children looked up at teachers. Several conversations could be heard echoing in the large space.

Tessa and the other ladies went ahead of me through the room and out another corridor with an office on each side. A bespectacled, tiny woman stood with her hands clasped in front of her and flashed a spectacular smile.

Magda kissed her on both cheeks, followed by Tessa, the blonde whose name was Maria, and the charm-bracelet woman they called "Chi-Chi."

"M.R. Taylor." Magda waved me over. "This is Sonia Millar, the principal of the school and another big fan of yours."

Sonia took my hand in both of hers as her eyes welled up. "I am so honored you have come to meet our students. A real writer in the flesh." Her voice shook.

"It's a pleasure, Sonia." I let her hold my hand longer. The reach of my book surprised me at every turn. I don't think even Rose imagined it reached this far. *I may need to renegotiate my terms.*

"Everything is arranged." Another voice came from behind us, and we turned to see a thin man with a feminine air about him.

Sonia pulled me around her office, never letting go of my hand, and introduced me in Spanish to all her office workers, the big smile never leaving her face. I looked back at Tessa, who also smiled. A few photos were snapped with everybody posing and smiling. Magda whispered that they didn't have any WiFi to post to social media, but she and the book club were working on it for them and the students.

"*Señora* Taylor, I must ask." Sonia stopped and turned to me. A sea of smiling young women stood behind her. She turned back and one of them nodded at her. "We *must* know." She paused again and took a deep breath. "Will Jake ever forgive Sarah for marrying another man, or did she even marry him?"

"Or will she ever forgive herself for not waiting for Jake to come back?" the feminine man asked.

"You will have to see what happens" was my canned response to those questions. I'd gotten the same ones hundreds of times, and I would never reveal what it would be to my fans. "Just know if you are open to it, love will find you."

They all appeared satisfied with my non-answer. The next book was already finished and would be released at the end of the year, just in time for Christmas. I was sure they'd be happy Sarah did not get married. Romance novels are not as messy as real life.

A bell rang, and loud voices rolled down the corridor. We made our way back to the big room as the curtains were being pulled back and hundreds of young people chatted and pulled lunch bags from their desks.

One group of children ranging in age from about thirteen to sixteen walked ahead of us and back into the first corridor then to the right. We followed them into another good-sized room with long tables placed in a "U" shape with a chalkboard at the head.

My ladies led me to a row of chairs along the back wall, and we sat.

"They're all girls," I whispered to Magda. The students slumped into the room like they'd been forced to give up their lunchtime to listen to me drone on about a book they hadn't read.

"The boys go to work or join the gangs," she said, her murmur awash in melancholia.

Sonia stood at the opening of the "U" and waited as the students took their seats around the tables and settled, about twenty pairs of eyes on her, silent and respectful.

She spoke in English as she wrote my name on the chalkboard.

"We have a treat for you today. A best-selling writer has come to read to us from her book," she said.

My temperature rose. What part of my sexy romance novel was I going to read to these teenagers? *Shit!*

I shot a look to Magda, who took my hand and squeezed it.

"May I introduce M.R. Taylor." Sonia held up a copy of my book. The students clapped. Their applause quieted as I reached Sonia—there were crickets. I was sweating already. Sonia handed me the book and stepped aside.

I must distract. I don't want to corrupt these kids with the more intimate details of my book...blowjobs and sixty-nine sessions. I cursed Jason as the strawberry episode from earlier popped into my head.

"Hello." I choked on my saliva. "Are any of you writers?"

The students looked at one another. One hand rose—a heavyset, black-haired girl exuding confidence.

"Wonderful. What do you write?" I asked.

"Tell her your name first," Sonia instructed the girl.

She stood and flung her long, black hair over her shoulder. "My name is Maria and I write poetry." She leaned on her left side with her hip out as she played with the ends of her hair.

"Who are your influences?"

She straightened at my question and looked around. We all waited for her to answer. "Lewis Carroll. The Jabberwocky."

I almost fell over at the answer. This was an impressive young woman. "'Twas brilling, and the slithy toves...'" I stopped and waited.

She widened her eyes and smiled. "'Did gyre and gimblein the wabe.'"

"'All mimsy were the borogroves, and the mome raths outgrabe,'" we quoted together.

My ladies and the staff applauded. The students were silent.

"Amazing, Maria. Inspiration can come from anywhere." I launched into my writing journey, where I got inspiration. I paced, used my hands, answered questions...even got a few laughs.

"Read from the book!" Chi-Chi shouted from the back.

Oh, Lord.

Sonia approached me and opened the book, pointing to

highlighted paragraphs. I could've kissed her. I nodded and read. She'd chosen fantastic passages, reminding me I was a good writer.

While there were a few questions about the translation of some big words, for the most part they seemed to enjoy my presentation.

A bell rang, and Sonia dismissed the students.

Maria approached me. "Would you read one my of poems?"

"Yes, of course. I'd love to."

She took a small diary-style book out of her bag, opened it, and ripped out a page.

"I don't want you to lose your work, Maria. You can email it to me."

She shook her head. "I have so many revisions, I won't forget it."

I smiled and folded the paper and put it in my pocket. "I'll get this back to you."

A few more girls approached me and told me they wanted to be writers. I reminded them true writers are readers, too, and to support each other as women. All smiled at me as they left.

I felt so much love and validation for my life choices in that moment. The sacrifices made to my physical appearance and housekeeping. All the hours and days I'd spent alone for two years, making sure every word written was perfect.

Sharing my story with the kids was a euphoria I couldn't have imagined, and I'd had to come all the way to El Salvador to get that feeling. When I got back, I was going to ask Kenny to book me at more schools when I toured South America next year. This was a big piece of my heart that was missing, sharing with young people and helping them on their journey. Now I knew what Magda and the book-club ladies were trying to do with their money and influence, and I wanted to be a part of it.

Sonia led us to a lounge, which was just another room with long tables, fresh coffee brewing, and a vending machine. We sat and enjoyed phenomenal local coffee—rich yet delicate, with hints of chocolate. This wasn't the over-roasted Starbucks crap. Teachers floated in, and we discussed some of the chapters of my book and everyone's favorite parts. A smiling man, soaked from the rain, brought containers of food. Warm pupusas filled with gooey cheese and tamales filled with corn and beans.

We spent three hours at the school, ending with a tour of the building and a discussion between Tessa and Sonia about needs for WiFi, laptops, and a cell tower for the village. Tessa nodded. I could see the wheels turning in her head. Contessa Rivera and Magdalena Garcia would get this little rural school online and into the twenty-first century if it was the last thing they did. Pride swelled in my heart for these heroines. I had to write a book about them.

~ * ~

"I'm going to use the restroom before we leave," I announced to Tessa as we stood in the hallway of the school.

"I need to get back. Is it all right if we go ahead?" Blonde Maria asked.

"Yes, Go on." Tessa kissed her on both cheeks, followed by Chi-Chi.

"I am coming with *you*," Magda insisted. "I won't let you two have any more fun without me."

"My son calls that condition FOMO," I said.

"What's that?" Magda asked.

"Fear Of Missing Out—*FOMO*." I went to find the restroom, returning to find the ladies tapping on their phones.

"Still nothing?" Magda frowned.

"No," Tessa replied.

"No cell service?" I asked for clarification.

The ladies shook their heads. Magda shoved her phone in her jacket pocket.

"All right, let's go. I need to be back for dinner," Tessa said.

The rain had stopped, leaving pools of mud. We tiptoed to the Range Rover, climbing in the back.

"Hello ladies." A voice made me turn backward to the trunk. "Where's my cross?"

A pockmarked man with wet hair stuck to his forehead held a gun to Tessa's temple. Magda jumped into my lap, and we pressed against the inside of the car door.

So, this was who'd shot at us in Mexico.

The guards opened the front doors.

"Get out or I'll shoot her," the man warned.

They backed away.

"Climb over, and get in the driver's seat, *Señora*," he ordered Tessa.

She obeyed, and he followed into the passenger's seat. "Drive."

She shifted into drive with shaking hands.

Magda fiddled with her phone then shook her head.

My insides wrenched at the gun pointed at my sister.

"Where are we going?" Tessa asked when we reached the highway.

"To get my cross." He spit as he spoke.

"What cross?" Tessa said.

Magda and I looked at each other in surprise. *The Cross of Castillo.*

"It's at my house," Magda said.

He wanted the Cross of Castillo. He was American. I recalled the theft case—and Juan's nephew.

"David?" I asked.

He turned around with dark eyes glaring at me.

My stomach twisted into a pretzel. "I know the Morales family."

"It's mine." His voice sounded higher pitched. "It belongs to me."

Magda shot me a look. "You know him?" she whispered.

I nodded. Her expression changed from fear to anger, and she glared at the gun. I watched a metamorphosis as her eyes darkened, her jaw tightened, and her fists clenched. What was she thinking?

A banging noise came from outside, followed by a series of *flump, flump, flump.* The car bounced. Tessa tried to control the steering wheel, swerving to the side of the highway then shifting to park.

"We have a flat tire," she said to David.

He didn't move, still pointing the gun at her temple.

"I can change it." Tessa didn't look at the man.

David was silent, motionless, except for a twitch in the corner of his left eye. As we sat, his twitch worsened. The corner of his mouth joined the spasm. He was thinking.

We all were.

I'd been told when I was thinking too hard, I tugged on my bottom lip. It was never conscious on my part. This was the first time I'd caught myself doing it.

I glanced at Magda. She tensed; her dark eyes fixed on the gun. Was she going to jump him and wrestle the gun from him? Did she know some karate move or the Vulcan death grip? If she did something like that he could shoot. He could shoot Tessa or me.

Dylan and Connor would hear I died in the jungle, shot by a madman.

"Five years in prison. Solitary confinement." He broke the charged silence. "They didn't believe me. All that time, in the dark, he talked to me. He told me he was waiting. The Cross belongs to me. He told me to save him from evil—evil Juan Morales and his family."

We stayed quiet, shocked at his ramblings as rain pelted our vehicle. Outside, the sky darkened. The dashboard clock showed we'd sat for over an hour. No passing cars. No streetlights. Just darkness and a gun.

"He chose me to be his savior. Castillo. I was his savior, like

Christ himself, the Savior," David rambled like the psycho he was.

"Can I please change the tire?" Tessa asked, still not looking at David.

He got out of the car and closed the door behind him. My heart pounded harder than the rain—I felt it in my throat.

Magda and I both jumped when he yanked Tessa's door open, gun back in her face. He dragged her out and slammed the door.

The only sound besides the rain was Magda's harsh breathing. "He is *loco*. He thinks the Cross talks to him."

I nodded, numb.

"I can't just sit here." She leaned over the backseat to rummage through the trunk. After long moments shuffling things, she produced a three-foot metal rod.

"What the hell is that?" I asked.

"Who cares?" She climbed over me to open the door, weapon in hand.

"Magda, what are you doing?"

"I don't know." Her gaze fierce, she climbed down into the mud and skulked around the back of the car. "Hormones, maybe?"

My breathing got heavier. I'd heard stories of "hysterical strength," a phenomenon of inexplicable heroism in the face of distress of a loved one. A mother's passion to protect a child from harm spans the entire animal kingdom, like a big cat or mama bear defending her young.

Magda was in alpha-mode. No way was I getting in her way. Keeping my distance, I followed her into the pounding rain.

She charged the man looming over Tessa kneeling in the mud. Screaming, she raised the metal rod over her head. David turned and shot her in the knee. Magda collapsed.

My body flared with heat, and I measured the distance to the weapon in the mud next to my fallen alpha. Animal instinct kicked in. I rushed to the metal rod, took it into both hands, and swung it like a baseball bat. It smashed into the man's ear and launching him backward away from my sisters.

David lay motionless.

I froze.

"Magda!" Tessa shouted. "Shelly, help me."

I stood, still frozen. A breeze touched my neck, and chills ran along my arms. Hands numb, I dropped the weapon.

"Shelly!" Tessa hollered at me over the hiss of the driving rain. "Help me get her in the car."

Keeping one eye on David lying in the mud behind us, I dragged

Magda into the back seat and rested her head on my lap. Tessa jerked the drawstring from my hoodie, tied it around Magda's thigh, and knotted it. She'd cut off the circulation to stop the bleeding. I'd seen it in movies. Eric told me it couldn't stay tight too long, or the leg might have to be amputated. Nausea threatened. Adrenaline kept it in check.

Tessa jumped into the driver's seat. "Find something to press into the wound." She shifted into drive. Stomped on the gas pedal and roared back onto the highway.

I shrugged my jacket off and pressed it onto her knee where the blood had pooled.

Magda was quiet, breathing out through her mouth, like in Lamaze for childbirth, faster than Jason's tantric method.

I breathed with her.

Tessa fought the steering wheel. "I have to pull over. I think we're far enough away now."

She pulled the car over and jumped out. Rain pounding for a heartbeat. The trunk door flew open.

I continued to breathe with Magda and pressed my jacket on her wound. Tessa flung a tire out of the trunk, then a jack like they weighed nothing. Black mascara dripped down her cheeks and she clenched her jaw. She was the new alpha. Impossible strength and adrenaline had passed to her to save our pack.

"How are you doing?" I stroked Magda's hair.

"Childbirth was worse. I had my second at home with no drugs."

Her strength blew me away. "That's crazy. No drugs? I can't imagine."

"Don't imagine. It was hell." She winced.

My stomach lurched as the car lifted from Tessa changing the tire.

"I made a deal with the pain," she said. "I told it if it didn't kill me, it could have me. I wouldn't fight it."

"Did that help?" I asked, fascinated.

"I passed out." A short laugh escaped her, then stopped as she resumed her breathing.

I kissed her forehead and used my thumb to brush the smeared makeup from her cheekbones.

The car dropped, and Tessa jumped into the front seat. "Magda?" She pulled back onto the highway. "Which is closer, Libertad or Santa Ana?"

Magda's eyes fluttered. "I don't know, *punta*. How the hell am I supposed to know where we are? I'm bleeding."

Old married couple.

Chapter Thirteen

Jason

Roberto sat across from me at their kitchen table. Two camping lanterns and a smatter of candles held back the dark. The storm had knocked out the power, and the generator wasn't working.

The sky was black; our women, missing.

He slumped over his Mezcal, not speaking. What was he thinking? Did he suffer the same terrible thoughts as me?

Roberto had sent his men to retrace the route to the school, taking all three of their cars. All we could do was wait. Guilt swallowed me whole for bringing Shelly to this damn country.

We both stood when the large wood door opened in the foyer. The clunking, heavy footsteps weren't Magda's.

A panicked and soaking wet Caesar appeared. "Have you heard from them?"

"No." Roberto sank back into his seat. "Come, Caesar. Have a drink. My men are out there searching."

"Mine too." He took off his jacket.

A CB radio handset hissed next to me on the table, and we all glared at it.

My stomach burned from the smoky liquor. I'd been stripped of any power over my fear.

Roberto grabbed it and pressed the button. "Have you seen anything, Jorge?"

"Nothing yet," the voice said between static pulses.

He put the receiver down and retrieved another glass from the cupboard.

"They will find them." Roberto poured another glass of Mezcal. He was a quiet strength Caesar needed at that moment. His *divino* glowed, covering us in silent assurance they'd be found soon.

Here we huddled, an alliance of a vicious and feared gangster, an aging surfer, and the possible next president of El Salvador, sitting in anguished uncertainty over three headstrong women lost in some dirty mountain town.

~ * ~

Shelly

"Look." Tessa gasped.

Through the windshield, six pairs of headlights came toward us. We kept driving and passed them. My head whipped around to see every one of them peel out with screeching tires, turn around, and fall in line to follow us.

Tessa let out a cry. "Caesar!" she shouted and pulled the car over. She flung the door open as the first Suburban pulled up behind us. Tessa threw her arms around the first man who exited the car.

She ran back and got into the driver's seat. The Suburban pulled ahead of us, and Tessa followed.

"Hang on, Magda," Tessa said in relief. "There's a hospital nearby. They're calling Caesar and Roberto now to meet us."

The sight of a cavalry coming to save us was not lost on the fact the heroes were a gangster's bodyguards in American-made SUVs on a highway in the pouring rain in Central America. I was going to have to get all of this down on my laptop somehow.

~ * ~

Jason

I went up to the guest room I usually stayed in, deep in thought about what was going to happen if I'd ever get out of here. If Shelly wasn't too traumatized by my fucked-up life, would she even want to be with me after all this? Magda's Louis Vuitton signature weekender held eight million dollars and was heavier than I'd expected.

This money paid to Caesar was the last deal I'd ever make to get free of the threats and intimidation. The CIA wanted a coup, and they were willing to pay for it. As soon as Caesar got his money, it had nothing more to do with me. *I'm going back to Huntington. No more gangsters, arms dealers, or kidnappers.*

I could reconnect with my dad and introduce Jaz to Shelly. I couldn't wait to meet her boys and even her cats.

I still had three million in the bank from the sale of Endless Aviation. Matt Sutter assured me I'd be left alone, and the harassment would cease.

I hadn't anticipated the extra $500,000 for the cross, but it was a small price to pay to extinguish Caesar's fury. The man could hunt me down anywhere.

I was so done with Latin America, done with the corruption and anxiety of a new regime or gang leaders who at any minute could turn on me or my family. My mind went to Jasmine and her new life in New York. Time to return to the States. Back to California. Back to Shelly.

I ached for that quiet life with a good woman. Maybe I'd start a surf school or a board-shaping business in Orange County. I still had my reputation to fall back on in the surf community in Huntington Beach. I could call Old Man Tennant and see if I could work with them again. I'd be okay in an office. I'd been doing it for twenty years. I still had the nice suits and ties.

I thought about Shelly and her schedules and disciplined life and smiled. She'd be my new life.

The cross was in a wood box on the bed. I grabbed that too before descending the dark staircase. Now if only Shelly would have me.

~ * ~

When I returned to Roberto and Caesar, they'd already finished the whole bottle and were grinning at each other.

"Did I miss something?" I set the items on the ground by the doorway.

"Yes, *gringo*," Caesar said. "You'll miss everything around here, because you're never coming back."

"Fine by me." I exhaled and plopped back down across from the gangster and the future president. "I'll miss you both, especially you, Caesar, but I'm done with the South." I raised my glass of clear liquor, saluted the other men, and downed it in one gulp. *"Hasta la vista."*

"Don't worry." Caesar winked. "I'll FaceTime you every once in a while, keep you on your toes."

Roberto chuckled.

"You're done with me, Caesar. *They're* done with me. None of it is too soon." I glanced at Roberto. Did he know the coup could happen any minute? Armed rebels would storm the Capitol with Caesar's guns. What would he do? Like he didn't have enough to worry about with his wife missing, no power in his house, and a murderer sitting at his table.

We sat in silence, listening to the rain.

I glanced back and forth between the two men, on opposite sides of the law, in shared fear over their obstinate wives. I stayed quiet and listened to them talk about their kids and fatherhood like two old friends. There was an amiable guilt to their laughter as they traded stories about toddlers and teenagers. They went on and on, basking in similar memories of long-gone restaurants and nightclubs in San Salvador, how much it had changed since they were young.

They debated the same TV shows from Anthony Bourdain to Breaking Bad. They talked about golf—their equipment, the best courses in the region, where they'd fanaticized about playing.

I swore they planned a trip to Scotland together when the handset on the table hissed—two hours and three empty bottles of Mezcal later.

"We found them." Jorge's voice crackled. "Caesar's men are leading us to the hospital in Santa Ana."

"What? A hospital? Why?" Roberto asked.

"Magda was…" Static clouded Jorge's hesitation.

"*Jorge!*" Roberto snapped into the handset. "*What?*"

"She was shot."

We jumped up.

"My car's outside," Caesar said.

"We'll meet you there," Roberto told his man.

I flung open the back door of Caesar's Mercedes SUV and dove in. With Rob in the front, the gangster tore out of the driveway. The leather bag and wood box sat next to me on back seat, and I couldn't wait to get those items as far away from me as possible and to their rightful owner.

After we got to our women, I'd take Shelly away and never look back.

"Is Shelly all right?" My voice cracked like a teenager's.

Roberto spoke into the handset. "How are Shelly and Tessa?"

"I think they are fine. Tessa is driving. I spoke to Carlos. He said she seems to be…"

Roberto and Caesar glanced at each other with concern and waited for Roberto's security man to speak.

"*'Enardecer'* was his word," Jorge answered. *Fired Up.*

Caesar laughed. "Of course she is."

"Do you know who shot Magda?" Roberto's cheeks flushed red under his scruffy shadow of a beard, and his voice shook.

"Tessa mentioned some *loco gringo*," the voice said. "Okay, we're here."

"*Maldición*," Caesar cursed, "we're still thirty minutes away."

"I'll call you back." Static hissed as Jorge signed off.

Silence came over the men as I willed Caesar to drive faster. This whole thing was supposed to be over. I was planning on going home with Shelly and holding her until our last breaths. Now I was stuck in a racing car to some third-world hospital because of some psycho.

Chapter Fourteen

Shelly

A battalion of government security men, combined with the gangster's thugs, all looked alike to me. They all wore black suits and had buzzed, dark hair.

All eyes flew to the scene of twelve big men, one of them carrying a petite bleeding woman, bursting through the doors into the waiting room. Jorge cradled Magda as they disappeared through the swinging doors with two men and a woman in green scrubs. Tessa threw her arms around me.

"Did you have that crazy feeling of like a Pantera-Mama protecting her young?" she asked me, shaking with the adrenaline still coursing through her. "I had this clear vision of what I needed to do, and all of a sudden I was just doing it." She held her hands up to her face then extended them in front of her to show me her direct trajectory state of mind. "I have not changed a tire in many years, and never so fast. You know? Pantera-Mama protecting my family."

"Pantera? Like a panther?"

"Yes, panther or jaguar."

I nodded in understanding. "I just kept thinking, what if Magda was one of my boys?" Tears built and dripped down my throat. "I thought of her as one of my cubs, Tessa. Just like a Panther-Mama, I was protecting her and you."

Tears welled in her eyes as she stared at me. "You're a brave woman. He could've killed you."

All the air in my lungs whooshed out. *He could've killed me.* "I wasn't thinking about that."

"Pantera-Mama."

"Or hormones, but I like Pantera-Mama better." I took her hand. "Magda…"

Tessa sniffed her tears and wiped her eye with the back of her sleeve. "She is a viper, that one. Small and vicious."

We sat on a sofa on the far side of the waiting room, away from the entrance. A group of people watched TV. The image on the screen was hard to make out.

"It's starting," Tessa whispered in my ear. She knew about the coup. They carried Caesar's guns.

I focused on the image on the television. The cameraman ran— the image bounced about behind a group of camouflaged figures with matching brimmed hats. They jogged down the rainy street in flanked military rows.

"They are disciplined, like a real army." Tessa critiqued as if calling the strategies of a soccer game, not a *coup d'état*. "See the way they all hold their guns the same and step in time together?"

"How many of these have you seen?"

"Too many." She sighed and stood to walk away in disgust. I watched her pace.

A soaking wet Caesar bounded through the doors and peered around the room. All eyes shot to him as Roberto and Jason stumbled in right behind. Tessa ran and jumped onto the big man, wrapping her long legs around him and burrowing her head in his shoulder. The gangster squeezed her as tears ran down his face. The imposing figure who could have a man killed with a wink of his eye sobbed, holding his wife close.

Jason rushed to me and cupped my face, crashing his lips to mine. He breathed into my mouth, then pulled away, panting. "Are you all right?" His face was red and pained with such powerful emotion my body fluttered, and I sank into his arms. My knees buckled. I clung to his neck as he supported me.

When my head cleared, he still clutched me to him.

"Can I go home now?" I asked.

Jason exhaled and smiled at me. "I'll take you home."

"You will?"

He nodded. "I'm coming with you, and I'm staying with you for as long as you can stand me."

I pulled his head to me and pressed my lips to his. He was the most beautiful man I'd ever seen. Thirty years ago, and now, and all I wanted was to hold him close to me and bask in his beauty for the rest of my life.

"I should hope forever." I pressed my cheek to his chest.

"Are you sure you're okay?" He pulled my head away from him and stared into my eyes.

"I've hit my kidnapping quota for the year. I might experience some withdrawal, though. The adrenaline rush was pretty intense." I grinned.

Jason shook his head. "Maybe I'll have to kidnap you on the anniversary every year as a new kind of kink. I'll tie you up and…" He waggled his eyebrows.

We both laughed.

"Come on. We'll wait to see how Magda is."

We went to the opposite end of the waiting room and sat on a couple of armless chairs pushed up against the wall. The rest of the congregation watched the television in anxious fear. Tessa and Caesar stood in the middle of the room in an embrace, swaying like a dance, unaware of anyone around them.

"It's started," I said to Jason, motioning to the crowd around the television.

"I don't care." He touched my cheek, shoulder, arm, hand, then back to my cheek, full of nervous energy.

"I'm fine." I told him everything that happened, from Maria's poem to crazy David hijacking us. By now, adrenaline had cleared my system, and I was exhausted. I leaned on his chest and closed my eyes.

I withdrew the ripped piece of notebook paper from the pocket of my wet and bloody jacket and unfolded it. Submitting to the serenity of him rubbing my back, I read the poem with his breath tickling my head.

> *Fortitude is a hollow coin*
> *Thrown into the rising breeze too strong to be shattered*
> *Then drawn back from the binding in the hollow*
> *Hold silver as it cools in hot flesh*
> *Hand warms and heat pokes the hollow fire*
> *Hold, hold, hold*
> *Hold my hollow coin*
> *Withstand the heat*
> *Make it stay, fill the coin.*

Though I was no expert at analyzing abstract poetry, I interpreted her poem as the hollow coin was her love being dangled when all she wanted was for her love to be held close. I knew how she'd felt. I squeezed Jason body and raised my eyes to him.

"You said a young girl wrote that?"

He must have been reading over my shoulder. I nodded. "Do you get what she's saying?"

"She has a hollowness and wants someone to love her?"

"I thought something similar," I said.

"I feel it."

"Me too."

He touched his lips to mine. "Do you want to know why I came to Vancouver?"

I nodded my head.

"I'd had a small heart attack and was in bed for a month on heavy drugs. I started having this recurring dream. My mother stood in the doorway of my bedroom and said, "Go get her.'" He closed his eyes. "It was so clear and realistic. I woke up sweating and dizzy. The dream repeated itself in my head when I was awake. I needed—"

He stopped and took the poem from my hand. I lifted my head from his chest and sat up. He read the words, and his lips moved, then his glowing ocean-blue gaze rose to meet mine. This was a new expression I had never seen before. It was all strength and resolve.

"Você precisou de mim."

"What?"

"You needed *me,"* he said.

My mouth opened but no words came.

"When I looked you up online and read the article, then read your book, you were so alone. *You* needed *me."* He stood and held the poem to his chest with the teenage-girl scribble to face me.

Hold my hollow coin, fill it.

I scoffed. I'd never needed anyone. I'd raised my boys, worked, took care of everyone—Eric, my brother, my aging parents.

Jason stared at me with such purpose, I had to listen.

"You need me, Shelly. I'm never leaving you again."

He obliterated each of my barriers, incinerating them to dust with one simple sentence. My eyes welled. No one had ever seen me vulnerable, including myself. He wasn't taking advantage of my momentary weakness; he wanted me to admit it. Not one therapy session had led me to admit any vulnerability. It took Jason Mattis, my young and reckless paramour, who'd never belonged to me, to make me see what I'd needed.

I *did* need him. He brought out the best of me, then and now. The me who ate greasy pizza in bed and took chances with passion and love. I was getting a second chance. Yes, I needed him, and he needed me. I loved him for that, for all of it. The past was the past. This was the promise of a future with the boy I'd let go all those years ago. He was back, as a man, because *I needed him now.*

"I *do* need you," I said. "For so many reasons. For *all* the reasons."

He wrapped his arms around my waist and lifted me. I leaned into his lips. He dipped me back, pressing harder. We broke our kiss when we heard Tessa call my name.

Roberto came through the doors. We rushed to him. Tessa and Caesar were hot on our heels, followed by a few of the ever-present, black-suited men.

"She's fine. They've removed the bullet and are patching her up. The doctor said about six weeks before she can start physical therapy. She was lucky. Then again—" He smiled and looked down. "She always was, that one." He put his hand to his face and sobbed. Tessa put her arms around his shoulders.

He straightened and cleared his throat, stepping back from Tessa. "Thank you both for your quick actions." The calm leader was back. "She can go home in about an hour. Why don't you all go ahead?"

I cried—with relief, happiness, and love all at the same time.

Chapter Fifteen

Jason wanted to head straight to the airport from the hospital and fly home. The driver told him that was impossible—all airports were closed due to the coup. He took us back to Magda's, which was better. She needed us there.

I lay down on the big bed in my room about to fall asleep. But Jason told me I needed to call Rose and let her know I was all right.

She answered right away even though it was an unknown number. "Hello?"

Her blunt tone didn't surprise me. "Hey, It's Shelly. I'm fine. It was all just a big misunderstanding." I wasn't sure where I was going with that statement, and I'm not usually good at making stuff up on the fly, but I was getting better at it.

"No it wasn't," Rose snapped back. "You were in a lust-filled haze with *Mr. Hottie* and let it dictate your actions. Not that I blame you."

I exhaled at her candor and considered the story of ditching her for a night with Jason. She'd believe it. But I decided to tell her the truth.

"You're not going to believe any of this but, here it goes—"

It was close to midnight when I joined Jason in the den.

"Is your publisher angry?" Jason asked when I entered the cozy room across the marble foyer from Roberto's office.

A 70-inch TV showed hundreds of armed soldiers lined up in front of the capitol building in San Salvador, men and women in a military at-ease stance, rows and rows of them in straight lines. The scene hadn't changed in hours.

After Roberto got Magda settled, he'd gone straight to the city, leaving her in our charge. She was asleep on the couch, insisting on staying in the den, not alone in her room. She was anxious before the pain medication kicked in; we all were. Seeing her asleep calmed me a bit. I sat next to Jason on the big sectional, gazed at the image on the screen, and laid my hand on his thigh.

"So, was she pissed?" he asked again.

"At first—until I told her the whole story. She said she'd reschedule the appearances I'd missed. I was supposed to be in Dallas today."

Rose was very upset. I learned she's a very serious person over the few years we'd been working together, and she'd insisted on honesty. Even though it all seemed ridiculously close to one of my stories, I'd relented to tell her everything. She was a romance book publisher after all, she'd love it. And she did. But I also swore her to secrecy. The conversation endeared me to her, and I even felt like we were closer as friends than before.

"You told her everything?"

"Well, not *everything*." I winked.

We watched TV in silence. The rebels didn't move. Only the flags waving in the distance reminded me the actual image was live and not a snapshot.

The reporter on CNN International filled the dead space with chatter and conversations with experts on what to expect. Rumors of who funded the coup floated over the airwaves. Roberto's name was never mentioned.

"What happens now?" I asked. "With us—you and me?"

"You still have your tour, right?" He sat up and turned toward me.

I nodded, not breaking eye contact.

"Until when?"

"I'm scheduled for the rest of the U.S. and three more Canadian cities through the end of the year. With the weeks off for Thanksgiving and Christmas through New Year's."

"I could go with you."

I pulled my hand from his thigh. I hadn't thought about him being that serious about never leaving me. So serious that he would want to tag along on my tour. "What would you do when I'm at one of my appearances?"

"I'll find some trouble to get into. I've been all over the world. I've never been to Dallas or Chicago or Atlanta. I went to New York once to move Jaz. It's high time I explored my home country."

I never imagined Jason accompanying me. "That sounds

wonderful."

"Maybe I'll write a book." He raised his eyebrow.

"I think you could do anything you put your heart and soul into."

He pressed his lips to the inside of my wrist. Tingles rose from the kiss. I hoped his touch would always give me that feeling.

"We have word from the President," the reporter announced.

"Here we go." Jason sat forward.

A bearded, middle-aged man in a black suit, a vibrant cobalt-and-white sash across his chest, approached the podium. Flags with matching triband surrounding a crest with an amber triangle in the center, lush green volcanic mountain peaks, indigenous wood spears, and a peaceful laurel wreath, flanked the lectern.

His eyes appeared bloodshot. He slouched as he gripped the podium and did not speak. The camera panned to a group of soldiers onstage, wearing the same uniform as the ones lined up outside the building, then to a smattering of men in suits and more formal soldiers, with tailored jackets and medals on their chests.

The scene was somber.

"He's going to resign," Magda croaked from the other side of the sectional couch.

"How do you know?" I asked.

"The generals behind him told him to. It doesn't diminish his power at all. So long as his party holds the majority, they still run the government." Magda seemed as resolved as Tessa about what was happening. Knowing the playbook and maybe even a bit bored by it. Her face was relaxed from the painkillers, and she struggled to keep her eyes open.

"Where's Roberto?" Jason asked.

"In his office, watching TV like the rest of us."

"What will he do?" I asked.

"Nothing." She adjusted her position, her face scrunching with pain. I helped her reposition pillows behind her back and under her bandaged leg.

"He'll wait until a new election is announced," she said in a husky voice.

I could only read the subtitles. I needed my readers from my purse. Not wanting to miss what the President had to say, I moved closer to the TV.

"First, I want to assure people there will be no violence here today. I concede my position effective immediately."

"That was straightforward," Jason commented with the most bile-ridden sarcasm I'd ever heard from him. "I guess everyone can go home now with their fancy new guns." He got up and walked into the kitchen.

I followed. "You're upset there wasn't any shooting?" I hoped he heard the distress in my voice.

"Of course not." He pulled a beer from the refrigerator. "I just want to get the hell out of here."

"Until they reopen the airports, we're stuck. Magda needs us right now."

He popped the cap off and put his hands on the counter, staring at me.

"What?" I asked.

"Nothing." He grinned, took a swig from the bottle, and came around the island to me. "I'm selling the plane. It's too expensive to maintain."

"Jason Mattis is going to start flying commercial?"

He put the beer down, slid his arms around my waist, leaned forward, and kissed my neck. "I want to have a real Thanksgiving, with turkey, mashed potatoes, green bean casserole, and..." He bent down, lifted my shirt, and kissed my abdomen. "Cranberry sauce, all over you." He licked me up to my bra.

"No, it'll be sticky."

"Yeah, sticky." He kissed my mouth.

A beeping sound stopped us from going any further.

"Magda's pain killer time." I held up my phone.

Jason snorted and rolled his eyes.

Schedules are schedules. I pulled away from him and went into the kitchen.

"I'd like Jasmine to come for Thanksgiving, if that's okay with you." He leaned on the island, watching me.

"Let's get something straight. We're going to be together, right?" I filled a glass with water from the fridge door.

"Finally."

"We're going to be a family, right?'

"I'd like that."

"My boys and your girl and us. A family."

"Yeah...?" he said.

"Then don't ask me if it's okay for *our* daughter to come for Thanksgiving. As a matter of fact, it's a requirement for the kids to come home for Thanksgiving, Christmas, and Easter. Their friends, boyfriends, girlfriends are all invited. That's how it's gonna go."

Jason gave me that smile—all teeth and lighting bolts.

"*Your* girlfriends, however, are not invited."

Now he looked pained. "Shelly, I don't have girlfriends. My life has been dedicated to work and my daughter."

"So, you've changed." I'd known about his affairs, even when we were together. I'd seen him in several magazines with models and beautiful women in exotic locations.

"I never sought out women. I just took what they offered. I was young."

I nodded.

"I never cheated on Gabby in our eleven-year marriage, and I haven't wanted anyone else. Except you."

"It might take me a little time to trust you on that front."

"That's fair. I'll make you believe me every day." He moved closer to me until my breasts were pressing on his abdomen, and he leaned down to touch my nose with his.

We stopped the progression of whatever was coming next when we heard Magda shouting.

~ * ~

Jason

"No! No, no, no," Magda yelled. "You get him out of there now! *Mierda!*"

We ran into the den to see Magda throw her phone.

"What happened?" I asked.

"The police are holding Roberto in his office." She winced, trying to get up.

Shelly rushed over to help her. "President Ribero just resigned."

"He may have resigned, but the VP is still his pussy-man. They all are."

"What does this mean?"

"They arrested him for the coup." She grunted as she pushed herself up. "If they take him to jail, they'll beat him—even kill him."

"Where are you going?" I demanded.

"I must see the *gringos*. They have to take responsibility," she huffed. "Oh, I'm dizzy."

Shelly settled her back on the couch.

"You're not going anywhere, Magda." I whipped out my phone. If Magda knew my people were involved, they were going to do something about it.

"Matt, they arrested Roberto."

"I can't deal with you right now," Matthew Sutter snapped at me.

Matt was pissed at *me*. Again? He was annoyed I was asking questions? What would he have to deal with? He wasn't based in El

Salvador—he was my handler in São Paolo. There was a whole other team in San Salvador.

"They'll kill him if goes to jail. *Do* something!"

"Roberto knew it could happen."

"Roberto knew what could happen?" Saliva got stuck in my throat. There was something he wasn't telling me.

"Stay out of it, Mattis. We're done with you." He hung up.

~ * ~

Shelly

"Merde, merde." Magda shook her head.

The reporter on the TV announced breaking news. "We are getting reports the leader of the opposition party, Roberto Garcia, has been arrested. *"*

The scene changed to a group of black-uniformed officers, two of them holding a handcuffed Roberto, walking him out a building and toward the still-waiting insurgent army that hadn't moved from their place outside the capitol.

Magda picked up her pinging phone. "I know, Tessa. No, he can't. The Americans did this, and now they're letting Roberto take the blame."

She waited and listened.

I stared at Jason in disbelief. "The CIA is going to let Roberto take responsibility for the coup?"

He didn't answer. He pulled his phone from of his pocket and walked out of the den.

I sat next to Magda and watched the TV as the soldiers holding Roberto made their way to a waiting black SUV and shoved him inside.

"Get that license plate, Shelly!" Magda ordered.

I grabbed the remote and paused the TV. I had to get closer without my readers and took a photo of the license plate.

"Send that to me." It wasn't a request.

I airdropped it to her. "What the heck?" I returned to the paused image of the two large men who held Roberto's elbows. "Magda, is that Tessa's bodyguard?"

"Carlos?"

I recognized the man who'd put his arm around Tessa and looked right at me as we walked into the emergency room. His big brown eyes curved downward at the outside corners, making his face look like a little boy's, full of fear and concern. He'd asked me if I was hurt and given me his jacket. I'd never forget him.

"He's Caesar's nephew." She sat up. "Rewind it."

I did as she bid.

"Stop," she said. I pressed 'play.' We watched the entire scene again of the officers taking Roberto to the waiting SUV. Roberto walked with his chin up, looking resigned but defiant. He stumbled, and the officer on his left steadied him. He gazed up at the large man, and his face lit up. I paused it again. We had an excellent view of Carlos.

Magda gasped. "It *is* him!"

I stood, hands on hips, and stared at the TV. "What are you up to, Caesar?" I whispered, then turned to Magda. "You don't think that car belongs to the police, do you?"

"No."

"Who does it belong to?"

"Caesar." She looked at me with anger and fear.

Caesar was getting Roberto out of the city. But why?

Chapter Sixteen

Jason

"Luis, they're going to let Roberto take the rap?" I whispered into the phone.

"Stay out of this, Jason," Luis whispered back.

"Magda's freaking out here. Are they going to arrest her too?"

Luis was silent.

A pounding on the enormous oak doors made me jump, echoing in the foyer.

"Luis?"

Too many silent seconds went between my question and his answer. "Stay calm, Jason. We're working on it."

I slid the phone in my pocket and opened the door.

The porch light illuminated a small man in a trench coat and about a half-dozen uniformed policemen standing behind him. A light rain fell, glowing in the light. Where was the security detail?

"Is the lady of the house in?" the man asked, proper with a slight, fake British accent mixed with Spanish.

"She's recovering from surgery and not seeing visitors." What was happening? I peered behind him to see if Jorge or the other security men were around.

"We can ensure she does not leave, then." The man pointed to three police officers, who entered the house.

"Hold on, this is a private residence. You can't just barge in here without a warrant." I held out my hand, knowing it wouldn't stop the invasion. Things were different down here.

"A warrant? From a judge? During an insurrection?" The man

strolled into the foyer and removed his wet coat. "A hostile government takeover? Civil unrest? A *coup d'état?*"

"From what I saw, there's no insurrection, just a peaceful protest."

This clown played some kind of a game with me. I would've kicked him out on his fake Burberry trench coat of it weren't for the armed policemen.

"A protest, eh? In uniforms, with American-made M-16 rifles, *señor?*" He sauntered up to me. I stood a head taller than him—he had to crane his neck back to look at my face. "You are an American, are you not?"

"I have no knowledge of any of that."

"Roberto Garcia does, and we're sure *Señora* Garcia does too. So, *señor...?*"

"Mattis."

"So, *Señor* Mattis, we'll remain here until any confusion is cleared up. *Bueno?*"

"I didn't get *your* name, *señor.*"

The man strolled around the room, examining personal photos and mementos. "I did not give it, *Señor* Mattis."

Where the hell were Jorge and the other guards? The officers who'd taken position at the front door gripped their rifles, ready to use them. They could care less about killing some insignificant guy like me. Jason Mattis, former professional surfer, shot and left for dead in the jungle.

"You can call me *El Jefe,*" the man said.

I rolled my eyes and groaned. They all wanted to be called *El Jefe.*

We glared at each other for a second in silence. What was he looking at?

The man's expression perked up and he followed the sound of the television and female voices.

I charged up the stairs to get to Ricky, Magda's thirteen-year-old son. He was supposed to be asleep. He'd be up playing video games instead. I didn't want *El Jefe* or any of his men manhandling him.

I stopped just outside his bedroom door and heard him yelling. An ache pressed on my weak heart as it was beating too fast. Too many close calls in the past twenty-four hours. I needed to meditate and rest. I needed to hold Shelly close and taste her strawberry skin.

"Go, go! No man, you've got to use the shotgun!" Ricky shouted.

I opened the door unnoticed. The boy wore big green

headphones over his ears and sat with his back to the door—and me.

I walked up behind him and leaned over his right shoulder. "Hey."

Ricky yanked his headphones off with an annoyed expression. "What's up, Jason?"

"Your mom needs you downstairs."

"Give me a few minutes."

I adopted my best parental scowl.

"Yeah, okay." He relented and put his headphones back on. "I'll be back." He flung the headphones on his desk and rose. His chair rolled away from him. "This better not take long. It's mid-tournament."

We headed for the door. I held it open for the irate teenager.

"Just so you know, there are police officers downstairs with guns, so lose the attitude." Jasmine's adolescent days weren't so long ago. I was his godfather. We'd spent hours with his video games. He trusted me like a third parent.

Ricky stopped and gave me a skeptical look. We marched down the hall, stopping dead at the top of the stairs. When he saw the police, his face flushed with fear.

"It's all right. Just walk past them, and don't say anything. Your mom's in the den."

We descended the stairs. Ricky bounded toward his mother. I sped up to stay close to him, without making eye contact with any of the officers, and went into the den. The boy launched onto Magda, who threw her arms around him.

"Oh, there you are, *Señor* Mattis," *El Jefe* said. "You can now assist me in collecting all electronic devices in the house—all laptops, phones, tablets, and desktop computers."

"Ugh," Magda sneered. "All electronics are on a private server with an encrypted security passcode. I don't have it. Good luck with that, *El Jefe.*"

"Don't worry, *señora.* I am a gifted hacker."

"Are you *the* El Jefe?" Ricky asked. "The hacker who broke Fortnite?"

The man scoffed. "A child's game? That is ridiculous."

The man suddenly looked young, like he was just past adolescence himself.

Magda waved her hand. "Have your fun. Go and find them, *El Jefe.*" She lay back and closed her eyes. The Vicodin had kicked in.

Shelly sat on the couch next to her and took her hand.

"Let's go, *señor.* We will start in the library."

I led the man out of the den, trying to figure out how to get to

Jorge.

~ * ~

I opened the library's sliding double doors to the distinguished smell of leather and paper. An indescribable scent grabbed my senses, urging a mere mortal to rethink their entire purpose. The lingering essence of power occupied by the *divino* was apparent. Roberto and his magnetic attraction was all around.

El Jefe paused before entering, as if he knew he was unworthy. He tugged his ill-fitting suit jacket down, jutted his chin, and entered.

A laptop sat closed on the mahogany desk. He sank into the leather chair, opened the lid, and began tapping on the keys.

I waited arms crossed. "What the hell am I doing here?"

El Jefe glanced up at me in annoyance. "Nothing, *Gringo*. We are finished with you."

The air left my lungs. Those words were too similar to Matt Sutter's. "Finished with me?" *What the hell is going on here?*

The crash of the front door flying open and several men yelling caught *El Jefe*'s attention. He looked up toward the library opening.

Jorge appeared in the doorway. "Tell those *gilipollas* to stand down."

El Jefe rose from the desk. "Who the hell are you?"

"*Señor* Jason." Jorge ignored the small man. "We caught the *loco gringo* who shot *Señora* Garcia."

I followed Jorge to the front door, where two of his men held a bludgeoned, bloody man slumped between them. They dropped him on the ground.

A surprised *El Jefe* turned green and gagged.

"Arrest him." I pointed at the injured man crumpled on the floor.

El Jefe stood frozen. "I... Who is he?"

"He shot *Señora* Garcia and kidnapped Contessa Rivera."

"Caesar Rivera's wife?" *El Jefe* gulped and glanced at Jorge, going from green to white.

Jorge and I nodded, then the giant security man shot me a glance and waved his hand. "What is all of this? What is going on? When did you get here and how did you know we'd left our positions?"

"What?" I stomped toward *El Jefe* with my fists clenched.

"I got a call the *gringo* was just outside the gates, and we all went after him," Jorge answered me.

God, I wanted to deck this *El Jefe*. "You lured the Garcias' security out of the compound?"

"This is a government matter." *El Jefe*'s voice cracked. "Your men are free to stay as long as you do not interfere with my investigation."

What fucking investigation?

"What about him?" Jorge pointed to David, who struggled to raise his head.

"Handcuff him and put him in the back of the car." El Jefe motioned to one of the officers. "We will deal with him later."

I followed him. "So that's how you got through the gates. How did you locate him?"

He resumed his place at Roberto's desk. "Locate who?"

"The psycho."

"I don't know what you are talking about."

"You don't work for Ribero or the government, do you?"

El Jefe kept typing.

"Who then?" I persisted. "Caesar?"

The man pulled a gun from his breast pocket and pointed it at me. I'd had so many guns on me in the past two days I couldn't summon a bit of concern anymore.

"Sit down, *Gringo*," he said. "Shooting you will be like swatting an annoying fly. Shut your mouth and cooperate."

"Did Matt Sutter tell you to shoot me?"

El Jefe stayed silent and clacked on the keyboard.

"I don't work for them anymore." I crossed my arms.

He raised his gaze to mine. "No one stops working for them."

His cryptic comment made me shudder.

The hacker returned to his task.

~ * ~

Shelly

Magda slept. Ricky sat on the couch next to me. We watched the frozen army continue to stand outside the capitol.

"Tell me about the hacker, *El Jefe*," I said to the teenager.

"Two years ago, he hacked into Minecraft then into Fortnite and deleted Mr. Flipper's entire mod. Wiped all his work from existence. It was a big deal to the creator, and he wanted him arrested. No one could find him. He disappeared."

I was pulled back in time to Dylan trying to explain the world of video games to me. I'd taught myself to take keywords to ask simple questions to feign interest. I didn't want my son to think I didn't care about the things he was so passionate about, but I couldn't follow any of the intrigues.

"Disappeared?"

"Yeah, his entire existence vanished from the ether and algorithms. Nobody had ever done that. When you have a presence, it's forever."

"Nobody knows who he is?" I glanced toward the office.

"Rumor has it he's from Venezuela. I think—" he pointed to the doorway, "—that's him."

Magda's phone buzzed on the table, interrupting our conversation. Ricky pressed his mother's limp thumb to the button opening the textbox. Clever boy. He handed me the phone. "Tessa Rivera."

Tessa: *How are you Viper-Mama?*

Magda: *Viper is resting. It's M.R.-what's up with Carlos?"*

The reply dots danced for several heartbeats.

Tessa: *He is so handsome, is he not? Maria says she wants to climb him like a mountain. She is repulsive and too old for him.*

She was diverting my question.

I didn't respond.

The writer in me was dying to piece this story together. Caesar's men took Roberto out of the city. Government men were trying to hack into the Garcia family's private server. Jorge and the security team were missing in action, and before I could go on with my bullet points, the reporter on TV spoke.

Anchor: "We have a video message from the leader of the PNM."

The image changed to a young and petite woman, a teenager. Her black hair tucked under a camouflage brimmed cap, she wore the same camouflage uniform as the soldiers in front of the capitol except for a cobalt-blue band on her left forearm. She stood in front of the matching cobalt-and-white flags.

"A girl," I whispered to myself, remembering the girls I'd met the morning before at the school.

"She's just a baby." Magda groaned.

The girl spoke. "We are placed in our nation's capital from big cities, small villages, plantations, and farms. Families stand here together, mothers, fathers, sons, and daughters to protest a corrupt government who have bled our resources for their own benefit. What we ask is an election in two months' time for every elected office in the federal government. There will be a monetary limit to the campaigns of one hundred thousand dollars. Outside supporters of any candidate must gain a license to campaign and not engage in any hate rhetoric toward opposition candidates. Any abuse by a candidate or their supporters will result in the disqualification of that candidate. This is an effort by the people and for the people. We will not be endorsing any candidate or dissuade any current elected official from running in this election.

"We have set the date for November first. Each region will have a voluntary election committee. There is a website launching tonight to volunteer. This is the new century, and we will make new decisions by the people."

She finished and walked off-camera, leaving a view of the two flags.

The image on the TV went back to the rows of rebels, still standing.

~ * ~

Jason

"What are they up to?" I asked *El Jefe*.

"Fuck off."

I threw my hands in the air and marched back into the den. This guy was more infuriating than a hormonal teenage girl.

Shelly rushed to me, grabbing my biceps and leaning in close. "Caesar took Roberto out of the city. It was his men in police uniforms," she whispered.

"There seems to be a lot of uniforms missing today," I said, looking at the fake officers occupying the Garcia's house.

"What?" Her fingers dug into my arms.

"These aren't government guys, either...not Ribero's guys, anyway."

Shelly glanced nervously at the fake police officers. "They're ours?"

I nodded.

"Of course!" She stepped back and pinched her bottom lip with her thumb. "The hacker's erasing any and all connections between Roberto and the rebels."

Shelly's spy-novel conclusions were endearing—and correct. Her anxious but calm demeanor was in full regalia, and she glowed, more beautiful than she was at twenty-four.

"The government will try and get their hands on anything to prove Rob incited the coup. This is preemptive to make sure they have no proof." She paced. "But then why didn't Caesar just let him be arrested? Why did he take him out of the city?"

I glanced at the TV.

Ricky jumped up. "There they go."

"Oh god." I turned toward the doorway. "*Jefe*, get in here!"

The officers, security men, and the hacker all ran into the den and watched.

The rebel army charged, maintaining formation as they ascended the outer stairs of the capitol in a disciplined assault. They burst through the front entrance and disappeared into the building.

"I thought they said no violence?" Shelly asked.

The cameraman who'd been with the rebels from the beginning came back on, camera bouncing and following a group into the large domed-ceiling foyer. His voice shook as he described what he saw.

"We have entered the capitol. The group I am with will not speak to me. I am going to try and get to the battalion leader."

The camera image wove through the rebels, who'd stopped and resumed their stance. "I have the leader. Sir, can you tell us what is happening?"

The old man's expression was stoic. His gray beard and hunched shoulders made him look more like somebody's grandfather than the leader of a band of revolutionaries. He stared right at the camera. "The government has refused our demands, so we will now occupy the capitol until they concede. We have not been met with any opposition from police or military for this new action yet. We do not want violence," the elderly leader said. "This is a necessary response."

The camera panned the large room, showing the rebels standing still once again, just like when they were on the outside.

"When all the lawmakers are present to put the matter to a vote, we will vacate the building. We ask they reconvene immediately."

The anchor safe in the studio broke in. "Miguel, we are just getting word from the leader of the Assembly; they are ready to convene for a vote if their safety can be ensured to enter the chamber."

The cameraman repeated the information to the rebel leader, who nodded. "We are standing down to let them enter."

"There you have it," the reporter said. "The Assembly is to come to the capitol and vote on the imitative put forth by the rebels."

"This is different." Magda groaned from the far end of the couch. "Welcome to the new Salvador, rational and educated on procedures. It is about time."

I turned to *El Jefe*. "Did you get it done?"

He glared and spun on his heel. *"Vamanos."* They left out the front door.

The house fell silent.

~ * ~

Shelly

It was two in the morning, and still, we watched the rebels. The news anchor filled dead space with several call-in guests and in-studio expert analyses of the situation. Magda and Ricky slept on the other end of the couch, wrapped in each other's arms. After Eric passed, I slept like that night after night with my youngest, Connor. He'd been about the same age as Ricky at the time.

"This is an incredible show of organized restraint in a volatile country," a male guest said. "Salvador has educated their rural communities over the past few decades with privately funded initiatives. These rebels, if you can call somebody's Abuelita that, know how the government should work, and the world is watching."

One man in crisp white shirt, black trench, and dark slacks stopped at the beckoning of the reporter. "Infrastructure Chairman Tomas Rodriguez, may I have a moment? *Señor*, are you here to vote on the rebel initiative?"

The man nodded. "It is my job, and my pleasure to do so. This is the will of the people. Excuse me. I have a vote to cast."

Another man appeared in front of the camera. "This is insurrection and will be treated as such. These rebels are guilty of treason."

"*Señor* Gonzales, will the military retaliate?"

"Let's hope so." The lawmaker scowled. "This is disgraceful. Just look at them, taking over our most sacred institution of democracy. They should all be arrested."

"*Punta.*" Magda croaked, half-conscious. "I hate that guy."

"Will you be voting for new elections, *Señor* Gonzales?"

"Of course not. There's no point. Our government works fine with our current leadership."

Tomas Rodriguez appeared back in front of the camera in Gonzales' face. "It's because of crooked men like you we even have this."

Gonzales threw up his hands in defense.

Rodriguez rolled his eyes. "Let's go vote and stop being such an egomaniac."

"You are going to lose, Tomas."

"As you can see," the reporter said, "lawmakers will have a heated debate on the floor of the assembly. Stay tuned."

The men walked away from the camera and disappeared through the large double doors.

"Magda?" Roberto called from the foyer.

"*Cariño?*" Magda winced as she sat up.

He rushed into the den and kissed his wife.

Ricky threw his arms around his father.

"Are you all right?" Magda said. "We saw Carlos, and—"

"I'm fine. I'll tell you everything later."

Magda's phone pinged, and she answered it. "Lara? *Si*, we're fine. He's here." She handed the phone to Roberto.

Jason leaned over to me. "Their daughter. She's away at school in Argentina."

I nodded.

Roberto's phone rang. He handed it to Magda.

Jason pulled me out of the room and put his arms around my waist in the empty foyer.

Without words, he pulled my head to his chest. I could hear his heartbeat and intermittent flutters along with his deep breathing, and we swayed.

"Are we dancing?" I asked.

"I am. You're just swaying off-beat."

"What beat?"

He pressed my head tighter to his chest. "Hear that?" he whispered. "We synced our heartbeats together."

I could hear it. We *were* synced. The warmth of his body engulfed me.

"I love you, Shelly. I always have," Jason whispered in my ear. "This time I'll get to show you every day."

Jason Mattis loves me. "I love you too, you crazy person."

This was the moment I had to choose to allow myself a happily ever after.

Chapter Seventeen

Capistrano Beach, California, two days before Thanksgiving
Shelly

"Dylan's flight comes in at eight-twenty-five tomorrow morning." I pointed to my iPad with my stylus. "He wants to take an Uber from John Wayne Airport and should get here around nine, ten at the latest." I adjusted myself on the couch. "Connor's driving down from San Luis Obispo today with friends, so who knows what time they will be here." I rolled my eyes. "Jasmine will be in by ten-forty tomorrow morning. So, from LAX, you should be able to get here...with traffic... Oh, I don't know," I said, exasperated.

"Whatever," Jason said from the kitchen. "Does it really matter?"

"We can just order pizza when you're on your way back, I guess."

Jason had his back to me at the kitchen counter.

"What are you doing?" I asked.

He looked over his shoulder and grinned. "Are you done with our planning meeting?"

"Yes." I huffed, taking off my readers and putting my tablet on the coffee table.

"Good." He turned back away from me.

Having him with me was blissful. I hadn't realized how lonely I was until he filled my life. We'd been together day and night except when I was at my book signings.

He'd flown with me from Seattle to Dallas to Phoenix, going off on his own to explore. He'd bought gifts for me and Jazzy and found restaurants for dinner, making friends wherever he went. Cuddling with me each night in strange hotel rooms made the experience more comfortable and familiar.

We spent Thanksgiving week in my townhouse on the beach, where he cooked and cleaned for me and gave me so much good loving. Happiness exploded. He had minimal belongings, and the things he'd brought from his house in Brazil were in storage.

There was no way to know if it would last, or if he would grow tired of my structured, schedule-driven life. But if he'd had any anxious tendencies, he didn't show it.

He'd fallen in step with my OCD and was so laid back and agreeable. Each time I'd have stomach-wrenching episodes that he would just leave one day, or he'd get sick, he'd acknowledge them with a shoulder rub or big hug. He knew how to calm me. "The Zen Shredder."

He came out of the kitchen and strolled over to me with a wicked look in his eye.

"What's going on?" I asked.

He pulled my T-shirt over my head, then kissed my chest.

"Oh," I said.

He shook his head, still grinning, and picked me up with a little grunt.

"Honey, your shoulder." I worried about him carrying me.

"You're right." He put me down on my feet, took my hand, then pulled me up the stairs into the bedroom. "Strip and get on the bed."

I smirked at him.

"I'll be right back. You'd better be naked."

"Fine." I removed my bra and pulled my leggings down.

He trotted out.

I groaned as I climbed on the bed and lay on my back. I didn't like the view he'd get when he returned. I flipped onto my tummy. No, my big butt. I turned on my side and propped my head on my hand. The scrunched comforter covered my saggy bits like a Renaissance painting. I waited.

He stopped in the doorway with a bowl in his hand and an unlabeled can sticking up out of it. He sauntered into the room and with his pinky in the air he pulled the top of the can up, shimmying it as a solid red, can shaped, gelatinous object appeared.

"No way." I smiled.

He nodded and took two fingers and pressed the red mound flat into the bowl, then swirled around. "Happy Thanksgiving, Shelly." He climbed up on the bed and straddled me as I turned onto my back.

"I can't believe this," I said. "You were serious about the cranberry sauce?"

"Mmm hmm." He hummed and pulled his fingers out of the bowl, setting it on the bed next to me. He circled my left nipple with his fingers and licked the sweet, sticky gelatin off, making me squirm with pleasure. He repeated with the other.

"This tastes terrible. Who likes this stuff?" He stuck his tongue out. I giggled. "You, on the other hand, taste amazing." He licked down my belly. "Like strawberries. But something is missing."

"Missing?" I peered at him as he sat up.

"Yeah. What's better with strawberries than…?" He pulled a can of whipped cream from his waistband.

"Oh no." I grabbed at it.

"Oh yes, baby."

"Oh my god." I threw my head back as he pushed my legs open.

He squirted a little inside me and licked me clean. The sensation was so erotic and sweet I had to brace myself, holding onto the sheets and laughing out loud.

"Mmm…strawberries and cream. That's you, Shel."

I couldn't speak or catch my breath. The action made me lightheaded. He squirted and licked and squirted and licked. I laughed. My body flamed. He squirted one more time and sucked, and I exploded.

"Jason!" I shouted. "Oh my god!" The orgasm did not leave, it just kept going and going as he ate me harder and harder.

He pulled his face from my legs and landed on top of me, pushing his loose pajama pants down and he slid himself inside me. I huffed and moaned. The orgasm continued. I was an out-of-control speeding train barreling toward the light at the end of a tunnel that kept moving farther and farther away. It was exhilarating, and my whole body buzzed, my muscles pulsed around him, and my consciousness faded in and out.

This was either multiple orgasms or one of the longest ones I've ever had. My head thrashed from side-to-side, and I couldn't get enough air into my lungs, the feeling humming my entire existence powerful and exquisite.

"You're still going?" He asked as he lay on top of me propped up on his elbows, still inside me. I hadn't even noticed he had come already.

"Yes, I am still…" I huffed.

"Excellent." He rolled his hips, watching me.

The feeling slowed and stopped. Still felt great, him inside me.

"Was that a record?" he asked.

"For me it was." I threw my hand over my eyes. "I'd read women my age could have prolonged orgasms."

"Hmm. A new challenge, how exciting." He got off the bed and extended his hand. "Shower?"

"Yes, please. I'm sticky." I followed him to the bathroom. "There will never be cranberry sauce on my Thanksgiving table ever again, thank you."

"Or whipped cream?"

"I'm going to keep a can by the bed." I got on my tiptoes and sucked his bottom lip.

The two of us in our fifties with such a healthy and imaginative sex life was inspiring my writing. I'd embraced the whole "older romance" genre, and we were having so much fun giving me constant material.

~ * ~

Capistrano Beach, CA, Thanksgiving Day

The headline read *San Salvador: "Assembly and Rebels Hold Joint Session After Peaceful Protest"*

All that seemed like an eternity ago.

Tablet on my lap, I sipped coffee in pure euphoria, sitting on my patio looking out at the Pacific Ocean. The sky was gray. Most people would complain about that. I loved it. It made everything a silvery monochrome, from the water, to the sand, to the sky. All glowing and ethereal, like an Ansel Adams photograph in black and white. Two of my favorite scents permeated my nose—Salvadorean coffee and morning calone from the ocean.

Inside, the smells of the turkey in the oven, rosemary, and braising meat, made me deliriously happy. Thanksgiving dinner preparations were organized and ready with two bags of russet potatoes, peeled and ready for boiling then mashing. Green beans, snapped, soaked in ice water and the table was set with my grandmother's china.

The best part about the morning was my home filled with the most beautiful people in the universe.

All our babies were under one roof, and Jason was elated. We'd watched three Marvel movies, ate pizza, and made margaritas last night.

Jasmine, our guest of honor, was much more extroverted than I had expected, and really funny about her experiences looking at schools in the U.S. She was a born storyteller, and I'd fallen in love with my new daughter.

"Everyone told me to at least look at the University of Miami." Jasmine had rolled her eyes as she told us after dinner. "I already decided on Columbia, but Mama wanted me to see it." She took a sip of her

Margarita.

"So, Mama had just hired a new assistant and instead of booking us at a hotel in South Beach or an Airbnb downtown, she got us a house near the school." She held her fingers up in air quotes and hesitated for effect. "Near the school." She hesitated again and looked around to make sure everyone was riveted. I was.

"In a swamp." She sat back and looked just like Jason with that same smug look on her face.

"A swamp?" Dylan repeated.

Jasmine nodded. "My mother was in hell. The humidity, insects, weird smells, and creepy sounds." She leaned into Dylan. "Have you ever been to a Florida swamp?"

Dylan laughed. "No."

"There are critters," she whispered. "Oh yes, there are critters."

"There are alligators, right? I've seen videos of those things swimming in people's pools and eating people's dogs," Connor added.

"Thank goodness we did not see any gators," Jaz said to him. "But have you ever seen an armadillo, like not in the zoo?"

We all shook our heads, except Jason. He grinned but stayed quiet, letting his daughter be the center of attention. I squeezed his knee under the table.

"Armadillos are fast," she said. "The landlord sent a 'specialist.'" Air quotes again. "This sweaty, balding, butt-crack-showing guy showed up to get it out of the house, and my mother barricaded herself in the bedroom."

We all roared with laughter at her description.

I didn't see a girl with insecurities, I saw an extraordinary young girl with sharp wit and a comfort in her own skin. She was beautiful. I saw Jason in her eyes and facial expressions.

"He chased it around the house with a paper shopping bag for a half an hour." She took another sip of Margarita. "It was like the Coyote trying to catch the Roadrunner. I was hoping to see him set up some elaborate trap or something."

"Did he?" Conner asked.

Jasmine shook her head. "He was sweating and panting. When the animal hid under a cabinet by the front door, he'd gone into the kitchen to throw water on his face. I opened the front door. He yelled at me not to, but I did anyway. The thing just ran out."

She sat back and threw her hands in the air in victory.

"Since Mama was still hiding in the bedroom, I told the man I would give him ten dollars for efforts and sent him on his way. 'Bye, Felicia.'" Jasmine finished with a shit-eating grin and a wave of her hand.

Jason looked at me and rolled his eyes. We'd obviously thought the same thing about the ending of her story being a slight stretch of the truth. But I liked it. She had a great skill for riveting storytelling and descriptions.

It seemed my boys loved her too. They began discussing the intrigues of Marvel Superhero films, and she was a self-professed expert.

They'd debated for an hour about who was the most powerful superhero of the Avengers before all agreed Dylan's well-thought-out argument for the Scarlet Witch had won with a four-to-one vote. Connor being the only holdout since I'd just voted for Dylan's choice after the delivery of his litigation.

Connor followed Jason into the kitchen to make popcorn for our movie marathon like a star-struck fan, asking him a thousand questions in one breath.

"What's your favorite brand of board? Longboard or shortboard? Did you ever surf in Thailand, Portugal, New Zealand?"

I thought my youngest son was about cry when Jason insisted he come surf with him in the morning.

When Jason left to go to his storage unit, the kids and I settled on the couches for the movies.

He'd returned a half an hour later with four of his surfboards, a few dusty photo albums, several framed wall posters of him from Tennant Surf Co., and three five-foot trophies from his World Champion victories. He left them in the entry hall. We'd discuss that later.

Dylan opted out of the early morning surf session as he was the sleeping-in, non-athletic type, so he stayed behind. Although he was just as enamored by Jason, surfing was not his thing. I'd let him sleep in.

The dining table was set, and a folding table for the kids was set up in the living room in anticipation for us, my parents, Jason's dad and new stepmother, along with her fifteen-year-old daughter, for Thanksgiving dinner.

My brother Ben hadn't answered my calls or texts for about a week. Not out of the ordinary for him. I wasn't sure if he was coming to dinner. The past three years, he'd only called to ask for money. It broke my heart to say no.

When his last girlfriend had gotten pregnant, he'd pursued a relationship with her, even planning a wedding. But after her father fired him from his motorcycle-parts shop, Ben's anger issues flared. She claimed he'd hit her. She kicked him to the curb and now wanted child support.

Three silvery silhouettes carried surfboards over the sand about two-hundred feet away. The two tall figures and a shorter apparition approached.

Only a painting could freeze the moment. I'd hang it on my family room wall. I settled for capturing the scene with a snap of my phone's camera.

Jason had the top of his wetsuit down over his hips and because he was still out of my focus, I saw the stunning young man who took my breath away all those years ago.

The unattainable and elusive legend who would never be mine was here with my son and his daughter. I was in love with them. *All* of them.

~ * ~

"Do you think he'll remember meeting me?" Jason asked later that morning after he'd showered and dressed, looking handsome in a heather gray T-shirt and skinny Nike joggers slung low in his hips.

My father had been battling Alzheimer's for quite a few years. It'd been a stress on all of us like no other illness could have prepared us for, especially my brother, who'd avoided him in the past few months rather than deal with his emotions.

"I doubt it," I said. "But he'd asked me about you a lot back then."

In 1992 I'd taken the World Champion of Surfing to meet my parents.

"So, let me get his straight, Jason," my father said at dinner, holding his woven fingers to his chin. "You do not have a residence?"

"That's correct, Sir," Jason replied.

"Where do you get mail delivered?" my father prodded.

"I have an accountant here in Huntington who handles all of my bills, Mr. Stringer," he said and smiled at me, "and the public relations folks at Tennant Surf handle the fan mail." He took a big forkful of rice and hummed in approval.

"This rice is delicious, Mrs. Stringer. How did you get so much flavor into it?" Now Jason was being annoyingly sweet.

"Oh, well." My mother had gotten giddy. "I use chicken broth," she answered proudly.

I cringed. Jason had been all over the world many times and he'd eaten in hundreds of restaurants in dozens of cities. Chicken broth in rice was pedestrian, at best, for his sophisticated palate.

"Well, it works very well." He winked at me.

My father scowled all through dinner and kept making snide remarks as to having a "real job" and a "real home." He was an old-fashioned soul who would've been more comfortable in the 1950's with his sense of humor and ideas about who I should marry, and soon.

Roger Stringer liked his lawn, his bowling league each Friday, and happily sold commercial elevators.

Anyone: "How's the elevator business, Roger?"

Dad: "Oh, you know, it has its ups and downs."

Laughter ensues

Ellen Stringer, an elementary school nurse with incredible empathy, a love for antique embroidered handkerchiefs, and a terrible cook, smiled at Jason all through dinner. I think she was less embarrassed by my dad's attitude toward a guest and more blissful in the fact I had brought a guy home for the first time in my life.

I loved them both dearly; they were good parents, and I had never wanted for support, love, and affection from either of them. I was their dream child, the good one.

My younger brother Ben, however, was the rebellious one—motorcycle, tattoos, high school drop-out, and on probation for aggravated assault at eighteen.

I was glad he was not at the dinner, although Jason would have charmed even my tough-skinned brother, I was sure of it.

"How long have they been married?" Jason asked me in the car on the way back to my apartment. He'd settled in as usual, my once-a-year roommate for a week.

"Uh, well, I'm twenty-three, so twenty-four years?"

He shook his head. "Crazy. That's a lifetime."

"Yup, high school sweethearts." I agreed.

"Mine too," he said contemplatively.

"Couldn't imagine that," I said, wincing.

There was no boy in my high school who I would even consider marrying. They didn't understand me. I was weird, reading all the time, listening to jazz, and not wanting to get drunk and make out.

For some crazy reason, Jason didn't mind those things about me. He'd ask what I was reading, and I'd caught him a few times reading my current book. He even liked my jazz music, bobbing his head when an upbeat tune came on. He'd also tried to put things back where I liked them to be. Mugs, face-down on the second shelf, dishes washed and put away right after using, and counter wiped down in the bathroom after each sink use.

"Believe it or not, I like your dad," he'd said. I must have shown surprise on my face because he chuckled. "He reminds me of my dad, all disciplined and boring, but he knows what he likes and what makes him happy, and that's all he needs. So, it's cool, I guess. It's simple but it works...for him. The same house for the rest of his life, wife, kids, all of that—simple, stable, and boring." He paused and our eyes met. "Yeah, *it works for him."* He shifted his bottom on the passenger seat of my Toyota Corolla. *"Yeah, not me though."*

"Me neither," I said, not knowing if that was true. I knew white picket fences were never going to be in Jason's future. But I was starting to think that might be mine.

"Oh yeah? He asked about me?" Jason asked as he opened the refrigerator door and stared into it, I assumed for some answer of what to eat that would not fill him up and spoil our early dinner. "He didn't like me, huh?"

"Just have some eggs," I suggested. "You know, I think my dad was just confused about your lifestyle. It didn't make sense to him."

"He and my dad could have sat around and wallowed in *that* forever." He took out the carton of eggs. "Although, what a hypocrite my dad was when he spent forty weeks a year on the road in his truck."

"He did what he had to do, Jason." I waited for a response.

"Is your brother coming tonight?" Jason pivoted the conversation.

I sighed. "I don't know. If he does, he'll just ask for money again."

"So *that's* the deal with him, huh?"

"That, and a whole lot of pent-up anger issues." I shrugged. "He's got a kid now, but he's as flaky as he ever was. I wanted to be an aunt, but he's never introduced me."

A knock on the door surprised us both as it was too early for our guests to arrive.

"I'll get it." Jason opened the door to find three boys I'd recognized as Connor's buddies from high school. Their faces lit up, and they stood motionless and speechless in the presence of their hero.

"Connor!" I shouted.

My son appeared and ran to his friends, bumping fists and shoulders. "Can we go down the beach, Mom?"

He'd been a sweet, polite boy with lots of friends. He was like Eric that way. In contrast to Dylan, who preferred his computer video games and only had a handful of lifelong friends. Just like me. I waited to get him alone to hear about a new girl he'd been seeing. I'd heard him late at night talking to her.

"Okay, just be back by four, your grandparents are coming."

Before the boys left, they'd taken photos with Jason and walked out the patio door, tapping on their phones.

I'd heard Connor tell the boys he'd gone surfing with Jason and his new sister.

My heart thumped at the "new sister" comment.

"Did you hear that?" Jason said.

I nodded and put my hand to my chest to calm the thudding.

"That's one of the best things I've ever heard," Jason said. "He already thinks of her as his sister."

"Yeah, that's so cute." I went back to my onion chopping.

"What do you think about making us an official family?"

"We already are, right? I mean, it feels like we are anyway."

"Maybe we show these kids we're serious about it."

I turned to him, confused.

"Marry me, Shelly. Like tomorrow." Jason didn't touch me, he just leaned against the counter and waited, twirling a spatula. Eggs popping in the pan was the only sound for a heartbeat.

"Tomorrow?" My brain scanned a virtual calendar in my head.

"Or whenever. Next week, next month. Just tell me you will."

"You're ready to stay put? Let your roots dig in?"

He came to me and took my hand. "Let me hold onto your hollow coin." He kissed my wrist, then took the other and kissed it, too.

"I'm not hollow anymore."

"Good," he whispered into my ear, then kissed the spot just below it, giving me a tremor. "Something simple, here on the beach, just us and our family."

Chills ran up my arms. *Our family.*

"Say yes, Michelle."

I bit my bottom lip, thinking it would stop me from shaking. I was a grown woman, for heaven's sake. But Jason Mattis just asked me to marry him. *Shit yes!*

The thought was exhilarating. My wedding to Eric was a big, traditional church thing, bridesmaids, reception with a band, more for our parents than for us.

"What's that reaction?" he asked.

My eyes welled, and I couldn't speak.

He turned off the burner. "Shelly, where are you right now?"

"Yes. Yes!" I burst out. "So, on the beach, like right here?" I pointed out the sliding glass door to the beach.

He took my hand, opened the door, then led me outside.

"Right there, I'm going to make you my wife." He pointed to the water then pulled me in for a lip-pressing kiss, the thankful kind, the forever kind.

A simple ceremony on the beach was just so Jason, and now so me to do something like that, so spontaneous and romantic.

We went back inside.

"What was your wedding like?" I asked as he plated his eggs.

"Remember the wedding in The Godfather?"

I nodded.

"Like that." He grimaced. "It felt like I was a guest and not the groom. I didn't know anyone. Gabby was already pregnant, and it felt rushed, too."

Now I felt sorry for him. Magda was right. He had so much to give and was a true romantic. Different than most men I'd known and far from my rational Eric, who could be life of the party—fun, but not what you'd call romantic.

Spontaneity wasn't something I was used to, but Jason made me want to try.

Chapter Eighteen

Shelly

The kids cleared the table, loading the dishwasher as we ordered them to. They were good kids, but they still needed some drill sergeant treatment. The grandparents had left after a wonderful Thanksgiving dinner, just like Jason had wanted. Everyone talked and laughed and made wonderful declarations of what they were thankful for.

The doorbell rang.

"I'll get it," Dylan shouted.

Jason and I were in the office, discussing permanent homes for the things he'd brought from his storage space.

"Uncle Ben," Connor called.

I stomped down the hallway in a rage, ready to launch at my inconsiderate loser brother who'd blown off my first Thanksgiving dinner with Jason and Jasmine. I'd texted and left him messages for weeks with no response. I could tell my mother was disappointed he hadn't shown up. She'd even asked several times if I'd spoken to him, then justified his lack of respect with ridiculous excuses like "Maybe he lost his phone?" or "He must have been on his motorcycle and didn't hear it ring?" I wanted to shout he was a flaky jerk who didn't care about anyone but himself.

Jason yanked me back before I reached the den. "Let me talk to him." His sapphire gaze bored into me. "You're too angry with him right now."

"Jason..."

He pushed past me and was already shaking Ben's hand before I could protest further.

~ * ~

Jason

"Beer?" I asked Ben as I opened the refrigerator. He looked just like I thought he would. Hair dyed black, flat billed hat, and covered in tattoos—layers of ink that had been corrected many times, revealing too many bad decisions commemorated by indelible art on his skin.

"Sure." Ben fidgeted with his keys.

"Come on." I handed him a bottle of *Eisenbahn* and headed for the glass door to the patio.

Ben looked at the bottle with trepidation.

"It's a Brazilian Pilsner. Come on, let's talk." I opened the sliding glass door and waited for him to go through it. I adjusted two deck chairs to face the beach.

I groaned as I sat down and put my feet up on the half-wall facing the beach. It was dark in the distance except for the glowing whitewash, followed by the soothing crash of high tide. Ben sat in the other chair and put his feet up, too.

"Happy Thanksgiving, man." I held my beer bottle up.

Ben clinked it with mine. "Sorry about dinner."

"That bit you're gonna have to deal with your sister. But first, we're going to have a chat. How much do you owe?"

Ben squirmed. "I've had some bad luck, and I got fired, and then this fucking guy—"

"I asked how much." I turned my head to Ben and waited.

He stared out to the beach, and his hazel eyes got glassy. "Sixteen thousand." He exhaled and lowered his chin like an ashamed child.

"I'll give it to you this one time, don't ask again. This is between me and you. You don't discuss this with Shelly, understand?"

Ben nodded. We sat, looking at the waves in silence.

"Now you're going to launder your karma," I told him.

"My karma?" He scoffed.

"Yeah, man. Where I've been the past thirty years, there's a hierarchy. When someone's in debt to the boss, he pays his debt." I took a swig from my bottle and winced. The beer was flat. "Payment isn't always money."

"So, what? You're the boss now?"

"You want your debt paid?"

"You're serious?" Ben scoffed again.

I turned my whole body to him. "Are you?"

He shook his head. "What are we talking about, here? Am I going to be your slave or butler or something? Like on an old TV show?"

"More like an assistant." I chuckled at the old TV show reference, like the Brady Bunch or something. "It's a job, Ben. You know, *work*?"

Even I was ready to work. I'd called the Tennant Surf Co. folks to pay my respects to the old man. I'd made Gus Tennant, my former sponsor, a rich man. But he'd been gone for over two months. Most likely on one of his world surfing escapades and just forgot to tell his family. Gus' son and daughter had taken over. They were in financial ruin after their father dropped everything and left them to carry the business. My heart broke for Brad and Lisa, struggling to keep the company afloat. I'd watched the two of them grow up. Brad used to follow me around like a puppy dog. I wanted to help them so, just like Ben, I'd made them a business proposal to be a silent partner, investing a good amount of money into the business.

Lisa, the daughter, proposed a clothing line for me to design and asked if I'd be their model in their ads. It was a great offer, and now I needed an assistant.

I glared at my future brother-in-law.

Ben shifted again, his fists and jaw clenched.

"Relax man. I know you've had trouble keeping jobs, and I'm offering you one."

"Yeah, to be your *pussy-boy*," Ben snapped.

"You'll need to chill around me. I'm not supposed to be around stress. It's a medical condition."

"What the fuck are you talking about?"

"Do you surf?" I looked back at the waves.

"I'm from Huntington." Ben took a swig of his beer.

"How long has it been?"

He sighed. "Forever."

"I took Connor out this morning. It was epic."

"I taught Connor how to surf."

"Yeah?"

"Yeah. Shelly's ex wasn't much of a surfer. He was from Chicago."

"He's not her ex. He was her husband. Dying doesn't make him an ex." I had no problem with Eric's photos with the boys around the house, no matter what Shelly said. It didn't bother me. That was her past. I was her future. He was still the boys' father, and from what she'd told me, he'd been a good one. They were nice kids.

"Yeah, okay. That's cool." Ben stared at me for a long time. "*Fuck*, Jason Mattis. I'm having a beer with a legend. The Zen Shredder." He snickered. "Let's Dance!"

I smirked and let out a huff. "Been a long time since I've heard that."

"I gotta tell you, man. I saw you shred. You were the master. The best."

I held my smirk.

"Now I see the Zen part." Ben held his bottle to me to clink.

Clink, drink.

"So? What about your karma?"

"Do I have a choice?"

"You still don't get it, do you?" I glared at him. "You have had all of the opportunities to get this right, and now you're too old for the same mistakes, man."

"Opportunities?"

"Yeah. You have a great family. I've met your parents. They're good people, and they love you and Shelly."

"My dad sold fucking elevators for forty fucking years."

"Yeah? My dad was a truck driver. So what?" I shook my head. He still didn't get it. "You rebelled against the fact your life was boring? Shit, man, come down to South America. Selling elevators is a privileged life—nice house, two cars, cable television."

"I don't want to be like my father." Ben's face darkened.

"I get it. But you've got responsibilities now. Shelly would like to meet her niece or nephew. How old is the kid now?"

Ben sat back and peered at the waves, not drinking or blinking. "Sofia is three," he whispered.

"Bring her over. Make your sister happy."

"I will." Ben blinked. "Dude, I've got to ask." He turned to me. "What do you want with my boring-ass sister? I mean, you're...well, you're you. You married a Brazilian supermodel. You're a three-time world champ."

I had to grin at the thought of my sweet lady. "Shelly isn't boring."

"All of her schedules and organization? She's a bore, man."

"Your sister is sexy as hell."

"Ugh, don't even." He faked a gag.

I kept smiling, thinking about her crazy blowjobs.

"Forget it. I don't want to know." He turned back to the ocean.

"We're getting married."

He stared at me in confusion. "Shit, really?"

I stood and poured my flat, stale beer over the wall into the sand.

"Come surfing in the morning. Let's get that karma straight."

"Yeah, okay."

I glanced up to the glass door and was not surprised to see Shelly leaning on the frame in silence, holding her cardigan wrapped around her.

"How much did you hear, Shel?" I sat back down.

Ben shot around to look at his big sister.

"Just about me being sexy as hell." She sauntered outside and sat on my lap, staring at her brother.

He rolled his eyes.

"Something about getting karma straight?" Shelly took Ben's hand and put her head on my shoulder.

Life was good.

Chapter Nineteen

Capistrano Beach, CA, December
Shelly

I should've been in pre-wedding bliss. I should've been happy to be marrying the most beautiful man in the world. But I was stressed and lashing out at everyone.

"Shel, you're giving off bad vibes here." Jason sighed as I climbed into bed with my teeth clenched.

"My mother asked what flowers I'm getting, and I freaking lost it."

"Flowers?" he asked in disgust, removing his sexy, black-framed readers. He looked like a professorial wet dream sitting with his back against the headboard, shirtless, holding his iPad with my big ginger cat tucked under his arm.

"Yeah, flowers. She got all weird about the fact I am not inviting her cousin Stan." I sat next to him, stiff as a board, staring into nothingness. "This was supposed to be simple. You and me on the beach, right?" I stared at my reflection in the dresser mirror across from the bed, picking at my gray hairs.

"Nothing's simple when it comes to family, sweetheart."

"We're up to thirteen people. No food, no space, no Cousin Stan." I sank down and rested my head in his lap. He stroked my hair.

My skinny black cat, Loki, came and curled up near my chest, and Ginger-Thor grunted from the other side of Jason. We were a little family all in the same bed. My cats had taken to Jason as if he was one of their own. Thor even groomed him with his tongue like he did with Loki.

"This *is* about us—you and me," Jason told me.

I grinned at him. "Can I tell everyone to go to hell?"

"Yes." He kissed my forehead.

He was so good at calming me. When he did, more often than not, I realized whatever I was freaking out about at the moment was silly.

Two purring cats and a purring fiancé made my existence more peaceful.

I woke the next morning to a warm hand between my thighs, then fingers teasing inside me.

"Mmm…" I was not awake yet.

"Stress relief," Jason whispered in my ear.

"Mmm hmm," I agreed.

He removed his hand from inside me and pulled my leg back over his hip, opening me up. His hardness slid inside me. A pulse of electricity shot up my thighs. I'd never been taken this way. He put one arm under my hip and the other on top, pulling me closer to him as his hips pressed into me.

It was dirty and porn-like, and I loved it.

When his thumb found my clit and pressed and rubbed, my breathing got faster, and an orgasm was building, his thrusts got harder. My body buzzed, and a hot wave crashed to our joining.

I huffed, making a high-pitched sound I didn't recognize. He chuckled.

"That good, huh?"

"Oh my god, Jason." I moaned and pushed his hand down harder on my clit.

He huffed several times into my hair then his body stiffened as his orgasm came at the same time as mine.

"Yes, so good." He hissed. "Shelly, my *wife*."

My eyes welled, and I laughed.

"Yes, my *husband*."

We didn't move, his arms wrapped around me, his front to my back.

"Just me and you, on the beach." He sighed.

"Don't forget Bob," I added.

His body jiggled, laughing behind me. "Right, gotta have Bob there."

My parents' hippie next-door-neighbor-for-fifty-years was an ordained minister, consummate kook, and the sweetest man you'll ever meet.

He'd had two dead VW microbuses in his driveway for years and been a good friend to my parents. His wife—at least I think they were married—travelled with the Renaissance Fair selling fake flower crowns and showed up over the years. They had a son about my age who was homeschooled by his mother and travelled with her all over the country and eventually became a roadie for tour bands. They were weird but nice to us, and I couldn't think of anyone better than Bob to officiate my unconventional wedding.

~ * ~

December 28 was the warmest on record. The sky was aflame at sunset, red, pink, and orange fading into gray and blue.

We stood barefoot at the water's edge, small frigid waves ticking our toes. I wore a flowing white maxi dress, the sheer top layer billowing in a slight breeze. My mother's white-silk pashmina draped over my shoulders. Jasmine flowers crowned my head, my hair threaded with blue ribbon, Greek-goddess style. Jason wore a white linen button-down and jeans. His eyes were bluer than the ocean and glowed in the setting sun.

He slid his arms around my waist, and I did the same, so we faced each other. He had the biggest, goofiest smile on his stunning face. The world froze. All I saw was him. All I felt was his heart thumping against my chest. Bob spoke but I didn't hear him.

"Mom!" Dylan called.

I started and met his gaze. He jerked his chin to Bob. Cheeks burning, I glanced at the old, bearded hippie.

He grinned.

"I'm sorry," I said. "What?"

Jason tickled my hips, sending distracting pulses to my sex.

"I asked if you were ready," Bob said.

"Yes, of course." I smiled at Jason.

He gave me a squeeze.

Soft chuckles came from our kids, parents, my brother, and Jason's new business partners, the Tennants.

"You all know I'm ready." Jason's gaze never wavered.

More chuckles.

"Good. I'll make this quick so you can spend the rest of your lives together." Bob adjusted his silver silk scarf with Hebrew symbols on it and opened his ancient and tattered leather book with random folded sheets of paper stuck into different spots.

"This is a love story of two souls who found each other again. The universe would not let these two stay apart and found a way to bring them together again. Now they are here to make an everlasting promise to keep each other's souls safe and loved for the rest of their days."

His words were perfect. Tears welled. Jason's eyes shone so they reflected the red sky in them. He tickled me again and moved his hands farther down my back. My body tingled and my breath hitched.

Bob's words faded again as I got lost in Jason's eyes. He brushed a tear from my cheek. I finished the job with my own hand. My mother handed me a tissue. I wiped then crumpled it in my hand and wrapped my arms around Jason's waist. He pressed his forehead to mine.

"You're beautiful," he whispered and gave me another squeeze, this time closer to my bottom.

"Okay, okay!" Bob shouted. "Say yes then kiss already, for heaven's sake!"

Everyone chuckled.

"Yes," we said in unison.

"Oh, shit, the rings." Bob jumped and pulled them out of his pocket. "Here put these on each other, *then* kiss."

This was not a perfect or pristine ceremony, but we'd both had that already. Our minister smelled of marijuana, forgot most of the service, and was better than I could've imagined.

Jason grabbed my ass with both hands, dipped down and rubbed his hard cock in between my legs as he kissed me. I'd hoped our kids and parents didn't notice.

The sun sank into the Pacific with the green flash, and we both hugged Bob. Our family rushed us, my boys at me and Jasmine at Jason.

As we made our way back to the house, Jason kissed the back of my hand.

"I've got to get you alone, right now," he growled into my ear.

"Patience, husband. Let's give them a little bit of a party."

I'd had hired a taco guy with a grill set up on the side of the house. Jasmine and the boys hung fairy lights across the patio and built a bonfire in the sand. They ran ahead of us, excited to light it up. Connor offered to DJ on his laptop, and there were no flowers or Cousin Stan.

"Toast!" Brad Tennant shouted as we poured ourselves some champagne.

Jason jumped up on the half wall. "Thank you for coming, we love you all. Now please leave so I can be alone with my wife!" he shouted and took a sip.

Everyone laughed, but I knew he was serious.

We'd reserved the honeymoon suite at The Waldorf Astoria Monarch Beach only ten minutes away. Dylan offered to drive us and changed into a suit with a chauffer's cap. But there was one more thing we needed to do before we left.

I motioned to Connor to play the song for our first dance as a married couple. When "You Can Leave Your Hat On" started, Jason pulled me close to him and dirty-danced me on cue, dipping and grinding. My mother gasped and went in the house. Brad, Lisa, and Ben whopped, and the kids groaned and eww'd.

We left the house as Connor's friends showed up to resume the party with the promise to kick everyone out by midnight. I trusted him. He was a good boy.

"Keep an eye on your sister." Jason gave Connor a stern gaze.

"Don't worry, she won't leave my sight. I'm her big brother."

The suite was stunning, white and gold, with a huge glass wall looking out to the now-dark Pacific Ocean and sky. A bowl of strawberries sat on the small table with vase of white Calla lilies and an ice bucket with a bottle of pink champagne.

"It's perfect." I turned to Jason as he held a strawberry to my lips.

We were together for as long as forever lasted.

Chapter Twenty

Capistrano Beach, CA, December A Year Later
Jason

A man stood on the beach, shoes in one hand and the other hand in his trouser pocket, his jacket draped over his forearm. He watched me for a long time. I picked my board "Michelle" out of the water and tucked her under my arm. Matt Sutter's expression revealed awe and a hint of bitterness.

"Matt," I acknowledged the CIA agent. "You look like an asshole standing there in your suit. Let's get you out here. I've got the perfect board for you."

"Maybe next time."

"Where's your mask?" I wiped a towel over my face then wet hair. "I've got a pre-existing condition, man. Stay six feet, will ya?"

Matthew Sutter pulled a blue N-95 mask from his trouser pocket but didn't put it on.

I shook my head, leaving the towel over my head like a hood. My ears got the brunt of the chill when I surfed the icy Pacific.

He fell into step with me as I started back to the house. If he was here, something was wrong. I was just going to pretend like he wasn't here at all.

"We're going after Caesar."

"Caesar helped you get Roberto out of the city, among other things. Did you forget that?" I couldn't look at him.

"Caesar helped his wife's best friend, and Roberto benefitted as well."

"That's a bunch of bullshit, and you know it." I was wet and cold and didn't want to talk to him. My lips quivered, and my teeth chattered. "I don't work for you anymore. Why are you telling me this?"

"You heard *El Jefe*. You never stop working for us."

That stopped me. I pulled the towel off my head and scowled at Matt. "You had a wire on him?"

"Be in DC on Thursday for a Congressional hearing." Matt held out an envelope.

I didn't take it and started walking again. "If I plead the fifth?"

"You won't."

"Fucker," I mumbled and started walking again. The agent followed then caught up with me. "My wife's an attorney. I'll discuss this with her." I tipped my chin up to the empty patio in the distance.

"If you don't testify, she'll be the one in trouble."

I stopped and waited.

"We will cancel the charity and destroy her reputation."

"Cancel?"

"You've heard of Cancel Culture?"

My perfect world was being picked up and shook out like a sandy blanket. I looked up at the sky. "Fucking assholes." I took a few long breaths and then spoke. "That charity has raised millions of dollars for those rural schools. Got them WiFi... Hell, Elon Musk donated a fucking satellite."

"It's going down. Shelly could be arrested for conspiring with a terrorist organization."

Without another thought, I dropped my board, and as if in an outer body experience, my arm cocked back. I'd been a pacifist my whole life, a lover not a fighter. But my rogue fist delivered a blow to Mathew Sutter's chin with all the strength I had in my body.

The younger man's face flew to the side, and he took a step back, staying on his feet. His hand raised to the point of the contact and assessed the damage. He opened his jaw and rubbed the outside of it, remaining stoic.

"You have a choice. Either you testify against Caesar—"

"He'll have me killed!" I shouted. My insides liquefied and pooled at my feet.

"We can get you into witness protection near a beach, maybe in the South Pacific somewhere."

"What about my wife and daughter, you fuck?" I continued to shout.

Matt shook his head, still rubbing his chin.

"You're making me choose?"

"Either way, it's over. She'll either never forgive you for taking everything she's worked for or else you'll just have to disappear on her."

A thud landed in my chest, and I had to clutch my heart as the pain started. This wasn't my physical heart straining under the pain. This pain started in my head and then my stomach and the twin pains met at my chest with a punch to my lungs. This was the pain I'd felt when I'd found out my ma was sick, whenever Jasmine would cry, and when Shelly had a gun to her head. This was emotional heartache.

"You've left her plenty of times in the past. It's what you do best."

"Fuck you!" I spat, bent over, trying to breathe, rubbing my chest.

"I emailed you your boarding pass. Call me when you get to DC. I'll have a car and a hotel room."

Matthew tossed the envelope at my feet and left me on the sand, arching my back, looking at the sky, trying to catch my breath.

When I picked it up, Shelly stood on the patio with her arms crossed. I tucked my board under my arm and continued toward the house.

~ * ~

Shelly

The sight of Jason, through the glass doors, rubbing his chest, made me jump out of my skin. My worst fear was losing him just when we'd found each other again. The man he was talking to looked like a government agent, and the news looked bad. I didn't want to stress him out any further, so I waited.

He leaned his board against the half wall of the patio and came in through the waist-high gate.

"That was Matthew Sutter, my old handler." He handed me the envelope, as if I knew what that meant. He saw the confusion on my face. "He was in charge of my case in São Paolo."

"I thought you were done with all that."

"Me too." He pulled his wetsuit off and hung it on a hook on the south side of the patio. "Come on, its cold out here." He took my hand.

"You're freezing!" I squealed as his frosty hand shocked my skin.

When we got inside, he pulled me to him. His whole body was frigid. He put his arms around me, and I adjusted the silver chain around his neck and rubbed the hollow coin the chain threaded through. I gave it to him on our first anniversary, only two days ago. He'd given me a copy of Maria's poem etched in glass to put in my office.

"Mmm, you're warm." He sighed and rubbed his body on mine.

"Ah! Get in the shower!" I pushed him away.

"Fine." He trudged upstairs.

I followed him. "What did he want?" I opened the envelope. The Congressional subpoena looked just like a federal court one, short and to the point.

Jason went straight into the bathroom and turned on the shower. He leaned on the counter with his head down. "I have to testify against Caesar in DC on Thursday." He sighed and glanced over at me.

"No." I stopped reading and peered at his reflection in the mirror. "You can't. He's done so much for the children…the schools… What will happen to the schools?"

"I have to. They're giving me no choice."

"There's always a choice. I have a friend from law school. He's a constitutional lawyer in Washington DC. I'll call him."

Jason shook his head. "I don't know what good that's going to do."

"Plead the fifth. You don't have to testify."

He approached me as steam covered the small space. "Caesar can take care of himself, and you can keep the charity going without Tessa. It'll be fine."

"What about you?" My stomach retched. "Will he come after you?"

He gazed down at me. his eyes turned liquid. "Maybe."

"Don't do it."

Coming closer to me, his hands rested on my shoulders. "I don't have a choice."

I was missing something. Something he wasn't telling me. When it hit me, the air left my lungs. "They're going to come after *me*, aren't they?" I stepped back out of the steamy bathroom and into the doorway. A cool breeze wrapped around my arms and chilled me to the bone. "They're going to wreck me and the charity, aren't they?" My hands flew to my mouth. "I'll be arrested for being too close to Caesar's business because of Tessa, won't I?"

"Listen to me." He grabbed my shoulders again, tighter this time. "I'm testifying against Caesar. You'll be fine."

"What about you?"

He took a deep breath. "I won't let anything happen to you."

"That's not what I asked. Hold on." I stepped back again. "No. You are not leaving me again."

I couldn't get enough air, and my breathing became labored. A panic attack loomed. I've had many of them; I knew what to do to stop it before it got bad, but this time I was too far gone. It consumed me.

"They'll take you away. They'll hide you." I leaned on the side of the bed. My head spun.

"I don't have to go into witness protection." He approached. "That *is* a choice."

"There *are* no choices here!"

He pulled me to him, wrapping his arms around me and pushing my head to his chest. His heart struggled, thudding and shuttering. It terrified me.

He held me close, a life preserver in a violent storm. "I promised you. I promised."

The rest of the night we talked about what we thought might happen when he got to DC. Both of us speculating, neither knew. We lay in bed, exhausted.

"I should warn Tessa," I said.

"You can't."

I sighed. "I love her like a sister. This will break her."

"She's lived this life for a long time." Jason took my arm across his chest. "They both knew the risks. Caesar's got lawyers. He'll be fine."

"He'll go to jail."

"Maybe. We can't be sure."

"Why'd they turn on him?" Nothing I could fathom would bring this turnabout. Something still didn't feel right.

"I don't know." He turned toward me. "I will never leave you."

"Getting killed is leaving me." Panic at losing him ate away at me.

He tucked a hair behind my ear. "I'll call Sebastian to get us some protection."

I sat up and glared down at him.

"I was going to call Gabby anyway to get some guards for Jasmine," he continued in his relaxed zen way.

How did he remain so calm? "Will she do it?"

"Of course. She still loves her daughter, even though she's a terrible mother."

"Don't say that. It's the hardest job in the world."

"I'm not going to argue with you on that." He turned me on my side with my back to his chest. He spooned me and squeezed. "Get some sleep. We won't figure this out tonight anyway."

I relaxed in his arms but couldn't sleep.

What if they forced him into witness protection after he testified? What if Caesar sent guys to kill him, and me too? Could the CIA wreck my reputation and my work? Too many questions assaulted my brain.

Jason's hold loosened, and I listened to his breathing until he started his purring. I got out of bed and went to my office, to my desk, and opened my laptop.

My first thought was to email Magda and tell her everything. She was always willing to help Jason.

Instead, I started writing questions, one after the other, until I had about thirty questions, ponderings, and scenarios.

The writing morphed into an article of sorts. After I proofread it at 4:00 AM and was satisfied I had all the pertinent information correct and my voice was crystal clear, I posted it to my website and my social media pages. No names, no mention of Caesar, Tessa, or Jason. This was all about me and how I refuse to be *Cancelled*. It was a preemptive strike to stave off any negativity my wonderful government had in store for me.

I still didn't know what Jason was going to do, and I didn't think he did, either. But we both knew for sure he'd do everything he could to stay with me. I knew. This time, I knew.

Chapter Twenty-One

Washington DC, The Capitol Building, January
Jason

"Jesus, don't they have better things to do than waste their time with me and some gangster?" I asked Matt Sutter.

We stood and regarded the feelings of the sad souls, skulking around in facemasks, either rushing to get somewhere or dragging their feet looking pathetic. The air was thick with sorrow and anxiety as three more Congressmen went down with Covid, and the country reached over 300,000 dead.

Brian Heller, Shelly's friend from law school, stood on the other side of me in his ill-fitting navy suit. A briefcase engulfed the short, stout man. He was sweating and kept adjusting his mask. He'd met me at the airport and rode with me to the Hyatt Regency on New Jersey Avenue the afternoon before. He'd told me what to expect, thank God. His demeanor was matter of fact and sympathetic at the same time, like a doctor.

I told him everything about my interactions with Caesar over drinks at the hotel bar as he took notes on his phone. He kept it professional, and after I'd finished my second beer, he'd just finished his first.

"Don't worry. This is all procedural. You'll get through it." He left, reminding me to meet him at the top of the steps of the Capitol the next morning.

Brian was waiting for me in his camel-colored coat. It was freezing, and I wished I had something better than just a trench coat. We went through security just as Matt appeared, wearing his mask this time.

No handshakes, just polite nods.

"Somebody gives a shit about this right now, so here we are." Matthew Sutter sighed.

"Where are we going?" I asked through my mask, not knowing if my voice even carried through it, as no one answered me. The domed entrance of the capitol building echoed low conversations as it loomed above, and heels clacked on the marble tiles below. I'd never been to DC, and I gazed in amazement at the drama of it all, the etched marble, grand the dome, and the enormous paintings lining the walls.

"Through here." Matthew navigated the place like an expert. "We need to go down to the chambers floor and meet with the committee members for an initial interview."

I glanced back at Brian, who shuffled to keep up with us much bigger men with longer legs.

"Wait." I pulled on Matt's arm. "How many days am I going to be here?"

"I'm not sure. It'll be up to them."

I already wanted to be back with Shelly's warm body. DC in January was too cold for me.

It better not snow. I hated snow.

"Just give them what they want." Matt pushed the down button for the elevator with his elbow. The gloved, face-shielded attendant, whose job it was to push the button, cleared his throat at him.

"Sorry, man. We didn't see you there." I nudged Matt with my elbow when the man held out a bottle of hand sanitizer.

Matt groaned but held out his hands, palms up, to the man. I did the same, followed by Brian. We entered the elevator, rubbing the foul-smelling liquid into our skin.

"Give them what they want?" I mocked. "You should've prepped me with the questions. How do I know you aren't just feeding me to the wolves?"

"Who says I'm not?"

"You're a fucking jerk, man." I didn't look at Matt when he said that. I couldn't. I was in Hell, and he was Lucifer.

"That's why *I'm* here, Jason, to ensure your rights aren't violated," Brian interjected.

We exited the elevators to a poorly lit hallway with a musty, old-carpet smell.

Matt stopped at the chamber doors and turned to me. "Look, this isn't my idea of a Christmas vacation either, okay? I'm supposed to be in my cabin in Vermont, skiing right now."

"Vermont?" I hadn't heard anything personal from Matt in the time we'd known each other, I'd learned nothing about the agent except he grew up surfing in Oceanside and got migraines.

"Yeah, fucking Vermont with my wife and kids." He growled. "So, don't think for one second I'm enjoying this. Okay?"

"Fine." I relented and threw my hands up in surrender.

"Just listen, answer their questions, and let's get back to our families."

I nodded. "Let's get this over with."

Matthew opened the doors to a long table with six stern-looking people, four men in blue suits and two women in colored jackets.

"Go sit at the table. There." Matt pointed to a shorter table across from the bigger one.

I walked in, then had to stop when, out of the corner of my eye, I saw Matt hold Brian back and let the door close behind him out of my sight.

I sat in the chair on the right side of the table with a place card with my name on it and peered at the people across from me. Most of them I recognized from the impeachment trial on television and various cable news broadcasts. Plaques with their names and states sat in front of them.

Three bottles of water lined up in front of me. The lights above gave off a blearing surge of heat. I opened one of the bottles.

"Mr. Mattis?" A pretty brunette, who smelled of vanilla, leaned over me and smiled. "Feel free to remove your mask as you are a fine distance to do so." She scurried away, and I removed my mask.

I felt like I was in a TV show or movie about some schmuck who was a traitor to his country.

"Thank you for coming today, Mr. Mattis." A woman in her sixties, with an outdated hairstyle like an old church lady, said to me from the line of lawmakers facing my table.

Brian's cologne wafted into my left nostril. He took his place next to me with a reassuring nod. I felt better with him there. I knew five languages but for some reason felt like I wouldn't be able to understand a damn word that was going to be said.

I sat stoically for a few heartbeats and stared at the woman. She reminded me of old photos of my grandmother from the 1960s.

"Uh, yeah, sure. It's cool." My California drawl rolled out of my parched mouth. I downed the first bottle and snagged another.

"For the record, we are interviewing Jason Mattis for the closure of Operation Shedder. The first thing we will be discussing is the indictment case against Agent Mark DeSantos," the woman said.

My head shot around to Matthew, sitting behind me in a row of chairs against the wall. He smirked. I looked back at Brian, who'd nodded again. What was happening?

"I… I'm sorry, ma'am. I don't…" I stammered.

"Apologies, Mr. Mattis, but we have an order of things here we need to address. We will ask you questions as soon as the formalities are out of the way."

Brian gripped my wrist.

I glanced at him, and he nodded encouragement.

"All right." I shifted. The seat was hard as a board, sending pain shooting to my hip. "Order is good. I like order, just like my wife." Sutter scoffed behind me. *Asshole.* The rest of the folks smiled at me.

Brian hadn't prepared me to discuss DeSantos, the man who'd threatened me, blackmailed me, and made my life hell for five years. My cheeks flushed and burned with anger from betrayal, not just from DeSantos, but Matt, too. If Sebastian found out, I'd have another reason to keep looking over my shoulder for a hit.

I leaned over to Brian and whispered, "Did you know about this?"

"Madame Chairman, may I have a moment with my client?" Brian asked, surprising me with his confident and authoritative tone.

The woman nodded. "Five-minute recess."

Brian followed me as I pushed the doors open in rage. "What is this? No one told me *I'd* be on trial here."

"You're not." The small man used the back of his sleeve to wipe sweat from his receding hairline. "Agent Sutter told me they're going after your former handler first, then they'll get your testimony on Caesar. They just wanted a timeline and then they can pursue them both. It's just to close your case. You are not in trouble."

"I'll have to tell them about Sebastian's business? That puts me in a shitload of trouble, man, believe me." I paced in a circle.

"You're doing the right thing here, Jason." The sweating and uncomfortable man stood still. "You want to be free of all this, don't you?"

I exhaled and put my hand on my hip for balance. I wasn't privy to the organization's business, therefore didn't have much to tell.

Sebastian made sure to leave Gabby and me out of the organization's dealings. Brian stared at me in fear, not knowing I was zen, and wouldn't fly off in a fit.

I clapped the man's shoulder in a friendly gesture, to assure him I'd calm down.

"Tell me, Brian, did Shelly ever talk about me when you were in school?" I pivoted.

Brian's eyes looked perplexed. "Uh, not that I can recall."

I pursed my lips and took in a deep breath.

"Just answer their questions, huh?" I pivoted the conversation again—a nervous habit of mine to avoid discussions of anything too heavy or uncomfortable.

Brian nodded, and his stiff shoulders dropped. "She *did* turn me down for a date back then, if it makes you feel any better."

I chuckled and noticed Brian's wedding ring and pointed to it. "How long you been married, man?" *Pivot*

"Twenty-six years."

"Good for you."

"You'll get through this, Jason. I promise." This time, Brian clapped my shoulder, acknowledging the nervous pivoting. "Just be honest and know you can say 'I don't know' at any time."

He was good guy, a smart guy. I was in good hands with him.

~ * ~

Six hours later, we recessed for the evening. I'd just relived the past ten years of my life with trepidation and nostalgia. As I recalled small details about my interactions with Sebastian and Agent DeSantos, painful memories of the demise of my marriage flooded back, hurting my soul.

A text from Shelly washed away the pain.

Shelly: *"How are you holding up?"*

Jason: *"Just going down Memory Road with a hockey mask and a butcher knife."*

Shelly: *"That bad huh?"*

Jason: *"What's your word? Cathartic?"*

Shelly: *"That's a good thing. Good word, Babe."*

Jason: *"What are you wearing?"*

Shelly: *"Are you asking for a photo?"*

Jason: *"No, you're the writer. Tell me."*

Shelly: *"Think 'The Big Lebowski Chic,' your plaid pajama pants, T-shirt, cardigan, and slippers. Been two days now, same outfit."*

I smiled at the image of my adorable wife. I pictured her at her desk, a messy bun knotted atop her head with a pencil stuck through it, maybe more than one, black-framed reading glasses perched on the bridge of her nose, drinking her third cup of coffee from her favorite Endless Aviation mug. One or both cats asleep on her desk.

Shelly: *"The cats miss you."*

Jason: *"If they've already taken my side of the bed, I will begin the beatings when I get home."*

Shelly: *"LOL, I miss you."*

Jason: *"Me too, I'll call you when I get to the hotel."*

~ * ~

Three long days wearing a suit was a nightmare. My anxiety level was too high. I hadn't slept at all, and the third day would be the day they'd get to my interaction with Caesar.

I wasn't surprised to see two familiar, black-suited, sunglassed, black-haired men with black facemasks waiting for me outside the hotel. I'd wondered what had taken them so long.

"Caesar wants to talk to you." The fatter one handed me a phone.

"Caesar." I sighed into the phone.

"Today is the day, eh, *Gringo*?"

"For what?"

A chuckle came from the phone. The gangster knew I was joking. He'd thought after everything we'd been through maybe we were friends. *Shit no!* He could turn on me at any time. I knew gangsters, and I didn't trust the man any farther than I could throw him.

"You're going to tell our story."

"That's what they want me to do, yeah." I didn't even want to know how Caesar knew what day the testimony was.

"They don't want me, you know."

"Then, why am I here?"

"Oh, they want to hear what you have to say about me, but they will not come after me this time."

"Caesar, Shelly means everything to me. I know you understand. I will keep my promises to her."

"I know, *Gringo*."

"I have to tell them everything."

"Go ahead."

Go ahead?

"That's why you sent your *gambaros* all the way here? Just to hand me this phone?"

"Jesus and Ricardo's *abuela* lives in Baltimore. They were already in town." He chuckled.

"What's your game, Caesar?"

The big men had their backs to me, acting more like shields than attackers.

"*El Jefe*, you met him, yes?"

Of course. *El Jefe* would wipe Caesar's involvement clean. He still worked with the CIA, and this witch-hunt was aimed at ensnaring Mark DeSantos, or Sebastian, or both. Caesar sent his men to protect me. All of Shelly's spy novels were paying off.

"Yeah, Caesar, I know *El Jefe*."

172

"Talented guy, but what a *punta*." Caesar chuckled again. "Tessa misses your wife. Come meet us in Hawaii this summer."

We both knew that was impossible.

The gangster hung up. I handed the man back his phone with a nod then headed up New Jersey Avenue toward the Capitol with Caesar's men close behind.

I'd just learned, and was relieved, Caesar wouldn't come after me. The weight of the world lifted from my shoulders.

This would finish it for good. The last day of testimony, and I could go home to the beach, the waves, and the love of my life.

Chapter Twenty-Two

Capistrano Beach, CA, February
Shelly

"I just go off a Zoom with Tessa," I told Jason as he stripped the wax off his board with the foulest-smelling chemical and blasted Bush's *Everything Zen* on some hidden speaker.

I wasn't happy about him doing the wax stripping in the garage with toxic chemicals. At least the door was wide open, and he wore an aspirator mask. He pulled the mask down and smiled at me. A flat-billed hat on backward made him look like a sexy punk teenager. He pulled his phone from his back pocket and paused the music.

"We're going to do readings via Zoom for the students. We've got three authors confirmed and Telenovio is hosting the broadcast. This way all the schools can do the meeting at once. Isn't that great?" I held the hem of my cardigan over my nose.

"It is." He wiped the dust off the board with a big fluffy brush.

"Ugh. When are you going to be done with that?"

"I've got two more to do, then there will be five in total for my class tomorrow." He pointed to the finished boards lined up against the wall outside the garage door, in the alley behind the house.

He'd gone to Lisa and Brad Tennent to pitch them sponsoring a surf camp for underprivileged youth in Orange County. They'd jumped at the chance and helped him get the necessary licenses and permits. They'd also convinced him to be the face of their clothing line once more. New branding brought maturity to the line, with the theme of Endless Summer for senior surfers.

"Hey." I looked in the alley for my brother's motorcycle.

"Where's Ben?"

Jason scraped a long stroke over the top of the board, curling the wax into a tube. "He went downtown to pick up fabric samples...uh, swatches. I'm supposed to pick out some prints for the fall line."

"How's he doing?" I asked.

Jason stood upright and rubbed his lower back with a wince. "He's doing well." A wicked grin graced his stunning stubbled face.

"What?"

"He likes all the design stuff."

"Really?" I didn't hide my shock.

"Yeah, he stays at the factory for hours with Lisa and comes back with sketches or fabrics and he's like...giddy."

"Giddy? My brother? My motorcycle-riding, tattooed brother?"

"Yeah." Jason chuckled. "I've been letting him approve the designs and pick out the fabrics for months now."

"So, 'Tennant Endless Summer by Jason Mattis' has been designed by Ben Stringer."

No, Babe." He corrected me, grinning. "It's been *styled* by Ben Stringer."

I shook my head. "I'm in some bizzarro world."

"He's good at it. I'm serious. I told him to enroll in fashion school."

I laughed at his comment.

"See, that's why we haven't said anything, Ms. Lawyer-Intellectual-Turned-Romance-Novelist." He was being snippy.

Now I felt guilty for my snotty attitude. I nodded. "You're right. I have no place to judge him."

Jason sauntered over to me, reeking of formaldehyde and melted wax. "I like your books. They're pretty hot. You know I'm your biggest fan. I like the research we do for them." He put his tongue in my ear, and I shook. "That's new. Add that to your next story."

~ * ~

Jason's first photo shoot was right on our beach and attracted a crowd.

He wore a plaid flannel coat and dark gray cargo pants, standing shirtless and barefoot as the water licked his feet. The gray flecks in his hair and whiskered chin and cheeks sparkled in the sun. He was stunning, the distinguished epitome of a silver fox. The legend—"The Zen Shredder"—my husband.

"Ready, Jason?" the photographer asked.

"Let's dance," The Zen Shredder answered with a wink.

He looked over his shoulder at the camera, making me flushed with heat, just like the first time I'd seen him.

"Is that Jason Mattis?" one neighbor asked.

"He looks fantastic," another commented.

"Yeah, still so hot," a woman added.

Jason had finally asked me, as we lay in our bed in our house with our cats, why I'd let him in my life over and over again all those years ago. There was only one answer.

"You were on my schedule."

Acknowledgements

My mentor; Bethany Hensel, coach; Beth Barany and my fearless beta readers: Stefani Seltzer, Kami Papa, Sarah Larson, Michelle Miksell-Persell & Shelly Nichols. The team at Champagne Books—Cassie Knight and Kat Hall.

About the Author

I am a storyteller first and foremost. My writing journey began a little over a year ago after my 50th birthday and the lock-down provided me the opportunity to get my stories down. Some stories have been haunting my dreams for over forty years. But when the characters began shouting at me at all hours of the day and night I had to write them down, never having written before.

Some romance stories some women's lit stories, always steamy and full of colorful characters most set in the 1990's with pop culture and music references.

Two debut stories coming soon made me realize that writing has been my destiny all along.

A proud native-Californian, I live in Hermosa Beach, CA, a tiny beach-town in South Los Angeles County with my husband of sixteen years, two beautiful kids and two spunky-rescue kitties.

Cindy loves to hear from her readers. You can find and connect with her at the links below.

Website/Blog: http://cindykehstories.com
Facebook: http://facebook.com/cindykehagirasstories
Instagram: http://instagram.com/cmkehstories
TikTok: https://vm.tiktok.com/TTPdSu5kRX/
Twitter: http://twitter.com/cmkehstories

Thank you for taking the time to read *The Perpetual*. If you enjoyed the story, please tell your friends, and leave a review. Reviews support authors and ensure they continue to bring readers books to fall in love with.

And now for a look inside *Whiskey on Our Shoes*, a fun and quirky story about a woman hiding from the spotlight who learns, with the help of a new romance, that being in the spotlight can sometimes be a good thing by Tonya Preece.

TONYA PREECE

When the attention-avoiding daughter of a celebrity couple and a Texas cowboy college student with his own troubles fall hard for each other, they must face their truths together or be torn apart by a media storm.

Eva dodges the fans, media, and gossip that follow her supermodel mom and rock star family members by wearing disguises. After an aimless gap, she struggles to figure out what she wants from life. She moves in with her famous guitar god brother in Austin while he recovers from a drunken stage stunt accident and tries to stay sober. When a hot Texas cowboy named Alex takes Eva by surprise, she risks her safety and security of anonymity by letting him into her unconventional life.

Alex is captivated by Eva and promises to protect her privacy. Yet he has a secret of his own—the fling he had with an older woman is fraught with scandalous potential for him and now Eva. He broke free of that mistake months ago, or so he thought. As things heat up with Eva, his old flame returns and won't leave him alone.

Just when Alex thinks he has the reins on the situation, his ex teams up with a gossip reporter hell-bent on invading Eva's privacy. The resulting exposé, with a sly spin on a recent encounter with his ex, is Alex's worst nightmare, and Eva's unsure what to believe. Can she face the world with Alex at her side or will she return to her hidden life?

Chapter One
Eva

A thrill races through me as I decide to ignore the wigs on my dresser and run a brush through my own hair. I don't need a disguise when I leave the house today. I'm going out alone. No driver. No security. And no celebrity family members.

The opening riff of "Welcome to the Jungle" blasts across the upstairs landing from my brother's room. Lor's favorite Guns N' Roses song is a good sign his physical therapy didn't suck for a change.

Hopeful, I set down my brush and go peer through his half-open door.

He's sitting in his hospital bed, playing air guitar. I'm sure he misses playing for real, but I cringe at the memory of the last time he tried. He got so pissed at the pain and weakness in his hands that the acoustic wound up on the floor with its neck cracked.

The song ends, and I call from the doorway, "Hey, you must be feeling—"

"Fan-freakin-tastic." He gives me the smirk I know well.

Not much else resembles his former self, though. His face is thinner, and his shaggy blond hair cropped shorter. Last year, during the filming of a Polly's Poison music video, one of his drunken pyrotechnic stunts led to a spinal injury and burns. He's forty, twenty years older than me, but he looks even older from a hard and fast life as a guitar god.

He lowers the volume on the next song and motions for me to enter.

His room, like the rest of his huge house, makes me think of a Hard Rock Café. Concert posters, photos, and guitars hang on every wall.

"You're still going somewhere, right?" he asks.

"Desperate to get rid of me, huh?" Smiling, I perch on the edge of his bed. "I'm leaving soon, but I don't wanna be chauffeured. Could I borrow a car?"

His scruffy, unshaven face brightens. "Take the Lamborghini. It's a sweet ride."

"Too recognizable." I don't want to be spotted in one of his poison green custom cars.

"Dammit, Eva." He shakes his head. "Stop letting Mom's paranoia freak you out."

"I'm trying. See, no disguise." I point at my wigless head.

"Nobody in Austin's gonna bother you."

He's told me this more than once in the two weeks since I moved in with him, but it's not easy to let go of how our mom taught me to stay anonymous. One of her obsessive fans tried to kidnap me when I was three. Although I don't remember it, the story haunts me to this day. Besides, I *like* being unknown in this family of celebs.

"And, while Mom's gone," Lor adds, "you don't have to worry about Crazy Carla."

Carla's the latest celebrity gossip reporter who tracks Mom. She's probably in L.A. where Mom's doing a commercial for a new cosmetic line.

"I understand but let me take baby steps. I'll drive the

Challenger. It'll blend in better."

"Boring." He rolls his eyes and nudges me off the bed. "Go raise hell for the both of us."

"Ha! That's your style, not mine." I lean in and kiss his cheek. "Be back in a few hours."

"Take your time."

I stop in the doorway and glance back at him. He's looking at his phone and doesn't notice me pausing to watch him. For a moment, I consider staying. He's bound to be bored. I should keep him company, shouldn't I? We could play cards or watch TV.

No. I better go. When he asked me to live here, we made a deal: he'll stay sober, and I'll venture out on my own. This is my chance.

With a sudden surge of independence, I descend the long marble staircase and exit, leaving behind the safety and seclusion of Casa Lor.

Chapter Two
Alex

My classes are done for the day, and I head for my dorm, playing a voicemail from a missed call.

"Hi, Alex." The speaker doesn't identify herself, but I'd know the voice anywhere. It's the one that lured me into what I thought was the best time of my life—and left me in ruins.

I stop on the sidewalk. My gut churns, but morbid curiosity keeps the phone to my ear.

"I miss you," she says, low and sexy, like she thinks it'll work. "Call me, okay?"

"Not a chance, Angie," I mumble and block the unknown number.

What the hell would we talk about? We haven't spoken in months.

Revulsion ripples through me. I shake it off and check messages for my errand service business. There's one from a person named Lor, which sounds fake, but whatever, it's work.

I message the customer to say I'm available now, and they reply right away.

> *Hey, man, thanks for the fast response. I need you to meet with a guy at Kudos Café near Lake Travis. He'll give you a package to bring to me.*

This sounds fishy, but I send a response.

> *As long as it doesn't have anything illegal or hazardous.*

*No worries. What should I tell my guy you
look like?*

*I'll be the tall guy in a dark blue shirt,
jeans, and cowboy boots. Please confirm
your agreement to my terms and
conditions, and an invoice for prepayment
will follow.*

*Cool. I'll text further instructions once you
have the package.*

Within minutes, his credit card payment goes through and damn,
he included a twenty-*five* percent tip. I need him as a regular customer.

I arrive at the café early and order a soda, knocking out some
reading for my marketing class while I wait. Right on time, a guy
approaches me, carrying a plain brown bag with handles. He has spiky
blond hair and ear gauges. His neck tattoo is a…steampunk penguin? I
stifle a laugh as he eyes my boots.

"Are you picking up for Lor?" he asks, and I nod. The bag's
heavier than I expected, and the top's taped shut.

"Tell Lor I said hello." The guy leaves before I can even ask his
name.

I text that I have the bag, and he sends me a residential address
that's ten minutes away.

*Enter NINE9999 at the security gate. Drive
to the house, ring the bell & ask for Jojo.
Tell her you need to hand-deliver the
package to Mr. Jenson.*

I'm intrigued and make the short drive with the bag on the front
seat.

A little guardhouse is unoccupied. The code opens the gate onto
a long, brick-paved driveway lined with perfectly landscaped shrubs and
trees. A mansion ahead has a five-car garage and a balcony across the
whole second story. Most deliveries, often for older folks, are to quiet
neighborhoods and apartments. This place blows my mind.

Why didn't Mr. Jenson send a butler for this errand?

I park in front of the house, grab the bag from my passenger seat,
and ring the doorbell. Sweat trickles down my back. I feel out of place.
I'm a small-town guy in jeans and a T-shirt and have never stepped foot
in a house this big. The door's opened by a woman in a dark blue suit.

"Hello, you must be Alex."

"Yes, ma'am." I remove my cowboy hat with my free hand. "Are you Jojo?"

"I am." She waves me into a huge foyer. "Mr. Jenson only informed me he was expecting company a moment ago. Would you like something to drink?"

"Oh, no thanks. I don't want to impose. If you'll just take me to him, I'll—"

"Of course." She leads the way up a massive, winding marble staircase overlooking a living room where platinum records and guitars are on display. Maybe I should recognize who this Lor guy is, but I can't put my finger on it.

Jojo shows me into a room where a man's sitting in a hospital bed. His hands and arms are scarred. I've seen scars like those before, from burns.

He glances up from an iPad as Jojo and I approach his bed. "The biographer's here," she tells him.

I squint, taken aback. "Um, excuse me ... what do you mean, bio—"

"Excellent." He sets the iPad aside and eyes the bag in my hand.

"I'll leave you two gentlemen to the task at hand," Jojo says and leaves.

"What *task* was she talking about?" I ask the man, more uneasy by the second.

"Oh, don't pay any attention to her." He waves a dismissive hand. "You're kinda young, but this could still work. How are your acting skills?"

Chapter Three
Eva

I browse through a few clothing shops at a galleria but don't buy anything. My shoulders are so tense from this new, undisguised solo experience, there's no way I could enjoy trying anything on.

Heading back to Casa Lor, I stop at a place called Austin Creative Repurposing. I've read about it online, how they use recycled stuff to make art, and I want to check it out for myself.

A bell chimes as I enter, and a few people look my way. My skin prickles from the familiar fear of exposure. There's no way anyone here would guess who I'm related to. Too bad my heart doesn't understand that logic. It hammers away in my chest. I run my fingertips along the edge of my wig to check that it's on right, but *duh*, no wig.

I glance around to get my bearings. ACR is a furniture showroom and art gallery. The air's a bit musty, with a hint of tobacco. The scent, mingled with furniture polish, reminds me of pleasant days at my grandparent's house in San Diego, and I relax.

A tall woman in a red ACR shirt greets me. "Holler if you need help with anything."

"Thanks." I clear my throat, embarrassed by the waver in my voice. "I'm just browsing."

There's a wall hanging with piano keys mounted on a long, painted board. It's simple yet elegant. On another wall, several doors hang sideways with cutouts for photos. In between the doors, there are window frames made into shadowboxes. They're above a table display of vinyl records that've been heated and molded into cool decorative bowls. Mixed in with The Rolling Stones and Metallica records is one for my dad and uncle's band, The Fabulous Undertakers. Nobody here knows my connection to them either. I trace the familiar record label with my fingertip. The design accentuates the band's nickname, FU.

The tall woman, whose name tag says Nadine, walks around with another woman and young teenage girl. Mother and daughter, I assume. It sounds like Nadine's giving them a tour.

"Everything's one of a kind," she says. "Artists and furniture makers obtain supplies from our warehouse, create new pieces, and sell them on consignment." She points to a clawfoot tub. "This is the work of a volunteer." One side is sheared off, and it's lined with padding.

"Oh cripes, art skills aren't required, are they?" the woman asks. "Jenny has none."

The girl's eyes shoot daggers at her mom, and Nadine says, "No ma'am, but we do hope volunteers have an interest in repurposing things otherwise destined for a landfill."

The girl rolls her eyes, and her mom scolds her in a hushed voice.

"I'll give you a moment," Nadine tells them. Stepping in my direction, she grimaces.

"Yikes," I mutter. "Sounds like they don't get the point of this place."

"Nailed it." She sighs.

The girl breaks away from her mom, storming out. The mother huffs and calls to Nadine, "We'll have to get back to you later, okay?"

"No problem." Nadine waves. Once the mother's gone, Nadine introduces herself to me as the co-owner. "Since you seem to appreciate, or at least understand, our goal here at ACR, by any chance are *you* interested in volunteering?"

"Um…" Put on the spot, I falter, but I'm grinning. Something about this place makes me feel like I belong. "What would I be doing?"

"Come on, I'll show you the warehouse."

We exit through a back door and cross a parking lot between the showroom and another building. "These are donated supplies." She points to rows of shelves, neatly labeled, holding stuff like paint, bolts of fabric, and bins with craft supplies. "Volunteers sort and stock, rearranging as needed." Bricks, lumber, tiles, and metal are stacked on the other side.

"Everything's so organized." I'm impressed.

"Thanks. We try. My stepdaughter, Blair, did the setup. What do you think of joining us? We'd love your help."

This would take time away from being with Lor, but *he's* the one who insists I get out more.

I bite my bottom lip for a second, then say, "Yeah, I'll give it a try."

"Yes! Let's go to my office, and you can complete a volunteer application."

The simple form only takes a few minutes. Since I've kept my identity disassociated with the celebrities in my family, I don't worry much about using my real name.

Nadine schedules me to volunteer on Tuesdays and Thursdays and sets a red shirt on her desk. As I reach for it, her eyes zero in on my left hand and widen in shock. Surprisingly, a lot of people don't notice my left index finger's missing. I'm prepared to brush it off as a childhood accident, but she doesn't ask.

Instead, she looks away and opens a file cabinet. "One more form. A liability waiver. How old are you?"

"Twenty."

"Good, no need for a parent to sign."

Whew. That would've sucked. Mom's signature could end my anonymity. Sloane Silver is a household name, like Heidi Klum.

"Are you a college student?" Nadine asks.

"No." Fact is, one gap year led to another, and I have no clue what to do with my life.

On my way to the exit, Nadine takes me through an area of the showroom I didn't notice earlier. I stop dead in my tracks. There's a guitar on display, decorated with colored glass mosaic tiles arranged in intricate patterns. Nadine traces a green tile. "The artist found the guitar beside someone's trash near the lake. In the right hands, one person's trash becomes another's art."

I touch the back of the guitar's neck. The burred texture of cracked wood confirms it. *I* was the one who threw this guitar out, at Lor's insistence. And here it is, transformed.

Checking the price tag, I say, "I'd like to buy this."

Her eyebrows rise in surprise. "Awesome. I'll ring you up. Bonus, there's a volunteer discount, albeit small."

Once I've paid for it, I carry the guitar to the Challenger. The glass tiles make it heavier. I carefully place it across the backseat. Before starting the car, I check my phone for the time and see a message from Lor's personal assistant, Jojo.

> *Did you know your brother's having*
> *someone write his biography? The writer's*
> *here, meeting with him.*

Frowning, I reread the message. There's no way Lor finally agreed to let someone write his bio, not while Polly's Poison wants to keep a lid on his condition.

Abandoning plans for a drink at the nearby café, I hurry home. At Casa Lor, there's a black truck with a UT longhorn symbol on the bumper. I park beside the truck, grab my purse, and sling the ACR T-shirt over my shoulder on the way to the front door. Up the stairs, two at a time, I rush into Lor's room.

"Whoa, Eva." He sits up straighter. "You're back already?"

I take a deep breath, relieved he isn't drinking. "What's going on? Who's this?" I gesture at the guy in the room holding a cowboy hat.

"Alex," Lor says. "He's here to work on my biography. Alex, my sister, Eva."

A strangled sound escapes my throat. Lor must've lost his freaking mind, telling this stranger who I am. He's usually more careful, even if he doesn't agree with me wanting to stay unknown. His eyes widen. "Shit, I'm sorry."

Sorry doesn't help now. I could run out, but the damage is done. It's best to draw the attention away from myself. I set my purse on the bed and ask Lor, "A biography, huh?"

He says, "Yeah," but Alex shakes his head.

My body tenses, thumbnail digging into my scar. Lor is nothing if not consistent. Despite his good intentions, he's the king of self-sabotage.

Unfortunately, now we have an audience.

Out Now!

What's next on your reading list?

Champagne Book Group promises to bring to readers fiction at its finest.

Discover your next
fine read!
http://www.champagnebooks.com/

We are delighted to invite you to receive exclusive rewards. Join our Facebook group for VIP savings, bonus content, early access to new ideas we've cooked up, learn about special events for our readers, and sneak peeks at our fabulous titles.

Join now.
https://www.facebook.com/groups/ChampagneBookClub/

Made in the USA
Monee, IL
25 June 2023

37418998R00105